HUSBAND

BETROTHED #2

PENELOPE SKY

Hartwick Publishing

Husband

For My Husband,

Through the longest storm

the harshest winter

the darkest night

for better or worse

in sickness and in health

you said you were with me

you were always with me

you will always be with me

CONTENTS

1

SOFIA

THE WEEK PASSED WITH PAINFUL SLOWNESS.

I worked at the hotel, went home to my mom's impatient stares, and tried to pretend that my life wasn't about to change forever.

Hades didn't come to the hotel and catch me by surprise. He didn't stop by to leave any paperwork for me either. He just stayed away until I addressed the situation.

I was sitting on the main balcony with a cup of coffee in hand, wondering how different my life would have been if I were born into a normal family. Being rich wasn't worth all the stress. It wasn't worth being manipulated like this.

Mother was seated beside me, a cup of tea in her hand. "You're out of time, Sofia."

"I'm not doing it."

She sighed as she looked straight ahead. "We can have the same conversation again, but it's not going to change anything. This will happen whether you like it or not. If you don't want Hades, we'll find someone else. But truth be told, I don't think you're going to find anyone better than him."

"You don't know him."

"I know he's been keeping everything together at the hotel since Gustavo died."

"Uh, no. That's been me."

"Honey...there's a lot of stuff that happens behind the scenes that you don't know about. Hades does the dirty work and doesn't complain."

My eyes drifted down to my coffee.

"You're going to talk to him."

The idea of looking at him made me sick to my stomach. The years had only escalated our mutual hatred. I still remembered the night he picked up that model and made out with her right in front of me. It was low...really low. But it wasn't as painful as the time he bumped into me in the hallway and threatened me if I ever spoke to him again. "No."

"Well, he's here."

"Jesus." I set my cup down. "You've got to be kidding me—"

"I'll leave you two alone." She leaned toward me and patted my hand gently.

I didn't want to face him—and now I didn't even have time to prepare.

My mother walked away, her shoes echoing on the pavers until she was inside.

I felt the breeze move through my hair as I watched the summer sun sink below the horizon. I was rigid from his presence, aware he was right behind me, staring at the back of my head. Once I faced him, the conversation would begin...and I didn't want that.

His slow footsteps were audible as he approached the edge of the balcony. He stopped beside me, a couple feet away so he didn't invade my space.

I could see him in my peripheral vision, see his dark jeans and his black t-shirt. My pulse was so strong in my neck that I thought the artery would burst open. I wasn't sure if I was scared or nervous...or both.

He was silent, waiting until I was ready for the conversation before he spoke his mind.

I couldn't run from this. Just like any other problem, I had to face it. I had to grow a backbone and stand my ground. If I let him intimidate me, then it would prove my mother right...that I did need someone to protect me.

I finally got to my feet, lifted my chin, and looked at his side profile. "I had nothing to do with this—"

"I know." He turned to me, his muscular arms resting by his sides. He was the same strong man that he had been when we were together, still painfully beautiful, still so masculine that he was made of pure testosterone.

I crossed my arms over my chest, feeling awkward because we hadn't spoken even a few sentences since we'd broken up, since the night he'd asked me to marry him. Now we were both reliving that memory, both thinking the same thing. "Why would you even want this? You could have anyone you want. Why me?"

His eyes narrowed slightly as he considered what I said. The sky was a mixture of purple and pink behind him, and despite the unpleasant conversation, it was a lovely evening. He took his time replying, either because the answer was so obvious that he didn't need to explain, or he was trying to find a reason.

"Are you doing this to punish me?" I whispered, afraid this was all about revenge, that he would hurt me as payback for my rejection.

His eyes narrowed farther, clearly stung. "No. I told you that's not the kind of man I am."

"Then why?" He couldn't still love me. Too much time had passed. He'd been with too many women, had plenty of time to move on and forget about me.

"A lot of reasons."

"Such as?"

"I've been working with Tuscan Rose for a long time, since my early twenties. I have a vested interest in its livelihood. Someone needs to oversee it. Someone needs to keep everyone accountable. Your mother said fifty percent of that hotel is now mine. That's my biggest reason."

I was hurt that my mother gave away half of our company, but I suppose there was no other way. A man would only want to be locked into marriage if he was getting something out of it.

"My second reason is children. I want a family—and you will give me beautiful children."

That meant we had to screw...and we hadn't screwed in so long. Would the sex still be good? Would it be awkward and uncomfortable?

"My third reason...I want to fuck you."

Despite my indifference to him, my arms were covered with bumps like a cold breeze had just blown through. My pulse quickened further, and my tongue suddenly felt too big for my mouth. I even dropped my gaze because I was so uncomfortable by what he said. What was I supposed to say to that?

He stared me down like he expected me to say something.

I tucked my hair behind my ear then brushed my fingertips across my lips. When my arms were close to my body, I could feel my heart thudding against my arm, feel it trying to break through my rib cage. "I'm only having this conversation because my mother forced my hand. She didn't tell me you were here... just sprung it on me. And I'm confused because anytime we've ever interacted in the past two years, it's been extremely hostile."

"I'm a hostile guy...when you get on my bad side. That's exactly why you need me."

If he could scare me, he could scare anyone. "Well, is that how it's going to be every day? Hostile?"

His eyes shifted back and forth as he looked into mine. "No."

"So...you forgive me?"

"No."

"I don't see how we can be partners if you can't let go of the past."

"I've let it go," he said simply. "Doesn't mean I have to forgive you. We don't have to talk about it ever again. In fact, I'd prefer if we didn't."

Could I spend the rest of my life with a man when we had such a dark history? Our feelings were muddy and complicated.

There were emotions all over the place. "I don't want to do this. But I don't see any other way…"

"Your mother is right. Marrying me is your best option."

"Or I could run away and start over…"

"And leave your mother behind?" he asked coldly.

No, I couldn't abandon her.

"You're overthinking it. Don't fight it."

"But that's what I am—a fighter."

He stepped away and looked over the balcony at the city below. "We both know I'm the best man you're going to find. I'm an asshole, but a harmless one. Other bachelors out there are liars, abusive, controlling…the list goes on. At least with me, you know exactly what you're getting."

Hades was definitely the best choice by far. Despite our uncomfortable past, he wasn't like the others. The members of the board were jerks, and the criminals that came into the hotel wouldn't hesitate to shank me. At least with Hades, he kept the violence away from me and didn't hurt me himself. "I have conditions."

He turned back to me. "As do I."

"I don't want you to control me, to tell me what to do. In our relationship, you did that a lot. I told you I didn't want something, but you forced it on me anyway."

His eyes stayed focused on me.

"When you didn't get what you wanted, you manipulated me. I want your honesty, your integrity. I won't tolerate a man who strikes me. If you ever hit me, I swear I'll kill you in your sleep. I want you to treat me with respect."

His expression softened. "Sofia, you don't even need to ask that."

"I'm not so sure..."

"I will always be honest with you. And I'd rather kill myself than ever hurt you."

"That doesn't only apply to physical pain. You hurt me when we were together."

"Don't act like the victim, Sofia. You hurt me too. You hurt me a hell of a lot more than I ever hurt you."

"That was because you made me... That's the problem. You forced me to do that."

He looked away. "Let's not waste time arguing about the past. We obviously have very different views of what happened. I promise you I'll never hurt you. I will always be honest with you and respect you. Is that enough?"

"Yeah...I guess."

"Anything else?"

"My father used to have mistresses..."

"A lot of men do," he said quietly.

"My parents didn't love each other, and my mother was fine with it. But I still don't like it. That's not the kind of marriage I want to have."

He turned back to me, his brown eyes lighter in the gentle sunlight. "You have my fidelity, if that's what you're asking."

When I saw him with that model in the lobby, I almost threw up all over the counter. "I just think that's more appropriate, especially if we have kids at some point." I was already talking like this was absolutely happening, like I'd already decided.

"That's a two-way street."

"I know." Even if our marriage was just a business relationship, I felt odd sleeping with someone besides my husband. It still felt like a crime.

"And if I'm not fucking anyone else, I better be fucking you." He stepped closer to me, looking at me with those aggressive eyes. He crowded my space with his presence, exerting himself before he even owned me.

I'd been with other men since Hades and I went our separate ways. The sex was never as good as it was with him. It lacked the passion and the fire; it lacked that all-consuming chaos. It was just sex, dull from the condom. I did my best to forget about the best sex of my life because my hatred for him made me stubborn, but now it came back to me, exploding in the form of dirty images in my brain.

He lingered in front of me, as if he was waiting for my agreement. "Do you understand me?"

I gave a slight nod.

He walked past me in preparation to leave. "Plan the wedding. Just tell me when to show up."

I turned to watch him walk away. "I'm not sleeping with you until I say I do."

He looked back at me. "And you expect me to keep my dick in my pants until then?"

"No…" He didn't owe me anything until we tied the knot.

"Good." He started to walk away again.

"Hades."

He turned back to me, looking more annoyed.

"My mother needs to live with us."

His hands slid into his pockets. "She never mentioned that."

"She's too proud to ask. I know she doesn't want to be alone…"

"And that's my problem?" he asked, being a smartass.

"I'd be really grateful to you if you did this for me…and I'd show it." I didn't want my mother to live in this big house all alone. She didn't have many friends, and all her hobbies took place indoors. She wouldn't get married again, so I was her only companion. Besides, she could watch the kids while I worked all day.

His eyes softened slightly. "I'm holding you to that."

2

HADES

DAMIEN AND I RENTED OUT THE STRIP CLUB FOR A PRIVATE SHOW, watching the girls dance around the stage in skimpy thongs and tops that barely covered their nipples. Articles of clothing slowly fell to the floor, revealing more beautiful skin for us to gawk at.

He slipped a big bill into the thong of the woman who'd just given him a lap dance.

I drank from my glass of scotch.

The music boomed overhead, so Damien raised his voice to talk to me. "I'm ready for the whorehouse. How about you? Or should we hit a bar and do this the old-fashioned way? You know, alcohol and romance?" He slapped the woman's ass as she walked away.

Sofia agreed to marry me. I was a betrothed man, committed to a woman for the rest of my life. When I told her I wouldn't keep my dick in my pants, it was an empty threat. I just hoped that would change her mind about sleeping with me. "I'm gonna call it a night."

"What? It's eleven."

"Yeah...I'm just not feeling it."

Damien looked at the dozens of girls dancing in front of us then turned back to me—like I was fucking crazy. "Then you're gay. You've got to be."

I smacked him upside the head then left my chair.

He came after me and followed me into the parking lot. "What's the problem? You've been weird all week."

I hadn't told him the news yet, knowing he would shit a brick. I walked to my car then leaned against the door. "I've got something to tell you. It's not easy for me to say..."

"Alright...you're scaring me." He crossed his arms over his chest and stood in front of me.

"Sofia's mother came to my office last week and asked me to marry her daughter. I said yes."

It took him some time to absorb that information, to get it inside his brain and understand what it truly meant. His face slowly slackened when the revelation hit him. "Okay...I'm officially freaked out now."

"I've just come to accept it."

"Why did you say yes?"

I bowed my head, not wanting to answer.

"Hades. You asked her to marry you, and she said no. Why be with a woman who obviously doesn't give a shit about you? Why subject yourself to this torture? You know how long it took you to get over her last time."

"I know..."

"Then what the fuck are you doing?"

"If I don't marry her, someone else will."

"Which is a good thing."

I shook my head. "I don't want anyone else to have her. Even if she doesn't love me, she'll still be mine. And maybe someday... that will change."

"According to the gypsy, it never will."

It seemed like he believed in it after all. "A guy can dream, right?"

He shook his head. "Don't do this."

"I don't have a choice, Damien. No matter what I do...I lose. And that's how I know this is a curse. I'm perpetually miserable. At least I can be miserable with the woman I want instead of imagining someone else fucking her every night. At least I'll be the one doing the fucking."

Damien knew I didn't change my mind easily. Once I had my mind set on something, I stuck with it. "When are you getting married?"

"No idea."

"So you plan not to get laid until then?" he asked incredulously.

I was free to do whatever I wanted, but now that she was mine... in a way...it didn't feel right. I couldn't screw a woman without thinking about Sofia. It would be a pointless screw, and my climax would be weak. Now that I knew I'd be having the best sex of my life again, without a condom, that was all I wanted. I didn't want the cheap, watered-down stuff. "Yeah...guess so."

3

SOFIA

I was sitting at my desk in the office when one of the girls stepped in. "There's someone here to see you."

If it were Hades, she would have just said so. "Who?"

"His name is Maddox Stine."

I'd never heard that name before. "Did he say what he wanted?"

"Something about a business opportunity. He's in a black suit, wears a fancy watch…he looks the part."

"Alright. I guess I'll see him." Gustavo wasn't there to guide me through his former accomplices. I had to get acquainted with every part of the business, even parts I didn't like.

He walked in the door minutes later, in a deep black suit that was as dark as midnight. He had short dark hair, nearly bald because his shave was so close. He didn't greet me with a smile as he entered my office, but his blue eyes visibly approved of my appearance. He didn't restrain himself from looking me over. "Sofia." He said my name in his deep voice, the sound reverberating off the four walls of my office. It contained extreme power, but also malice. He had a fair face, but there was a noticeable scar along his jawline, like someone had dragged the tip of a blade directly across it, aiming for bone. He lowered himself into the chair, ignoring my attempt at a handshake.

The energy in the room was weird, like he somehow stole all the control with just his presence. I didn't know this man, but I got a strange vibe from him. Couldn't explain it...it was just instinct. "How can I help you, Mr. Stine?"

"Maddox is fine," he said quietly. His fingers moved under his cuff and adjusted his flashy watch. "Before Gustavo passed away, he told me you were looking for a husband. Said I might be a good fit."

My mother never mentioned Maddox, but maybe he was another man on her list. Being in his presence immediately made me uncomfortable. When the mafia came into the lobby and convened in the bar, I felt the same sense of dread. There was something evil about him, but I couldn't put my finger on it. It made Hades much more preferable...by a long shot. We had our differences, but I never felt unsafe. "I'm flattered by your interest, but my family needs to butt out of my personal life."

He smiled, showing all of his straight teeth. He was a handsome man, maybe a couple of years older than Hades. But there was still something off about him, especially the way he stared at me without blinking. "Annoying, isn't it?" he said with a laugh. "But they're trying to do the best thing for you. Not to sound presumptuous, but I probably am the best thing for you."

Wow...that was a little much. "With all due respect, I don't know you, and you don't know me."

His smile slowly faded, his gaze turning ice-cold. "I'm the richest man in this country. What else do you need to know?"

I found that hard to believe. There were a lot of rich men within a twenty-mile radius. Hades seemed particularly wealthy, but I never asked him what his net worth was...because it never mattered to me. "Then what do you need me for?"

"A beautiful wife. Isn't that what every man wants?"

I felt like a possession, a toy he could play with until he got tired of it. I could picture this man treating me more like a dog than a person. "Like I said, I'm flattered. But I'm marrying someone else." I'd been having cold feet about the idea all week, thinking about breaking it off with Hades. But now that I saw an example of what my mother had in mind, I quickly changed my mind.

"Oh, that's too bad." He glanced at my left hand. "I don't see a ring."

"It happened very recently."

He nodded slowly. "Who's the lucky man?"

"You probably don't know him."

"I know everybody." His voice lowered.

"Hades Lombardi." I wanted to wrap up this conversation quickly, to get this man out of my office so I would never have to see him again. The more questions I answered, the longer the conversation continued.

His entire body tightened at the name, like he knew exactly who that was...and didn't like it. He stared at me so coldly, it seemed as if he wanted to reach across the desk and choke me to death. He swiped his tongue across his bottom lip, letting out a deep breath that showed his disappointment. "You could do better."

Maybe. But Hades was definitely better than this guy. "I've got to get to a meeting, so thanks for stopping by." I rose to my feet and opened the door for him. "It's a beautiful day outside. You'd probably rather be out there than in here."

He took a long time to stand up, lingering as he faced my empty chair. As if he had something else to say but wasn't sure if he was going to say it, he took his time. When he finally stood up and looked at me, he was still ice-cold. He gave me a final look at the door before he walked off.

Thank fucking god.

I watched him walk around the corner before I relaxed. That man made me uneasy, like my soul could detect a demon living underneath his skin. It gave me the shivers. I returned to my chair and sat down, actually grateful I was marrying Hades. Now that my mom had gathered interest from suitors, they would probably keep pestering me until a wedding ring was on my finger.

Thankfully, I was already taken.

HOURS LATER, Hades appeared in the doorway of my office.

I was actually happy to see him—until I saw the scowl on his face.

He sat in the chair Maddox had occupied earlier that day then set a stack of folders on my desk. He moved paper around until everything was arranged to discuss whatever business needed to be addressed.

Since he was so irritated, I didn't mention the awkward conversation with Maddox. It might piss him off even more.

"You haven't given me a date." He sat upright in the chair and looked at me with impatience. He was annoyed and angry, but he didn't emit the same level of evil the other guy had. Hades seemed harmless...for the most part.

"You haven't given me a ring."

He cocked an eyebrow. "Didn't realize you wanted one."

"Isn't that a requirement for marriage? To wear a wedding ring?"

He didn't answer my question. "When were you thinking of doing this?"

"I don't know...people are usually engaged for a year before they tie the knot."

He immediately looked livid. "I'm not waiting a year. A month, at the most."

"You expect me to throw a wedding together in a month?"

"Your family plans elaborate parties all the time. Let's do it in the ballroom here at the hotel."

That was where I'd always imagined getting married—just not to someone like him.

"Unless you had somewhere else in mind."

"No..."

"Then make it happen." He turned to his paperwork. "There's a meeting with the board tomorrow, and I think—"

"I need a ring."

His jaw tightened at the request. "Don't interrupt me."

"Then don't change the subject."

He threw down the papers. "I'll get you a damn ring, alright?"

"I want it now—not at the wedding."

Now he just looked perplexed. "For hating me so much, you seem to be in a hurry to marry me."

"It's not that. I just want everyone to know I'm betrothed."

He raised an eyebrow. "Did someone bother you?"

I didn't want to talk about the creepy man who had made me feel uncomfortable in my own office. Hopefully, I'd never see him again. "A few men have taken an interest in me. If I were wearing a ring, that probably wouldn't happen."

Hades digested that confession, his jaw shifting as his teeth ground together. "I'll get one today. How about that?"

I nodded. "Thank you."

He sighed before he looked at the paperwork. "At the meeting tomorrow—"

"Aren't you going to ask me what kind of ring I want?"

His eyes turned hostile. "What did I just say about interrupting me?"

"Let's finish our conversation first."

"Why don't you just spit everything out so we can move on, alright? If you take this long to get your point across, imagine how you're going to handle the board members and everyone else at this hotel. Get to the goddamn point and be concise." His hand formed a fist, and he set it on the desk. His brown eyes were steaming like hot coffee, but he didn't undress me the way Maddox did. He was attracted to me, but he wasn't creepy about it. He was an asshole, but he didn't cross the line.

"I want a princess cut ring—white gold."

"Got it."

"But I don't want anything too fancy. I prefer simple things."

"I'm buying you the biggest diamond I can find."

"But I don't want that—"

"You'll be my wife, so you'll need to look like my wife. All people will have to do is look at your left hand and know you're married to a very powerful man. That's exactly what you want, right? To look the part?"

"Hades, this is the ring I'm going to be wearing for the rest of my life. I want to love it."

He sighed quietly as his fist relaxed. He looked away for a moment, wrestling with his thoughts before he looked at me again. "Alright."

"Thank you."

"We'll pick one out after work. That way, you'll get exactly what you want."

THIS WAS SUPER WEIRD.

I was in the passenger seat of his car as we drove to the jewelry store. It was a different car from the last one he'd had, an updated model with the same blacked-out windows. The paint job looked like the deep recesses of space had been plastered across the surface.

Music played through the speakers, drowning out the silence and replacing the conversation we weren't having.

I looked out the window and tried to pretend I was somewhere else.

He didn't try to make small talk either. He'd never had much to say, even when things were good between us, and now he was cold like frostbite—the kind of cold that could make your skin turn black.

And soon...he would be my husband.

He parked at the curb, and we entered the store. The door was locked behind us, so we could have all the privacy we wanted. The owner shook hands with Hades. "Congratulations, sir. Now comes the hard part...finding a diamond as beautiful as your future wife."

Hades gave a slight nod. "Thank you, Emilio."

I looked through the glass cases and eyed the sparkling diamonds. They were all beautiful, and I'd be lucky to wear any of them. I moved to the princess cut diamonds and found a simple one I liked. With a large diamond in the center and smaller ones along the band, it was exactly what I wanted. Not too big, not too flashy. "Can I try it on?"

Emilio pulled it out of the case and slipped it onto my left hand. "Perfect fit."

I gazed at my left hand and admired the way the diamonds caught the light. Beautiful rainbows illuminated my gaze because the clarity was phenomenal. There was no price tag listed, so I had no idea how much it cost...not that it mattered to Hades.

Emilio turned to Hades. "She's in love, sir."

Hades came to my side and looked at my left hand. "Is that the one you want?"

"Yes...if that's okay." I knew he preferred the biggest diamond in the display case, but bigger wasn't always better. At least not to me. I started to slide it off my finger.

Hades grabbed my hand and steadied me. It was the first time he'd touched me in years. I recognized the familiar heat of his body, felt the tremor as his skin touched mine. It was an authoritative grab. His hold suddenly loosened. "Leave it on." He let me go and pulled out his wallet. A black credit card was put on the counter, plain with nothing on the front.

Emilio took it. "Thank you, sir."

"How much is it?" I asked, feeling the extra weight on my left hand. I'd never worn jewelry, so it felt odd to have something squeeze my finger, to feel something weigh me down with commitment.

"Doesn't matter. I could buy this store and everything in it if I wanted to."

"I just thought I could—"

"No." He would never take my money. It seemed pointless to even ask.

He got his card back and slipped it into his wallet. Then we walked back to his car. "I never want to see you without that ring. You understand me?" He opened the passenger door so I could get inside. "That's one of my conditions."

"What does it matter?"

He cocked his head slightly. "It shows your loyalty."

"How would you feel if I made the same demand of you?"

He continued to hold the door, his body rigid as he stared at me in silence. "When I put on that ring, I'm never going to take it off. That's fidelity. That's loyalty. That's commitment. I shouldn't even have to explain that to you."

INSTEAD OF DRIVING ME HOME, he parked in front of a restaurant.

We'd been in the car for five minutes not speaking, and now I became even more tense when I realized he wanted to prolong our time together. I remembered how comfortable I used to be with him, like I could say anything without thinking twice about it, like I could tell him how much I wanted him and he'd never make me feel stupid about it.

But all of that was gone. "It's been a long day. How about we just call it a night?"

He ignored what I said and got out of the car.

I was hungry, so the idea of getting some actual food didn't sound bad. I just didn't like the company.

We took a seat in the restaurant, ordered a bottle of wine and our entrees, and then returned to the uncomfortable parameters of our relationship. There was resentment from both of us, anger about the past, but there was also mutual need.

He basked in the discomfort, practically thrived on it. He stared at me with his hands on the table, occasionally drinking his white wine, but still never taking his eyes off me. The heat was in his gaze, like he meant what he said when he told me he wanted to fuck me. But there was also subtle anger there, like he would always hate me for walking out on him. He'd asked me to spend our lives together...and I couldn't get away from him fast enough. It was humiliating, but it was also entirely his fault.

It was hard to look at him when he wore that expression of perpetual rage. He had such a handsome face, but that dark tint around his presence always made him slightly formidable. He'd come into my life at various stages, and I realized it'd been almost ten years since we'd first met. The more he aged, the sexier he became. Now he was thirty-one...and in better shape than he'd ever been.

I kept drinking. This dinner had to end sometime.

He still didn't talk, as if he expected me to do all the work.

In situations like these, it seemed like marrying him was a bad idea. How could we ever be compatible? But when I considered my other options, I knew he was the best I would ever find.

I looked at my ring, watching it sparkle even though there was low lighting in the restaurant. It was a beautiful ring, given to me by a beautiful man, but I still felt so empty inside.

When I looked at him, he still wore the same coldness. "Why are we here if you're just going to glare at me?"

"Not glaring."

"You definitely aren't smiling."

"I don't smile."

It only happened on the rarest occasions. I think I'd seen it happen twice. "Well, is there something you want to talk about?"

"Our marriage."

"That wasn't clear...since we've been sitting in silence for twenty minutes."

"You know I'm not much of a talker."

I decided to play his game instead of letting the discomfort fester. "Alright...where should we start?"

"You and your mother will move in with me. My place has enough space for all three of us, and it's much more secure than yours."

"And what will we do with ours? It's been in our family for decades."

He shrugged. "Doesn't matter to me."

"Why don't you move in with us?"

"No." He didn't give an explanation.

"You won't even consider it?"

He took a drink then gave the same answer. "No."

Asshole. "Fine."

"If you're going to be my wife, I expect you to behave a certain way—"

"I told you I wouldn't submit to orders. Don't expect me to do anything. I'll do whatever the hell I want, alright?" My mother was an obedient wife, but that wasn't me.

His eyes burned like frostbite. "Interrupt me again and see what happens."

"Did you just threaten me?"

"Yes." He held my gaze without blinking. "If you'd allowed me to finish, you would have heard me explain that you're marrying a powerful drug dealer. That means you need to be aware of your surroundings at all times and allow me to do my job to protect you. No late-night walks. No solo trips to the grocery store. Nothing like that whatsoever."

"So, I'm a prisoner now?"

"You can do whatever you want. Just do it right."

This felt like an agreement between two lawyers, not partners or friends. "When are you going to be kind to me?"

"Have I ever been kind?"

"Yes...you used to be."

"That was before you betrayed me."

"That wasn't a betrayal—"

"It'll take time for us to move past it. Don't expect it to happen overnight. I want to marry you, but that doesn't mean I don't resent you for what you did to me. It doesn't mean I've forgiven you. It doesn't mean I'm going to sit here and pretend it never happened. But as time passes, our relationship will grow. We will be partners. We will be loyal to each other. Maybe we'll even be friends. But you'll have to be patient."

At least he had an open mind about it.

"Let's talk about kids."

I stared at my wine for a few seconds before I lifted my gaze to meet his. "That seems premature."

"I have no idea when you intend to start a family. Enlighten me."

"I don't know...maybe in two years."

He gave a slight nod.

"You have no opinion about that?"

"No."

"Do you ever want kids?"

"I told you years ago that I did. I'll be thirty-three by that time, which is a good age because I don't want to be ancient when my sons are grown men."

"Sons?" I asked, my eyebrow raised. "How many kids are we having?"

"Two. Is that how many you want?"

"Actually, yes. But why do you assume they'll be boys?"

He stared at me for a long time, his eyes unblinking and his chest stationary. The answer he gave was a direct contradiction to the length of his pause. "Just do."

"Are you one of those men who would be disappointed if you had a girl?"

"No. I don't have a preference, honestly."

"Seems like you do."

"It's just a prediction."

Our food arrived, but my appetite had disappeared. All of this felt so real, that this man would really be my husband, that I might be buried next to him someday, our corpses rotting until we were nothing but skeletons. "I want to keep my last name."

He stilled at the request, about to take a bite of his dinner but having a sudden change of heart. "That's funny." He took a drink of his wine, washing away his bitterness. "No."

"No?" I asked. "Taking a man's name is so archaic—"

"The answer is no. Take my name, or don't marry me at all."

Damn. "Then a hyphen."

"No."

"You won't even compromise?"

"My last name will protect you more than a bulletproof vest. Wear it like armor. And my sons won't be using a fucking hyphen."

I shouldn't have expected anything else. "I feel like I'm the one making all the compromises…"

"Because I'm the one doing you a favor."

"Oh, really?" I spat.

"Most men would treat you like a dog. Trust me on that. You know I never would."

After meeting Maddox, I believed him, but I still wasn't happy.

"And I have compromised."

"No, you haven't."

"You asked me to be faithful. That's a big sacrifice to make. I won't sneak around behind your back and do my best to keep it a secret. I'm a man of my word, and if you want to be my only, I'll give it to you. That's a lot to ask of a man like me."

I poked my pasta with my fork. "Well…have fun fucking as many women as possible before that day arrives."

He stopped eating his food altogether. "I haven't been with anyone since your mother asked me to marry you."

"Why?"

"It feels wrong."

He didn't owe me anything, so it was a sweet gesture. "I haven't been with anyone either..." I had been in too foul a mood to take a man home, and since I would be sleeping with someone else very soon, it seemed strange.

"Then are you still going to make me wait?"

I could feel his heated stare across the table, feel the copious amounts of desire leak through his skin. I was the target he wanted to claim, the woman he wanted to dominate. "Is this revenge? Do you want to marry me because I said no? Do you want me so you could lose that battle but win the war? Is this some toxic masculinity bullshit?"

He continued to stare at me. "Does it matter?"

"It does to me."

He leaned forward, lowering his voice so no one could eavesdrop on the conversation. "I want to fuck you. I want to own you. And I want the world to know I fuck you and own you. That's all." He leaned back and grabbed his glass of wine again.

It was a power play. If I'd said yes to him in the first place, my marriage would be much better. He would be kind, affectionate, and respectful. But I took the wrong path, and even though I ended up in the same place, this time...I got the monster.

4

HADES

I walked with her up the stairs to her front door. She was in a black dress with matching pumps, sterile in her work attire but still sexy in anything she wore. Her ass shook from side to side as she walked, her long legs carrying her like a queen without a crown. She occasionally brushed her hair behind her shoulder with her fingertips, showing her fair cheeks and painted lips.

I didn't want to wait.

She stopped at the large mahogany doors and faced me. "Goodnight."

"Thought I'd say hello to your mother."

"You can say hello when we move in together." She grabbed the handle to open the door.

I wanted to grab her and keep her close, but I refrained from touching her. "You never answered my question."

She halted and turned back to me, still significantly shorter than me despite her formidable heels. Her long brown hair was in wavy curls, and her thick eyelashes were curled with dark mascara. Even after a full day at the office, she looked just as fresh as she did in the morning. "What question?"

"Are you going to make me wait until our wedding night?" It'd only been a week since she'd become my fiancée and my celibacy had begun, but it was already destroying me. I was a man who needed sex on a regular basis, and while I could get laid whenever I wanted, I preferred to wait for the best pussy I'd ever had. If I was going to screw someone, there was only one woman I had in mind.

She looked away when she couldn't handle the desire in my eyes. "Yes." She opened the door.

I swallowed the disappointment, fought the demon living inside me. Sitting across from her over dinner was torture because I wanted her so much, wanted to fist that hair and take her roughly. I wanted those hot, passionate nights, when she grabbed me by the front of the shirt and kissed me deeply. I didn't want any more cheap one-night stands. I didn't want a stranger in my bed.

I wanted the woman I loved.

If only I could tell her that. If I did, it would just chase her off again.

I was committing myself to the torture the gypsy promised me, but I'd rather be tortured every day with her than be miserable without her.

She stepped inside and shut the door.

Just when I turned away, it opened again.

"Hades, please come inside." Maria grabbed my arm and

ushered me into the entryway. "Please excuse my daughter. I raised her to have better manners, but she never listens to anything I say."

Sofia stood with her arms over her chest, visibly annoyed by her mother's intervention.

"She does," I said. "She's just stubborn." I kissed Maria on the cheek. "How are you holding up, Maria?"

"I've been better," she said with a sigh. "But I'm thrilled by this gorgeous ring you gave Sofia." She grabbed her daughter's left hand and examined the diamonds. "Perfect clarity...and the perfect size for her slender hand."

Sofia kept up her attitude.

Maria turned back to me. "I spoke with the manager of the hotel, and the ballroom is free in two weeks. How do you feel about getting married on such short notice?"

"Two weeks?" Sofia asked incredulously. "That's way too soon—"

"I'd marry her tomorrow if there was availability." I looked at Sofia as I said those words. She would be mine soon, whether it was in a few weeks or a couple months. I already owned her in so many ways.

"That's so sweet," Maria said. "So, we'll do two weeks."

"How am I going to get a dress by then?" Sofia asked. "Or drop a few pounds?"

I couldn't control the chuckle that escaped my lips. She really had no idea just how perfect every damn curve was.

"I can get any designer you want to create your dress," Maria said. "I've already talked to the florist and the caterer. We can pull this together with no hiccups at all. It'll still be the wedding of the year."

The sooner I married her, the sooner I could peel off her dress and fuck her.

Jesus Christ, I couldn't wait. A thrill ran down my spine just thinking about it.

Sofia looked horrified. "This is happening too fast. I literally just got my ring today."

"Because you wanted one," I reminded her. "The sooner you're my wife, the sooner you'll get to run that hotel exactly how you want. The sooner we'll get everything we want. This is a good thing."

Maria turned to Sofia. "He's right. We'll get to work on your dress tomorrow."

Sofia stopped arguing, but she ran her hand down her cheek as she struggled in silence.

I turned to her mother. "Sofia and I agreed to live together at my place in the city. I would love it if you accompanied us. The entire second floor is unused, and my staff are the best."

"Wow...that's such a generous offer." Maria rested her hand against her chest, genuinely surprised I would extend that invitation. She glanced at her daughter then turned back to me. "I'd love to, but you two should have some privacy, especially as newlyweds."

We would be doing a lot of fucking. "I insist." Of course I didn't want my mother-in-law in the house. I was marrying Sofia—and that was the only part of the package I wanted. Now I had another person to be responsible for. But since it was important to Sofia, who was important to me, I caved.

And she said I didn't compromise...

"Well, then I would love to," Maria said. "It'll be nice to see my daughter often and be there for my grandchildren. That's very kind of you, Hades. I'm so glad my daughter chose a good husband."

I looked at Sofia, an arrogant grin on my face.

She refused to look at me.

She could look away all she wanted, but when she was my wife, she'd look me in the eye every night I fucked her.

"I should get going. It was nice to see you." I kissed Maria on the cheek then turned to the door.

"Sofia, aren't you going to walk your fiancé out?" Maria asked, audibly embarrassed by her daughter's coldness.

Sofia was so stubborn, she still refused to look at me. "He's a strong man, Mama. He doesn't need me."

Maria brushed off the tension and walked me outside. "I'm sorry about her. She's just—"

"Don't apologize. I like her exactly how she is." I gave her a gentle pat on the arm.

"I'm lucky you're smitten with my daughter's looks. It'd be impossible to get anyone to marry her without her beauty."

I wanted her for more than just her appearance. "That's not the only reason I want her. Your daughter is smart, strong, and loyal. She's just a little rough around the edges. I am too...and I think that's why we go together so well."

A WEEK HAD PASSED, and Helena prepared the house for my new guests. Maria would get a guest bedroom on the second floor, private quarters that were luxurious and spacious. Sofia would be sharing my bedroom, so I made space in my closet and my bathroom. Knowing her, she would probably try to get her own bedroom.

Not gonna happen.

Damien walked inside and glanced at the pile of my clothes I was donating. "You're just going to throw these out?"

"I have too many suits."

"Yeah, but these are, like, thousands of dollars each."

I shrugged. "It'll do someone else some good." I took a seat at the table. "I know Sofia has a lot of clothes, so I need to make room for her."

He sank into the chair across from me. "Haven't changed your mind, then?"

I shook my head.

"And I can't talk you out of it?"

I shook my head again. "Even if I agreed with everything you said, if she marries someone else, they'll treat her like shit. And I can't allow that to happen. I wouldn't be able to sleep at night knowing some asshole is talking to her like a dog."

Damien still looked disappointed. "Alright...then I'll let it go."

"Good. Because I want you to be my best man."

He smiled. "I figured. You didn't need to ask."

I didn't have family. I didn't have any friends either. Damien was all I had.

"When's the show?"

"Saturday."

"As in, a week from today? Is she pregnant or something?"

I wish. "No. Her mother is impatient."

"And how does Sofia feel about it?"

"She's pissed. But she's always pissed, so I don't notice anything new."

He chuckled. "We've been through some crazy shit together. Survived against the odds. But the most detrimental thing that ever happened to you was falling in love with the wrong woman. I hope the same thing doesn't happen to me..."

"She's not the wrong woman. She's exactly the person I was supposed to fall in love with...that's why the universe sent her to me. She's the one woman I can't resist, so she's the best person to torture me. God knows how to punish sinners."

"You really think God is doing this to you?"

"After all the shit I've done? Yes."

Damien stared at me for a while. "You're not the evilest man in the world."

If only he knew. "I've done a lot of shit you don't know about. And if you knew...you would know I deserved this."

WHEN I STEPPED into the hallway, she was in front of me. Her hair was in a high ponytail, and she wore snug black jeans that showed the perfect heart shape of her ass.

In just a few days, that ass would be mine.

She wore a skintight black blouse with pumps, and she looked through papers as she walked back to her office.

I took my time walking down the hallway—enjoying the view.

I stepped into her office and saw her sit behind her desk, her chin tilted down as she read. She hadn't noticed me yet, so her face was tight in a focused expression. No matter what mood she was in, she was beautiful, but she looked particularly erotic right now. With red lipstick on her mouth and gold earrings in her lobes, she looked like a model rather than a manager.

And her engagement ring was the sexiest thing of all.

It was a leash made out of diamonds.

I cleared my throat as I entered the room.

She looked up, and instantly, her guard was up. She was uneasy around me, still the recipient of my resentment. Her timid nature was synonymous with guilt. She knew her rejection of me had been wrong, that she was responsible for our untimely demise. She said she'd never wanted it, but I believed that was a lie. She just couldn't bring herself to trust anyone.

I was the one person in the world she could actually trust.

I sat in the chair facing her desk. "I'll notify the board of our nuptials this afternoon."

"Why? They don't give a damn."

"Yes, they do. You won't have any problems with them from here on out."

"You're just going to snap your fingers and make them respect me?" she asked incredulously.

"No. I don't need to snap my fingers."

She was probably impressed, but she chose not to show it. She sighed like my statement was ridiculous rather than a spot-on prediction of the future. "You came all the way here to tell me that?"

"We're getting married in five days. We still have things to talk about."

"Like?"

"Money."

"I have my own money, and you have yours," she said. "I don't want your assets."

No surprise there. "My lawyer has drafted a legal agreement. What's yours is yours. What's mine is mine."

"Good."

"But you will have access to all my accounts, and you're welcome to spend any of it."

She folded her arms on the desk. "I don't need your money."

"Never said you did. But what's mine is yours."

"Why are you giving it to me?" she blurted. "Now that the hotel is mine—"

"Ours."

She couldn't bring herself to repeat the word. "I have all the money I need."

"You're my wife. I want you to have everything that I have. I'm completely transparent with you."

Her venom started to fade away. "I don't understand…"

"We have our differences, but we're a team. We need to act like it." I would always resent her for what she did to me, but it was time to leave the past behind us. If I wanted any chance to have something real with her, I needed to put all my cards on the table. "This isn't just a marriage. It's a partnership. Your success is my success, and that's a two-way street. You will be the mother of my children. I want you to have all my power in your hands to do with whatever you want."

For the first time, she was speechless. She stared at me like she had no idea what to say. "I still don't want your money, but I appreciate the gesture. And for that, I'll do the same with you."

"That wasn't my angle. Keep your money. I'm your husband. I'll provide for you and protect you." Her assets were marginal compared to mine. I wouldn't even notice they were there. She probably had no understanding of just how rich I really was. If she knew, she'd probably lose her marbles. "I want to start moving your stuff over. My men will come back and collect whatever you want to bring."

Her eyes dropped to the surface of her desk. Her expression was easy to read; she was dreading this, like she'd made a deal with the devil. "Alright."

"Do you want to go on a honeymoon?"

"No. I have too much work to do."

We could have our honeymoon in the bedroom.

She lifted her gaze again. "I've known you for years, but I feel like I don't know you at all."

"What do you want to know?" I'd never discouraged her from asking questions. I'd been an open book from day one. But she'd wanted our relationship to be nothing but sex, so all the deep conversations lovers usually had were missing. She tried to keep our relationship sterile so I would never mean anything to her... but she ended up with me anyway. It was ironic.

"I don't know where to start."

"Have dinner with me tonight. We'll talk then." I couldn't wait until she was mine, until I could rip off her clothes and take her as my wife. Fantasies played in my mind on a nightly basis, dreams so vivid I could actually feel her pussy around my dick. Other women felt like trolls compared to the woman I actually wanted. I was committed to a woman I wasn't even fucking, and it caused me to lose my mind.

Maybe dinner and some wine would loosen her up, would get her to drop her walls and let me in. Maybe she wouldn't make me wait until our wedding night. Maybe she'd let me have her sooner.

It was the longest I'd gone without having sex...so I was hard anytime I was around her.

She took her time before she answered. "Alright."

I ALWAYS HAD shit to do, so I walked into the meeting late.

Members of the board were talking to each other quietly even though Sofia stood at the front, going over different ideas she had for the hotel. The energy in the room was chaotic, with people's thoughts in different places. It had a casual feel—like no one was taking it seriously.

Sofia continued to do her best, even though only two men were paying attention. "Most of our restaurants are outdated and designed to attract an older clientele. I think we need to breathe new life into this place, possibly turning the main bar into a hipper space. There're a lot of locals who would love a new hangout spot."

One man made notes on his paper, while Charles and Tim spoke about golfing this weekend. It wasn't Sofia's fault this was happening. For several decades, they'd been dealing with authoritative men, and Sofia was a poor substitute in their eyes. She belonged at home, taking care of the cooking and cleaning.

Sofia had never had a chance to be successful...not on her own.

"Charles." I stopped at the head of the table, making my presence known. "Tim." I stared at them both for a few seconds, my irritated tone conveying my displeasure at the situation. "Gentlemen, maybe you haven't heard the news yet, but Sofia has agreed to be my wife. After this Saturday, you will address her as Mrs. Lombardi."

Sofia didn't cop an attitude like she normally would.

"We had no idea," Charles said. "Congratulations."

I buttoned the front of my jacket. "Thank you."

"Does that mean you'll be running the hotel from now on?" Tim asked, unable to mask his eagerness.

"No. My fiancée can do a much better job than I ever could." All she wanted was her family's legacy, to take pride in her work. Her gender had made that impossible, but that was all about to change. "If anyone has a problem with that, I suggest you sell your stake in the company and excuse yourself. Otherwise, your family can inherit your share instead. Do we have an understanding, gentlemen?" They knew exactly what I was capable of, and death threats weren't handed out as jokes. I'd killed men for much less. I scanned the faces of every single one of them, seeing them go rigid as my threat seeped deep into their bones. "I asked you a question."

"Yes," Charles barked.

Tim straightened in his chair and pivoted his body toward Sofia.

One by one, they took their attention off me and focused on my fiancée at the front. With eager eyes, they waited for her to continue her presentation.

I crossed my arms over my chest and looked at the beautiful woman standing at the front, so sexy in her jeans and blouse that it was hard to take her seriously. How could a woman so stunning be so intelligent? Be a strong leader for a company as big as this? But she could. I had no doubt about it.

Now Sofia could witness my influence firsthand, how I could step into a room and make shit happen. If she had cold feet about marrying me, I was sure those doubts disappeared. I could give her exactly what she wanted.

She gave me a slight nod then turned back to what she'd been saying before I'd stepped inside.

Like I'd never been there at all, I walked out.

I SAT on the balcony and watched the sunset. A bottle of wine sat in the ice bucket, and there was a single red rose in the small vase in the center of the table. I was in a black t-shirt and jeans, my muscular arms stretching the fabric. She liked me in a suit, but I knew she preferred this dressed-down look, where my ripped physique was truly noticeable. If it weren't completely inappropriate, I would be naked.

Helena let Sofia into the bedroom a moment later.

She was in jean shorts and a black tank top, choosing to go casual too. At work, she dressed more formally, but this look was much sexier. The shorts went all the way up to her thighs, showing off her sculpted muscles and her tanned skin. Her curled hair hung down her shoulders, and her black tank top showed off her nice cleavage and her flat stomach.

Fuck. I could picture her in just that tank top, getting fucked with her ankles locked around my waist.

She stepped onto the balcony, her posture rigid like she was recalling the last time she'd been there. She probably noticed the bed had been changed out and that some of the furniture in the room had been replaced. She looked at the splashes of color in the sky before she took a seat.

I didn't get up and greet her, and I didn't make small talk either. It was nice that we didn't have to do that, that we could survive the heated silence without getting unnerved by it. I opened the wine and poured two glasses right before Helena came outside and dropped off the appetizers.

When she left, Sofia spoke. "I'm glad Helena is still here."

"I'll never let her go."

"I guess it's something for me to look forward to..."

Among other things.

She placed a few pieces of bruschetta on her plate before she took a small bite, the bread crunching under her small teeth. She washed it down with a sip of wine.

Hypnotized, I stared at the beautiful woman across from me, feeling the desperation roar inside my chest. I'd never been infatuated with a woman like this, so obsessed that I could barely think straight. I'd been with beautiful women all around the world, but none of them compared to Sofia Romano. Her perfect skin, her full lips, that dark hair...I wanted all of it. I'd wanted her since the moment I saw her, and I never stopped.

When she grew uncomfortable by my stare, she looked away. "Thank you for what you did today. I wish I could handle it all on my own, but you definitely made my life a lot easier."

"I'll fix all your problems. That's my job."

"But I wish it weren't your job..." Her eyes filled with self-loathing, like she'd lost self-respect because she couldn't control those assholes.

"It's not you, Sofia. It's just the way men are."

"If only that weren't true..."

"It doesn't matter now. They'll be easy to work with from now on."

"Couldn't I just get rid of them?" she asked. "I hate having to answer to someone. I want to do what I want without needing approval."

"Since they invested in the company, you could only accomplish that by buying them out."

"Okay...could I do that?"

"Yes. But it'd cost you a lot of money."

Her gaze drifted away as she considered it. "I hope someday I can make that happen. I could run that place entirely on my own and cut ties with all the weasels my family has associated with."

That was unwise. Those relationships had been built over decades. It'd be stupid to mess with the structure, to provoke the underworld. "The hotel has been successful for several decades. I wouldn't change anything if you want it to remain successful."

She took another bite of her bruschetta. She seemed a lot calmer around me, probably because I'd done her a huge favor without her even having to ask me. I'd proven my worth to her, and now she realized how useful I could be.

I could be really useful in the bedroom too...which she already knew. "Is your mother going to give you away?" I couldn't wait to see her in her wedding dress, to see how beautiful she was as she glided toward me. I wanted the world to be envious of me, to watch the most stunning woman in the world agree to be my wife.

"Yes." Her eyes moved back to mine. "So...most of my stuff is already here."

"Helena hung up your clothes."

She glanced through the open doors even though the closet wasn't visible. "Will I be getting my own room?"

Silence was my answer.

"You expect me to sleep in here every night?"

"I expect you to do other things here every night."

She shifted her gaze away once more. "I think I need my own space...at least sometimes."

"No. We're husband and wife. We sleep together."

"What happened to compromise?"

"Your compromises push us apart. Give me a constructive compromise, and I'll consider it." She wanted to keep her last name. She wanted to sleep in different rooms. "I know you'll never love me, but I command your loyalty, commitment, and friendship. I need to trust you the way I trust Damien. You need to feel the same way about me. So, let me be your husband. Stop trying to half-ass this."

"I'm not. It's just a big change and—"

"Get over it." My coldness froze the summer air around us. "On Saturday night, you will be my wife. You will behave like my wife. You will come to *our* home, and you will fuck me like my wife."

She didn't appreciate what I said, but she didn't argue with me either. "This is exactly what I didn't want...to be owned by someone."

"That's too bad. I own you. But trust me, you're going to like it." My goal had been to get between her legs tonight. Instead, I was pissing her off and pushing her away. I'd always been a dick, but right now wasn't the best time to behave that way.

She turned her view to the city, which had become darker with every passing minute. Soon, only the nighttime would surround us.

Helena set dinner in front of us before she walked away.

Sofia hardly looked at her food. "You said you would tell me about yourself."

I took a long drink of my wine. "What do you want to know?"

"You've never told me about your family."

"Not much to tell."

She picked up her fork and took a few bites, but I suspected she was just doing it to be polite. Our conversation made her sick, made her angry at me, but also forced her to respect me at the same time. A woman like her wouldn't want to marry a gentleman. She needed a monster. "Are your parents still alive?"

Even after all these years, it was still difficult for me to talk about. I'd be honest with her because this would be the deepest relationship I would ever have with anyone. She would be my wife, be closer to me than even Damien was. "My mother is. My father is gone."

"I'm sorry about your father," she said. "It's rough..."

"Yeah." I felt sick to my stomach just thinking about it. My breathing increased, and I could feel my pulse in my neck.

"Are you close with your mother?"

"No." My fingers rested against my bottom lip as I looked across the city, admiring the lights from the church.

"May I ask why?"

"Because she doesn't remember me."

Sofia stiffened in her chair, her eyes slowly showing understanding. "I'm sorry."

"She's in a home in town. I stopped visiting her because it felt pointless."

"Jesus…" She set down her fork. "That's terrible, Hades."

"Hades isn't my real name." Confessions spilled out of my mouth without restraint. "But I'd rather not say what my real name is."

"Why?"

"That's not who I am anymore."

She left it alone. "Well…if you ever change your mind, I'd like to know."

I probably wouldn't.

"How old were you when your father passed away?"

"Twenty-six."

"At least you had a long time with him. Were you close?"

"No. Not at all."

"Oh…" Dinner was abandoned because our conversation took hold of everything. "I can tell this makes you really uncomfortable, so we don't have to talk about it if you don't want to. You can share as much or as little with me as you want. It doesn't change my decision to marry you."

"It might."

Her green eyes showed fear because she took me seriously.

"I killed him." I couldn't meet her gaze as I confessed my sins, as I told her I'd killed my own flesh and blood. I'd aimed right between his eyes and pulled the trigger. It had to be done...but it'd haunted me ever since.

She was speechless. What else could she be?

"I have an older brother. We don't speak." Mentioning my brother seemed anticlimactic after what I'd said about my father.

She was still quiet, clearly in shock. "Why would you do that?"

"I didn't have a choice."

"What does that mean?" she whispered.

I'd invited her over in the hope of rekindling our physical relationship. Obviously, that wasn't going to happen at this point. I'd have to wait until Saturday. "Ever since I was young, my father has been a human trafficker. He captured vulnerable girls from all over the world and forced them to work in whorehouses. Sometimes he sold them to men who turned them into slaves. It wasn't until I was much older that I understood what he was doing."

Her hand covered her mouth.

"When I realized what he was doing, I asked him to stop. He refused. I turned my cheek for the longest time until he took a woman I knew. I confronted him, asked him again to stop, and when he didn't...I shot him." I took a deep breath before I continued. "I thought that ended the organization altogether, but my brother picked up the pieces. He runs the operation to this day—and he hates me for what I did. And to be honest...I hate myself for what I did." I stared at the ground because the guilt had been eating me alive for the last five years. I did what I thought was right, but it'd been haunting me ever since.

I killed my own father.

If he were another man, I wouldn't have felt bad about it. But I'd committed a deadly sin. The operation was still running, so the murder didn't make a difference. I already had my father's blood on my hands; I couldn't stand holding my brother's too. "Damien is the only family I have. He's the only friend I have. I've done a lot of other terrible things in my life, but that's definitely the worst thing I've ever done. So...now you know me."

THERE WASN'T MUCH TALKING after that, especially since she didn't ask any more personal questions. She seemed to have had enough of me. Her dinner was untouched, and the candle in the center of the table eventually burned out. We sat together in the darkness.

There were times when I wanted to justify my actions, but I knew it didn't make a difference. I killed my own flesh and blood, the man who raised me, who took care of me until I became an adult. We disagreed on a lot of things, and I should have just let it be. That night still tortured me.

And I wondered if that was why the universe was punishing me.

I killed my father...so I didn't deserve the love of this woman.

That was fair.

When it became late and the conversation remained stale, I got to my feet and prepared to walk her out. "I'll walk you to your car."

She stayed in the chair a moment longer, her mind elsewhere. When she pushed herself up and faced me, there was a new look in her eyes, a complex web of emotions I couldn't even begin to describe. She was clearly about to say something to me, possibly yank that ring off her finger and call the whole thing off.

But the gypsy said Sofia would marry me, so I didn't think that was likely.

"I've been trying to think of something to say for the last hour. I've still come up with nothing." Her green eyes shifted back and forth as she looked into mine, her full lips sagging in a slight frown.

"You don't need to say anything." I was a horrible human being —message received.

"But I do." She moved into me, getting closer than she'd been in a long time. Anytime she interacted with me, there was an invisible line she wouldn't cross. There were always at least three feet in between us.

Now there were nearly none.

Her hand moved to my arm, her thumb resting in the crease of my elbow. "You were trying to do the right thing, and I admire you for that. Most men wouldn't have cared about those girls, but you did. That makes me want to marry you...and not because I have to."

My heart started to race inside my chest, started to bounce against my rib cage. She was the only woman on this planet who could do that, who could change my heart rate, who could raise the temperature like she had a thermostat in her pocket. It was hard to stare at the sincerity in her gaze and not grab her by the hair and kiss her. I wanted to marry her now, to take her to bed and make her feel the same way.

"I can tell it kills you inside that you did what you had to do, but don't let it destroy you. If it were another man, you wouldn't have hesitated to kill him. Just because he's your father doesn't mean he deserved special treatment."

That decision had ruined my life, acted as a catalyst for all the other bad shit that had come after. It didn't matter how many times I confessed to a priest, I never felt vindicated for my sins. I should have found another way to end the operation. I should have kept my father alive. I should still have a relationship with my brother. I should love a woman who loved me in return. "It doesn't matter if my actions were justified. He was my father..." I was grateful my mother didn't have her mind long enough to know what I did.

"What he did was way worse than what you did."

"He didn't kill anyone."

She squeezed my arm. "There are worse things than dying." Her fingers slowly released me, and she pulled away. "You and I have our differences. I've chosen to stay in the dark in regard to your criminal affairs. But this makes me see you with new eyes... makes me proud to call you my husband."

I closed my eyes because I didn't deserve her praise. "It's still going on..."

"But you did everything you could to stop it."

"I killed someone, and it made no difference at all. Don't misunderstand me—I want your praise. I want you to take off all your clothes and kiss me to make me forget. But I don't deserve it. What I did was unforgivable, and I've been punished for it ever since."

"By whom?"

I looked into her eyes and almost considered telling her the truth, telling her that all of this was preordained. Neither one of us had any say in the future. I didn't know why her future had to be intertwined with mine, why she couldn't fall in love with someone and get married. Why did she have to be a pawn in my punishment? Or was being unconditionally loved by a man who would die to protect her a good thing? "By me."

"How do you feel?"

I sat in the chair with a scotch in my hand. The liquor killed the nerves, but that wasn't why I drank so much of it. Today was an exception. I was thrilled to be getting the woman I wanted, but I was dismayed by the price I'd paid for it.

My father's life.

This was all a sick punishment, all a twisted game for the universe.

Even if she never loved me...at least I got to love her.

Damien kept watching me. "You're ignoring me. So you must feel amazing...or feel like shit."

"I'm not sure what I feel." I set the glass on the table beside me. "It's a strange feeling to look forward to your punishment...to be addicted to the pain."

"If your pain is Sofia Romano...there are worse kinds of pain."

"True."

He pulled back his sleeve and looked at his watch. "We should get out there." We both got to our feet, and he straightened my tie before we moved to the door. "You know, it's a shame there was no bachelor party. If I ever get married, I'm not gonna pussy out like you did."

"You say that now…" Sofia didn't give a damn if I went to a strip club. She didn't care if I fucked someone the night before our wedding. But I found it dirty, especially after the moment we'd had on my balcony. I was in this fully, loyal to the end.

We moved up the rows until we stood at the front of the room, the glass windows behind us. A thousand people were there, friends and acquaintances. Sofia had a large extended family, and I did business with a lot of people.

Once everyone was seated, the music began.

The wedding party was small, so only a flower girl came down the aisle along with a few bridesmaids. Then the wedding march began, and everyone rose to their feet. Instead of picking the traditional wedding march, Sofia chose a quiet symphony, something with a dreamlike quality. It fit her perfectly.

With her arm interlocked with her mother's, she glided toward me like an angel without wings. Her tight dress highlighted her hourglass frame, and the small veil in front of her face made her so traditionally beautiful. The dress was low-cut in the front, showing her porcelain skin and a bit of her womanly chest. The long train dragged behind her, brushing up against the rose petals that had been sprinkled earlier.

Damien leaned into my ear and whistled quietly. "Damn. I think I get it now."

My eyes never moved from her face, never moved from her outstanding beauty. She was divine, commanding the envy of every single person in that room. The young men wanted to be her lover. The women wanted to look like her. Everyone wanted something...because she was so magnetic.

And now she was mine.

When her mother arrived, she placed Sofia's hand in mine.

I took an involuntary breath as the static moved through my veins. My fingers closed around hers because I never wanted to let her go. Now that I had her, I wanted to bust my ass so she would never leave.

I wanted her to love me...somehow.

I lifted the small veil from her face and looked at her, stared at her in a paralyzed state. And to my joy, she smiled at me.

And it was fucking perfect.

I took her hands in mine.

Then married the woman I loved.

SOFIA

HADES TOOK MY HAND AND GUIDED ME INTO THE CENTER OF THE room. Our song played overhead, and he wrapped his arm around my waist and held my hand as we danced back and forth, slowly rocking, looking at each other and forgetting everyone else in the room existed.

"It's ironic. I said no, but I married you anyway."

His eyes didn't narrow in anger. They stayed neutral, that dreamy look in his eyes. "It's not ironic. It happened exactly the way it was supposed to happen." His hand gripped the fabric of my dress, and he pulled us tighter together, our foreheads touching.

The music continued to play, and we swayed together, everyone watching us while they drank champagne and dined. Maybe everyone thought we were in love. Maybe they knew it was just an arranged marriage.

Hades was handsome in his wedding suit, with a freshly shaven face and beautiful brown eyes. He kept staring at me like I was the sexiest thing in the world. He gripped me like he didn't want anyone to steal me away from him. Despite our differences and the times he annoyed me, I knew he would be a good man to me. I knew he would be honest with me. That he would protect me. And he would give me beautiful children. Come on, look at him. If I had to be forced to marry someone...there were definitely worse options.

"What are you thinking about?" he whispered, his eyes trained on me the entire time.

"You."

"And?"

"I've only been married to you for a few hours...and it's not so bad."

IT WAS SO warm in the ballroom that I went outside to feel the cool air. It was almost midnight, and most people had already left. Hades got tied up making small talk with the people he knew, probably talking about business...because he never stopped talking about business.

I let the air lick away my sweat, let the quietness of the night slow my racing heart. Another band had been added to my wedding finger, and I was officially a married woman. Sofia Lombardi...it had a nice ring to it.

I walked across the patio and stared at the spot where Hades and I had first spoken. A cigarette had been in my mouth, and I'd forced a bad girl attitude I couldn't pull off. I'd laid eyes on Hades and wouldn't let him go until I had a piece of him. Then we fucked right against the wall years later.

And now I'd married him.

This man had been haunting me for a long time; I didn't realize it until now.

Hands wrapped around my waist and a hard chest pressed against my back. His familiar cologne enveloped me, smothered me with his smell. His arms squeezed my frame, reminding me I was his.

His face rested against my neck, and he held me close, no longer putting on a show because there were no witnesses. Now he grabbed me because he wanted to, pressed the firmness of his dick into my back so I would know what came next. "Let's go home."

HE DROVE us to his place.

I mean, our place.

With one hand on the steering wheel and the other in his lap, he drove down the quiet streets and parked in the underground garage underneath his building.

My heart started to pump harder the closer we came to our destination. I'd slept with him before so there would be no surprises, but a part of me was still afraid of what it would mean. It would consummate our union. It would bond me to him, make me permanently his. I wouldn't go home afterward like I usually did. That was my home...that was my bed.

I would never sleep with someone new again.

The engine died, and I continued to stare out the windshield, my enormous dress filling up all the free space in the car. My veil had been left behind, but I was certain my mother got it. When our children were grown, they would ask me about this night.

Would I look back on it with fondness?

Or regret?

He didn't get out of the car, sensing my trepidation. He looked forward then rubbed his fingers across his lips, his black wedding ring visible in the lights from the dashboard. He had a clean jaw, and while I preferred the shadow, he looked as handsome as ever.

The silence continued, tensions rising. Once I stepped into that house, there was no going back. That was my life.

I wanted to hold on to my independence for just a moment longer.

Hades didn't push me. Instead, he grabbed my hand and twined our fingers together before he got comfortable in the seat. He leaned back and brushed his thumb over my fingertips, comforting me with the affection he used to smother me in.

We sat there for fifteen minutes, saying nothing.

I finally released his grip and stepped out of the car.

He joined me. Together, we took the elevator to the ground floor. Helena wasn't there, and it was quiet. The main lights were on, but the kitchen sounded quiet. My mother planned to stay at our place for the weekend so we could have our privacy.

I started to slip off my heels because I didn't plan to walk up two flights of stairs in killer pumps.

Hades scooped me into his arms and carried me instead.

Without giving any sign of exertion, he took me to his bedroom on the top floor and carried me over the threshold. The door shut behind us.

We were alone.

He kicked off his shoes then loosened his tie from around his neck. He yanked it off then moved to his vest underneath. Piece by piece, he undressed himself until he was in nothing but his black boxers.

His body was different from the way I remembered him. Now he was so ripped that his muscles practically popped out of his skin. His tanned arms were covered with cords, and his muscular thighs were so cut. His chest was the best part. It was a solid piece of concrete, an indestructible wall. The grooves underneath looked like small mountains, abs of power. His bulge was visible in his underwear. He was fully erect, charged full of desire.

I turned my gaze away and tried not to stare. My eyes looked at his bed, the comforter already pulled down so we could get naked on the sheets. The second nightstand had been completely cleared so I could add my things. He picked the left side of the bed and gave me the right.

His bare feet thudded against the rug as he came for me. He approached me from behind, like a predator about to attack his prey. When he was right against me, I felt his breath fall on my bare shoulder, inhaled his scent deep into my lungs.

I was so still, I didn't breathe. I didn't know why I was so nervous, why I was on edge. I wasn't afraid of him. I knew this night would happen. I'd slept with him before and enjoyed it. I was still attracted to him...especially now that he was in even better shape.

I guess I knew how much he wanted me...and the thought scared me a little bit.

His hands moved to the back of my dress. One by one, he popped each button, working the delicate fabric as it came loose around my body. Slowly, it started to sag, started to shift down my frame. When he reached the last button, he let my dress fall to the floor on its own.

His powerful arm hooked across my chest, and he pulled me tight against him, his mouth lowering to my shoulder. His entire body flexed when he had me, as if he were about to take a bite out of my neck and suck me dry.

Instead, he kissed me...so damn hard.

He kissed me everywhere, my neck, the back of my ear, my shoulder, and then down the nape of my neck. His arm continued to grip me tightly as he practically devoured me, turned me into his next meal.

I closed my eyes and let him have me, let him claim his prize. His hot breaths fell across my skin everywhere as he worked up a sweat just kissing me. His hand groped my tits, and he yanked me hard against his chest, showing off his strength as if it weren't obvious just how powerful he was.

One hand moved to my white thong, and he pushed it over my ass, letting it slide down my legs until it reached my ankles on the floor. I could tell he dropped his boxers too when I felt his bare dick against my ass cheeks.

I felt like a prize for a king, a concubine for a count. I didn't feel like a partner or a lover. I felt like a piece of meat this animal had ripped from my bones.

When he turned me around, all of that changed.

His arm rested in the deep curve of my back, and he pulled me into him, bringing me so close that my hard nipples poked his skin. His other hand moved up my neck and into my hair, sliding through the soft curls as he pulled them away from my face. His look was still predatory and his touch possessive, but at least I saw a bit of human in him.

His thumb brushed across my bottom lip as he stared at my mouth, as he eyed me with so much lust. One of his reasons for marrying me was to fuck me. I could tell he meant that. Every single word.

He leaned in and kissed me for the first time in two years. His lips were warm and eager, and he kissed me like no time had passed at all. After the bitter way we'd left things, I was surprised he wanted to kiss me at all. I expected him to bend me over the bed and fuck me like a whore.

But he kissed me with passion, breathed deeply into my mouth before he gave me his tongue. His hand moved to my ass and squeezed one cheek as he guided me backward to the bed.

I was still rigid, but I was definitely aroused by this man. When he'd ruined our relationship, I hated him for taking away the best sex of my life, for bringing our connection to an end when we still had so much unfinished passion.

Now I had it back.

When the backs of my knees hit the frame, he pulled his lips away. "On your back." When he made the command with that heated gaze, I knew things weren't exactly the same. He warmed up to me a bit, but he still resented me for hurting him. Now he wanted to fuck me like he owned me.

The night would only end one way—so I obeyed. My back rested against the sheets, and my head found the pillow.

His heavy body moved on top of mine, and he widened my thighs with his knees. His thick arms hooked under my legs, and he spread me wide apart, his chiseled body hanging over mine with sculpted perfection.

His dick seemed bigger than I remembered. Or maybe he was just harder than he'd ever been in his life. He pushed on his shaft and pointed his drooling head at my entrance. He must have assumed I was wet because he didn't bother to moisten his dick before he slipped inside me.

He was right. I was slick.

When he felt that rush of moisture meet him, he moaned and sank all the way inside me, diving deep inside and erasing all evidence that another man had ever been there. He moved until his balls slapped against my ass.

I hadn't had a big dick like this in a long time. I hadn't felt a man stretch me so far that it seemed like my body would cave in. My breathing increased, and my nipples became so erect they actually ached.

Then he fucked me hard.

He pounded into me at a quick speed, like he couldn't slow himself down to appreciate every strike, every wet sensation. His ass worked hard to buck inside me, to dig me farther into the mattress while he fucked me with enthusiasm. "Fuck yes." He fucked me like a man who hadn't had sex in years, like I was the hottest pussy he'd ever found. He closed his eyes and clenched his jaw, enjoying it as his face began to tint.

Watching him enjoy me like I was the best he'd ever had chased away my fear, eradicated my insecurities. The past was irrelevant. Now we were just a man and a woman, enjoying the carnal sensations our bodies created. He wanted me so much, deep down into his soul and bones. His hips bucked like they had a mind of their own, and his anxious dick kept sinking deep with every thrust. The sound of his exertion filled the room as he fucked me like a teenager getting laid for the first time.

It was so hot.

I could feel him claiming me with his dick, consummating the hell out of this marriage, banging his wife and filling her with seed that would seep onto the sheets. Some of his previous traits had returned, like his possessiveness and his raw sexual magnetism.

All I did was lie there with my legs open, letting him take me with as much aggression as he wanted. My pussy ached because he took me so roughly, but it felt so good that I didn't want him to stop. Just when I was about to come, he beat me to the finish line.

He groaned so loud that his sounds must have filled the hallway outside the bedroom door. His cock twitched inside me as he filled my pussy with an enormous load. His face buried into my neck as he writhed on top of me, his sweaty chest rubbing against mine. His ass tightened as he pressed deep inside me, making sure my cunt got every single drop of him.

His performance was definitely a sprint, not a marathon, but I knew Hades well. He wouldn't leave me hanging, and feeling all that come deep inside only turned me on more. It would give me a stronger climax, make me feel sexy knowing I made him explode like that.

He kissed my neck and made his way along my jaw until he

reached my lips again. His cock softened slightly inside me, but it didn't dull his desire. He kissed me with the same passion as before, his dick slowly hardening back to full mast. "That's what happens when you make me wait." He started to thrust again when he was hard, sliding through his come and my slickness.

"I didn't ask you to wait." My fingers dug into his hair, feeling the sweat in his strands as I held on to him. My other hand gripped his back, holding on as he rocked me back and forth.

His eyes watched mine as he fucked me deep with every stroke. "No. But you made me want to." He took a deep breath and groaned as he kept enjoying me, balls deep in my pussy. "And fuck, baby." He moaned again. "You were worth the wait."

IT WAS four in the morning, and lights from the city were visible through the small crack in the curtains. I lay on the right side of the bed, stuffed with come and so sore that I needed a break for a while.

Hades was beside me, sleeping on his back with the sheets bunched around his waist. His left hand rested on his stomach, his black wedding band so strange but also fitting on his finger. His chest rose and fell slowly as he enjoyed his deep sleep.

He'd taken me over and over again all through the night, fucking me in the exact same position. He wanted to feel me at the deepest angle, give his deposits in the most intimate way possible.

The sex hadn't changed much in two years.

Other than the fact that it was better.

I disliked the idea of being married for gain, of forging an alliance for bullshit purposes, but at least my husband was good in bed. It might make me overlook all his other flaws. Most people were in love but having mediocre sex. That wasn't the case for me.

That was something I wouldn't miss about being single...finding a cute guy, only to be disappointed by his skills in the bedroom.

There was nothing disappointing about Hades.

It'd been a long day so I should be deep asleep, but my eyes continued to stare at his bedroom, to see my clothes hanging on the left side of the closet. My wedding ring was still on my finger. My wedding dress was visible in the sliver of moonlight that snuck into the bedroom. Our quarters were spacious and plenty big for the two of us, but it was still odd to share everything, from money, to space, and even a bed.

Fifty-fifty.

I pulled the sheets back gently and slipped out of bed. His white collared shirt had been flung onto the armchair, so I slipped it on and buttoned the front as I made my way outside. I stepped onto the balcony and was overcome by the silence. There were no cars on the road at this hour. No sirens. No bells. The city was asleep. I gripped the rail and looked at the city I knew so well, feeling different now that I'd changed my address as well as my last name. My fingers rubbed my cheek and corrected the smeared mascara I'd never washed away.

The door shut behind me, his footsteps echoing a moment later. His bare feet tapped against the pavers of the patio as he approached me, his size audible in the way he disrupted the energy around him.

He came directly behind me, his bare chest pushing against my back. His arms gripped the rail in front of us, his body acting as a cage that locked me in. His lips slowly moved into my hairline, pressing gentle kisses against my warm skin. He moved down until his lips were pressed against my ear. "Want more?" His hand pushed my hair over the opposite shoulder. "Because you can get on top of me whenever you want. Wake me up—I don't give a damn." He kissed my neck again, his tongue tasting the sweat from my skin.

"I just couldn't sleep..." I closed my eyes, feeling his lips suck my skin.

He pushed down the front of his boxers and let his cock move to my entrance. He grabbed my shoulder and bent me over slightly, making my ass pop. Then he pushed inside me, shoving himself deep and hard.

I gripped the rail and moaned, feeling the pain from all the soreness. He made me feel like a virgin, making me ache like I'd never taken a man like that before.

His large hand wrapped around my neck, and he kept me still as he fucked me, fucked me like he hadn't enjoyed me all night long. It was another possessive fuck, reminding me that I belonged to him.

Like he'd ever let me forget.

IT WAS nine in the morning when I woke up to him getting dressed.

He stood in jeans and a t-shirt, clasping one of his watches onto his wrist.

It was way too early to wake up after the night we had, so where was he going that was so important? I sat up and pulled the hair from my face, my eyes so tired, I could barely keep them open. "Where are you going?"

"Work." He grabbed his wallet and phone and slipped them into his pocket.

"On a Sunday?"

"Every day. I'll be back in a few hours." He headed out the door.

"It's the day after our wedding, and you're going to run off?" I didn't expect anything romantic, but I was surprised he would take off and leave.

He stood in the doorway and stared at me. "Don't worry. We'll fuck when I get back."

"That's not why I'm—"

He shut the door and left.

I lay back in bed and felt the fatigue overtake me. I fell back to sleep within minutes and slept until past noon. I showered and got ready for the day even though I didn't have any plans. Since it was my bedroom, I tidied up the place and fixed the sheets. They were dirty, but if we changed them after every night of sex, we'd need an endless supply.

I headed downstairs to see if Helena had anything for lunch. She made me a sandwich and a salad, and I sat at the kitchen table and ate my food while scrolling on my phone. It was nice to have space from my mother, but it was also strange to start over in someone else's home. Technically, it was mine now...it would just take some time to get used to.

Esme texted me. *Sore?*

Yes, actually.

Ooh...good for you. He really must have a big dick.

Sometimes it's too big.

Girl, don't torture me. You want to go out and do something?

Sure. Hades went to work, so I'm home alone.

Wow...what a dick.

It's not like we married for love...

Then let's meet at the bar. See you in twenty minutes.

I finished lunch then prepared to leave. But on the doorstep, I came face-to-face with my mother. "What are you doing here?"

"Moving, obviously."

"I thought you were giving us the weekend."

"Yes, but I called Hades, and he said it was okay." She would never admit she was lonely, that she couldn't stand to be alone for even a single day.

It annoyed me that she'd immediately asked Hades for permission when this was my home too, but since she was a grieving widow, I let it go. It wasn't like Hades and I were home doing it all over the furniture. "Need help with anything?"

"No. The staff is bringing in my suitcases." She was in a skirt with a buttoned jacket, looking like the prime minister's wife. She stepped inside, examined the grand entryway with approval, and then turned back to me. "So, how was last night?"

I raised an eyebrow. "Private."

"That's not what I was asking. I just meant, did you have a good time?"

"Yes." I hadn't been fucked like that in two years. It felt goddamn amazing.

"Where is your husband now?"

It took me a second to understand her question because that title took some time to settle into my bones. Hades was my husband now. That was how everyone would refer to him...as my husband. "Work."

"Wow, he's dedicated. That's a good trait in a man."

"He's a drug dealer," I said sarcastically.

"He's more of a distributor."

"Whatever," I said. "I don't think that qualifies as a good trait."

She rolled her eyes. "Give that man the respect he deserves. It's easy to break the law, but it's not easy to build the billion-dollar empire he's started entirely on his own. That takes guts. That takes brains. And it takes big balls too."

"YOU'RE SERIOUSLY GOING to hold out on me?" Esme asked as she sat across from me. "Come on, that gorgeous man took you to pound town, and you ain't gonna share the details?" Her third glass of wine sat in front of her, and she pried more than usual because her blood alcohol level had spiked.

"We had sex. That's it."

"You've told me some personal stuff about your lovers over the last two years. And then with this guy—"

"This guy is my husband now. It feels weird to share intimate details."

"If they're positive details, I doubt he cares. Every man wants a woman to say how amazing he is in bed."

He was amazing. With top-notch skills and desire that burned the room around us, he was the best lover I'd ever had. But now we were in a partnership based on trust and loyalty, so sharing details felt like a betrayal. "He's good in bed. I'll leave it at that."

"Is that why you're so tired today?"

"Yes...we didn't sleep much."

She smiled. "Well, thanks for giving me that."

"What about you?"

She shrugged. "No one new on my radar."

"There were a lot of bachelors at the wedding."

"Yeah. But the only man I liked didn't even know I was there."

"Who?" I didn't know every name on the guest list, but I could probably figure out who she was talking about.

"The best man." She swirled her wine before she took a drink. "That man is gorgeous."

"Damien."

She shrugged. "Never got his name. Every time I tried to talk to him, some other woman beat me to the punch. He had so much pussy handed to him that he didn't even need to look around."

Damien was a handsome guy. With a built musculature and a classically handsome face, he reminded me of Hades in a lot of ways. "He and Hades are really close. I could ask Hades about him—"

"God no," she said with a laugh. "I don't chase."

My phone started to vibrate on the table as I got a call. It was Hades. Since we were out in public, I ignored the call and sent him a text instead. *I'm out with Esme. Be home later.* It was hard to believe that four-story mansion was home now, that my husband was the biggest drug dealer in this part of the country.

Is that a joke?

I ignored his message. She and I changed the subject and started to talk about work. I hadn't walked into the hotel since I'd gotten married. Wasn't sure if it would be any different now that I was married to the man who laundered all our money.

Ignore me and see what happens.

I didn't ignore you. I said I'll be home later. Bye.

He didn't text me again.

WHEN ESME GOT cozy with a guy, I paid for my drinks then drove home. I expected to face my husband's wrath when I walked in the door, but there was nothing I couldn't handle. I headed upstairs and stepped into my bedroom.

He was sitting on the balcony in his sweatpants, the phone pressed to his ear as he talked quietly. His building was the tallest one in the vicinity, so he didn't have to worry about anyone staring at him as he enjoyed the view.

I slipped off my heels and placed my jewelry on my nightstand. It'd been a long day, and I was ready to wind down for the night.

Hades finished up his conversation and set down his phone. His defined back faced me, the muscles rippling with any little move he made. A bottle of scotch was beside him, along with an empty glass. "Get your ass over here." He only raised his voice loud enough so I could hear his command.

I didn't like being bossed around, so I ignored him.

He spoke again, this time with a lethal tone. "Don't make me ask you again."

It was our first day in marital bliss, and we were already bumping heads like rams. I moved outside and faced him, ready to set the parameters of this relationship. My arms crossed over my chest, and I didn't blink at his intimidating physique. "I told you not to boss me around. You're my husband, not a dictator." Did he expect me to abandon my social life just because I had settled down? The only thing that would be different in my life was the man in my bed. Everything else would stay the same.

He didn't speak a word, but the hostile gaze gave an entire speech. His jaw was clenched tightly, and his fingers balled into a fist onto the table. This was the version of Hades I didn't see often—the king of the underworld. He stared at me like he couldn't decide how he would punish me—but either option was equally cruel. His muscles swelled with blood, and his frame turned rigid like a piece of steel. There wasn't a hint of attraction in his eyes, as if I were nothing but an enemy to him.

He rose to his feet.

And I stepped back, instinct kicking in.

He cocked his head slightly as he studied me, brown flames

dancing across the surface of his eyes. "As husband and wife, our bond is sacred. Our loyalty is unbreakable, our trust is undoubtable." He took another step toward me. "When you call me, I will answer—always. We're partners. We're accomplices. We're family." He backed me up farther. "Don't you pull that shit ever again." When my back hit the stone wall and there was nowhere for me to go, he pressed his face closer to mine. "When you see my name on the screen, you don't fucking hesitate. You take that call like it's life and death. Disrespect me like that again, and this won't last." His nostrils flared before he backed up. "Our bond needs to be stronger than the mafia's. We need to be loyal like fucking gangsters." He turned around and walked into the bedroom, his body still tense with all the rage that hadn't dissipated.

I'd been expecting a different argument, bullshit about jealousy and possessiveness. Now I felt humbled by his speech. I'd brushed him off like this was a normal relationship, but it was anything but typical.

I followed him inside but didn't know what to say. Once I apologized, he would have all the power again—and I didn't like giving up a single ounce if I didn't have to. I stared at his muscled back as my tongue tasted the words before they came out of my mouth. "I'm sorry..."

"Don't be sorry." He turned around and faced me once again. "Be better."

There he went...pissing me off again.

"There's no one in the world you can trust more than me. I'm the man who will die for you, who will kill for you. Other people will talk shit the second you turn your back, and I'll be the man that sticks up for you. Through thick and thin, through better or worse, I'm the man in your corner. Your allegiance is solely to me. I don't give a shit if you're out having a good time. I'm more important than anything you could possibly be doing. My life could change in an instant, so you better take my fucking call because you never know when it might be the last time we'll speak."

"I said I was sorry…"

"I don't give a damn if you're sorry. I don't care about your apology. Just do as I say."

My arms crossed over my chest, and I sighed.

He stared down at me with those dark eyes, still pissed off. "I could have a gun pointed to someone's head, and I'd still take your call. You're the most important thing in the world to me… and you'll never have to doubt if that's true."

"Alright. Lesson learned."

He still seemed livid, like my cooperation wasn't enough damage control. "Take off your clothes."

"I said I was sorry and…what?" I didn't process his command right away. I assumed he wanted to continue to vent his frustrations. Once it became clear, my eyes narrowed, and I questioned everything I just heard.

"I said, take off your clothes." He pushed off his pants and boxers, his dick hard even though he'd been yelling at me for ten minutes. Sculpted and strong, he stood proudly with his feet planted into the ground, his cock pointed at me like I was a target.

"I thought we were fighting."

"And now we're done." He moved toward me to reach for the zipper at the back of my dress.

I thrust my palm into his chest. "Are you crazy? You're mad, and I'm in a pissed off mood."

"So?"

"So?" I asked incredulously. "I don't want to have sex right now."

"That's too bad." He grabbed my dress and got the zipper down before I slapped his hand away.

"Too bad?" I stepped back. "I'm not in the mood right now."

"I can change that in thirty seconds."

"Wow...fuck you."

His eyes narrowed in anger, and he moved toward me again. "Let me explain something to you. When I come home, I want to have a drink, fuck, and then go to sleep. I've already had a drink, so you're the next thing on my list."

"I'm not a slave, Hades."

"No. But you're my wife, and that's what wives do—bend over so their husband can fuck them."

"Asshole." I shook my head.

"Couples fight. They get angry with each other. Life goes on." His powerful arms hung by his sides, the cords in his skin prominent along his muscles. He had been much kinder to me yesterday, but once our clothes were off, he turned into this aggressive man. A man who needed sex more than anything else. "My wife is the sexiest woman in the goddamn world, and I'm not an asshole for wanting to screw her. It doesn't matter how pissed off you make me, I'm gonna want you as much as I did last night. So take off those goddamn clothes and bend over."

"You're still demanding me to do something—"

"You married me so I could protect you, preserve your hotel, and chase away the bad guys. I've upheld my end of the bargain— now it's time to uphold yours."

"That's so romantic..."

He raised his brow. "You don't think a husband wanting his wife is romantic? A man who wants one woman so much that it drives him fucking crazy? A man who will be faithful even when he doesn't have to because there's only one woman he wants? That's the most goddamn romantic thing I've ever heard." He grabbed the sleeves of my dress and yanked them over my shoulders so the material would slip down my body and land on the floor. "On the bed. Ass up. Face down." He moved into me, his face tilted down to mine with menace in his gaze.

I didn't want a man to speak to me that way, but my body responded to his command, my primal instincts kicking in. A part of me liked the way he spoke to me, the way he ordered me onto the bed so he could fuck me. And I also liked that there was no way out of this—that he would get what he wanted.

It was very conflicting.

When I turned down the covers and got onto the bed, he grabbed my ass and forced my face into the sheets. With rough hands, he yanked my thong off my ass and let it sit around my knees. A big cock pressed into my entrance, then slipped inside with a forceful thrust.

I moaned into the sheets.

He held on to my neck as he positioned himself at the edge of the bed, one foot on the mattress so he could deepen the angle. Then he pounded into me while gripping my hip, his dick so hard, it made my insides ache. Every thrust was deep and forceful, as if this were a punishment as well as a reward. "This is how you will spend your nights for the rest of your life...getting fucked by your husband."

6
___

HADES

"Consider it a two-for-one special." I tossed the two plastic bags of crystal across the table.

He opened a bag and inspected the contents, crushing a piece with the bottom of his cell phone. Once it was dust, he bent over and sniffed it like he had a runny nose. He leaned back and rested his head against the leather chair, letting the potency affect him instantly.

"I've got a hundred kilos waiting to be transferred to you...as long as we have an understanding."

"Chemically, it's pure. But the asking price is steep."

With my hands together on the table, I watched him with a callous expression. "If you want the best, you have to pay for it."

"I just took a hit of something similar. Not as good, but half the price."

I knew exactly where he'd gotten it. "Do business with Maddox if you want, but don't do it on my turf. You can sell the cheap shit for a marginal price, or you could sell the good stuff and make a fortune. The answer is clear to me, but if it's not clear to you, then perhaps I don't want to do business with you anyway—"

"I'm in. I just thought we could negotiate the price."

I stared at him without blinking. "I don't negotiate."

He placed the bags in his briefcase and excused himself from the table.

"I expect a drop every two weeks." I didn't turn around to look at him as he walked off, commanding the room without any exertion.

"Yes, Hades." His footsteps faded as he disappeared down the hallway.

I was sitting in a conference room at the hotel, Damien looking out one of the windows to the city beyond. His hands were in the pockets of his suit, and he leaned against the wall, far more entertained by the view than the deal that just went down. "Can we trust him?"

"Only one way to find out."

Damien pushed off the wall then made his way toward me. "Maddox is still our biggest competitor."

Sure, he undercut my prices, but he still couldn't match my product. He was a nuisance—not a threat.

"We should have killed him years ago."

"We'll get our chance. Be patient."

"Be patient?" He fell into the vacated chair. "If we don't kill him, he'll kill us."

"Not so easy."

"He still needs to be eliminated. He undermines us."

If I'd been able to track him down, I would have put him in the ground a long time ago. But he was always on the move, changing residences and guarding his property with enough ammunition for war. I wasn't hard to find, but he knew it would be a suicide mission to provoke me. So we both waited for the perfect time...the moment we could get the other alone. "We will. I promise you."

He looked out the window again, his fingertips drumming against the table. "How's married life?"

A lot of fighting. A lot of fucking. "Have you seen my wife?"

Damien grinned. "I guess that answers my question."

It wasn't the way I wanted our relationship to be, but it was better than the alternative. At least she was there every night when I came home. She was in that bed with me all night long.

"How does she feel about all this?"

"She's never really asked."

"Maybe she doesn't want to know."

I gave a slight nod. "I think so."

"It's better than trying to get you to change."

"It would defeat the purpose of marrying me in the first place."

"And what's it like with the mother-in-law?"

I wasn't thrilled about Maria joining us, but she wasn't the worst houseguest. "She respects our privacy."

"Good. It'd be hard to get frisky when your mother-in-law could knock on the door at any minute."

"She doesn't come to the third floor. I told her it's off-limits."

"Good." He continued to drum his fingers. "It's going to be weird not hitting the strip clubs and whorehouses with you."

"You'll find someone else to do it with."

"Nah." He shook his head. "You're the only guy I'd do that shit with."

"Looks like we'll have to find other things to do together."

"Besides selling drugs and killing people?" he asked. "I don't know...not very much tops that."

"Maybe we could take up golf?"

He chuckled. "Pass. Hey, does your wife have a cute girlfriend?"

I'd seen Esme before. She was cute, but I'd never paid much attention to her because all my dick could think about was Sofia. "I've seen one. She was in the wedding."

"That blond girl?"

"Yeah."

"She was pretty sexy...set me up. We'll go on a double date or something."

"I doubt Sofia wants you to sleep with her friend then ditch her."

"Maybe her friend likes that. You never know."

I packed up my things, and we walked out of the hotel together. When we entered the main lobby, my eyes scanned for the beautiful brunette who rocked heels like she was born to wear them, but she was nowhere to be seen. "I'll catch up with you. Just gonna stop by Sofia's office."

"If you want to fuck your wife on her desk, just say that." He winked then walked out.

I moved down the hallway and approached her office, my satchel over my shoulder.

She stood at her desk, her pencil skirt making her ass look juicy like a plum. She was flipping through papers, her curled hair pinned back with a few strands coming loose. Her white blouse was a classy choice, but it still hugged her sexy tits in a noticeable way.

I'd love to fuck her in the office, but she would never go for it.

I stepped into her office, my heavy footsteps announcing my presence.

She looked up, her body tightening when she realized it was me. She bunched the papers together then tossed them on the desk. Instead of making fake small talk, she just looked at me as if she expected me to tell her what I wanted.

Our relationship was still turbulent, with chafing attitudes and cold remarks, but as the years passed, that would all change. My arm moved around her waist, and I pulled her into me, watching the way her gold hoops shifted back and forth with the movement.

She let me hold her close, her red lips slightly parted.

"I'll be home late tonight, but I'll make it by dinner." My lips rested against hers, giving her a soft, gentle embrace. I tasted her mouth and felt her lips move with mine, tasted my property and noticed just how sweet it was.

She kissed me back, her eyes still open. We didn't kiss unless we were fucking, but that needed to change. We needed to act like husband and wife. She would fight it for a while, but once it became routine, she would stop opposing it. Maybe she would open her mind to other things too…like loving me. "Alright. See you then."

WHEN I WALKED in the door, Helena immediately took my suit jacket. "I'll serve dinner now, Hades."

"Thank you, Helena." I stepped into the dining room and saw my wife and mother-in-law sitting together, sharing a bottle of white wine while they talked quietly about the events of their day.

When Maria noticed me, she got to her feet to give me a warm greeting. "How was your day, Hades?" She turned her cheek and allowed me to plant a kiss on her skin. She'd treated me like a son instantly, grateful I took on the onerous task of taking care of her sassy daughter.

Best decision I'd ever made. "Great. Yours?"

"I had a wonderful lunch with a friend at La Balena. Such a cute little bistro."

Sofia didn't rise from her chair, drinking her wine like I was a stranger she didn't want to meet.

Maria turned to her daughter, visibly embarrassed. "Honey,

that's no way to greet your husband. On your feet." She snapped her fingers.

That just made Sofia more disobedient. "I see him at work all the time, Mother." She spoke in a bored voice, only responding to her mother to get her to shut up. "I kissed him goodbye just hours ago."

"Well, you should kiss him again," she argued.

"It's alright." I pulled out my chair and took a seat across from Sofia. "I mean, I wouldn't mind a kiss from my beautiful wife, but I'll live." I poured myself a glass of wine and stared at Sofia's stunning face. She was an enigmatic woman. She seemed to despise me one moment but then enjoyed fucking me in the next. She probably hated herself for it, hated herself for getting into this position in the first place.

Maria dropped the protest, but she gave her daughter a fierce glare in response. "What did you do today?"

Sold crystal to a new distributor in Portofino. "Lots of meetings. What about you, Sofia?" Maria Romano bent over backward to respect me and tried to make up for her daughter's rudeness. She was a good mother-in-law. I just wished I didn't have to see her over dinner on a nightly basis. I wanted to spend all my time with Sofia, cracking her external shell and getting to the soul underneath.

Sofia took another sip of her wine, drawing out the silence before she spoke. "Today was payday. So I had to handle all of that." She swirled her wine again and didn't give me further information.

Helena set dinner in front of us, tarragon chicken with roasted broccoli. She also set a basket of fresh bread on the table, along with homemade butter.

"Looks amazing," Maria said. "Your cooking is phenomenal, dear."

Helena excused herself and allowed us to eat alone.

Maria started talking again, hijacking the conversation. "So, I went to the farmers market downtown…"

My eyes focused on Sofia's, noticing the way her lipstick had washed off on her wineglass. Her makeup was still perfect in every other way. With ethereal beauty, she seemed to be an angel sent to torture me…because she wasn't real. I tuned out everything her mother said and directed all my energy on my wife.

Sometimes she met my gaze, but most of the time, she ignored me. She focused her attention on her food, but it was obvious she wasn't paying attention to a word her mother said either. My heated gaze stole all of her concentration, as much as she pretended I wasn't there at all.

I wanted this dinner to end already…so I could go upstairs and fuck her.

WE REACHED the third landing and walked to our bedroom.

"What did you really do today?" she asked as she glided on her heels, strutting in black pumps that made her legs look even sexier. She was still in her tight skirt that made her ass look juicy as hell. The second I'd seen her at the hotel, my dick wanted to slide between her cheeks and fuck her right in the asshole.

I almost didn't answer her question because my mind had wandered so far. "Met with a new distributor. He took a hundred kilos with him, but he tried to argue that my prices were too high. I have a competitor in the area I've been at war with for years."

"When you say war…"

"I mean we want to kill each other, but it's too difficult."

"That's not scary at all."

"Don't worry. He knows it would be suicide to come after me. And I know it's suicide to go after him."

"Why?"

"Because we're both protected. We'd have to catch the other one alone and off guard…but that hardly ever happens."

She reached the bedroom door first and stepped inside. Now that she had her privacy, she slipped off her heels and set them in the closet. Once her bare feet were on the rug, she sighed as the pain finally left her body. She tilted her head slightly and arched her back, like she was stretching everything to relieve the discomfort.

I tossed my tie onto the armchair and unbuttoned my shirt. "Long day?"

"These shoes are so cute, but they hurt."

"I'm sure there are other cute shoes that would be kinder to your feet."

"Unlikely."

I stripped down to my boxers then leaned against the head-board. "Come here."

She always gave me the cold shoulder when I bossed her around. "I'm going to take a bath."

"I didn't ask what you were doing. I told you to come here."

She turned to me, venom in her eyes. "Stop talking to me like you own me—"

"I do own you." I patted my thigh. "Now, take off your clothes and do as I say."

"How about you fuck off instead?"

I chuckled because she was cute when she was angry. "We can do this the easy way or the hard way. Which do you prefer?"

"The one where you fuck yourself."

"I can do that if it turns you on...but I'd rather fuck you instead."

She rolled her eyes and yanked off her clothes, letting them fall to the floor before she approached the bed. Her hips shook with attitude, and her eyes were fiery.

Exactly how I liked her.

I grabbed a pillow and tossed it to the foot of the bed. "Lie down."

With both hands on her hips, she cocked an eyebrow.

Her narrow waist and perky tits were so distracting, I almost changed my mind about what I was going to do. But I knew she would be more receptive when she relaxed, so I stayed focused. "Come on."

She crawled onto the bed, showing me her ass for a second as she lay down.

I grabbed her ankles and placed them on my chest before my thumbs started to dig into the balls of her feet.

She arched her back and sighed with pleasure, like I was releasing pressure everywhere.

My fingers worked her petite foot, applying pressure to all the places that were the most tender. I even rubbed her toes, gently glided my fingers down her skin and made her relax further.

She moaned like she was taking my dick. "Oh my god..."

I watched her writhe on the bed, my cock trying to break free of my boxers. She arched her back and rolled slightly, her nipples hardening because of the exquisite sensations she was experiencing. Her quiet moans filled the room, sounding identical to the noises she made when she was with me. "I can take care of you. I can make all your aches and pains go away. I can do anything you want me to do...if you just let me in."

I SAT OUTSIDE on the balcony with the phone to my ear. My wife was in the bathtub, soaking for hours after I gave her a massage that practically made her come. The heat in Italy was unforgivable because the humidity was killer, but this was still my favorite season, so I basked in the warmth after the sun set over the horizon.

Damien spoke over the line. "I'm telling you, I think he's hiding out in Tuscany. My guys spotted his vehicles heading to an estate in the countryside. It's difficult to see because it's surrounded by four hills. You wouldn't even know it was there because it's not visible from the road."

"You're making a lot of assumptions."

"But what if I'm right? What if he's there, thinking he's immune?"

"We still have no idea what he's got behind those four walls."

"All we have to do is camp by the roadside and wait for him to leave. Then we hit him."

As much as I wanted to take out Maddox, I wasn't willing to attack unless it was certain. "The windows will be tinted. There will be no way to know if he's in the car."

"Unless we get eyes on the house."

"And how do you suppose we do that?"

"I don't know...but there's gotta be something. Look, I'm tired of this asshole making us look like assholes. I'm tired of him siphoning off our business and making us look like pussies to the world."

"I assure you, they don't think that." My eyes shifted to my side when Sofia joined me on the patio. She held a piece of white lingerie, a lacy bodysuit with an opening in the crotch.

"Well, I think that—"

"I have to go, Damien. We'll talk tomorrow." I hung up and set the phone on the table. Now that my eyes were on her, her makeup gone and her hair still pulled back, I didn't care about business anymore. I cared about the sexy piece of lingerie dangling from her fingertips.

"This was laid out on the bed. Hope you don't expect me to wear it."

"I do." With my knees planted apart and a bottle of scotch

beside me, I stayed in the chair with the cityscape in front of me. But I'd been waiting for this moment all night—to fuck my wife.

It was the greatest high in the world.

She tossed it on the table. "I took off my makeup, and my hair—"

"Don't care." She looked better this way anyway. I could see her features much clearer, see the beautiful woman underneath all that makeup she wore. With her hair pulled back, I could see more of her face, more of the exquisite contours she possessed. "Put it on and lie on the bed. I'll be there in a second."

Her eyes flashed with anger. "You know, I'm getting really sick of the way—"

"Listen to me." I set my drink aside, my impatience getting to me. I was used to issuing commands that were obeyed without protest. But my own wife was the worst soldier I'd ever had. "I work all day. I make deals, kill people, and protect the things I care about. Sometimes I deal with bullshit. Sometimes I'm the one cooking the crystal in my lab. So, when I walk in the door, I want you naked on the damn bed so I can fuck you however I wish. That was the deal we made. I protect you, your family, and your legacy. In exchange, I get you. Have I made myself clear?"

She crossed her arms over her chest.

"In exchange for letting your mother live with us, you said you would show your gratitude. I'm calling in that favor now."

She sighed quietly and dropped her arms.

"So, get on the fucking bed. Now."

I ENJOYED another glass of scotch as I waited for her to get ready. I needed to let my anger fade away anyway. Teaching this woman how to be my wife was exhausting. Her disobedience was infuriating...but it also made me respect her. If she just gave in to every command, she wouldn't be nearly as interesting. Maybe that was why I'd fallen headfirst for her...because she wasn't like the others.

I finished my scotch and stepped into the bedroom. The lights were off with the exception of a couple lamps. She was on the bed, her hair out of her ponytail and across the pillow.

I shut the door behind myself and walked farther into the room. My cock slowly hardened as I gazed at her on the bed, her slender legs pressed together with her knees bent. The bodysuit fit her snugly, her tits visible through the thin fabric.

I dropped my boxers by the bed and let my hard cock get a little closer to her.

The anger was gone from her eyes. Now defeat remained.

I moved onto my knees and positioned myself in front of her, my large hands gripping her knees. This woman was my fantasy, the kind of partner I wanted to fuck every single night. On our wedding night, I couldn't control myself. I'd bucked into her hard and took her like I couldn't get enough. I didn't even last long...because it'd been nearly a month since I'd last had pussy.

And her cunt was dynamite.

For a brief second, I felt light-headed, the blood rushing to my dick so fast. I wasn't sure what was sexier, her beauty or her obedience. I controlled an uncontrollable woman, conquered a woman who refused to be conquered by anyone. Owning her gave me a thrill down my spine.

Maybe it didn't matter if she never loved me. Maybe owning her was enough. I had her fidelity, and she had my last name. She was still my property, and with our mixed blood, we would have a family that would keep us bonded forever.

Who gave a fuck if she never loved me?

No one else would ever have her.

My hands gripped her knees and gently separated them, opening her legs so I could see the cunt that my dick had claimed for himself. Her nub was visible, her pussy perfectly groomed to be fucked by her husband.

My cock twitched just looking at it.

My palm flattered against her stomach, and I slid up her body, moving between her tits before I reached the top of the bodysuit fabric. I grabbed a handful then tugged it down, letting her tits pop out. She looked so gorgeous, her long legs open and her pussy inviting. She was so beautiful that she didn't need makeup; she was fucking perfect.

My cock was so hard it ached.

My arms locked behind her knees, and I opened her wide as I lowered myself onto her body. My cock slid against her pussy, brushing up against her tender flesh as it moved over her clit. My face hung over hers, so close I could hear her breathing quietly. My stomach tightened as the arousal rushed through every single vein in my body. I wanted this woman so much that just being close to her caused my head to spin. Every screw was the best sex of my life...and now I got to have it every single night.

Her fingertips pressed against my hard abs, and she gently slid them up my body, moving over my pecs as she made her way to my face. Slowly, they slipped into my hair as her body relaxed in preparation to take me. Her hands cradled my face to hers so she could kiss me.

Fuck.

I loved kissing her.

Our lips met with mutual softness, a burst of static electricity erupting between us. We breathed into each other before we kissed again, exploring as we both got wet for each other. Our mouths opened farther and tongues were introduced. With charged energy, our bodies started to grind together.

She wanted me as much as she had before...and she hated it.

I pushed on the shaft of my dick to guide myself inside her.

Fuck...that was sweet pussy.

I slid through her tight wetness, expanding her channel as I dominated the territory. I sank deeper and deeper, surrounded by the best cunt in the world. She made other women look like hell. It was bittersweet to be reunited with her bare skin instead of being covered by latex while I fucked a woman I didn't give a damn about.

I loved fucking my wife.

I slid inside until I was balls deep, my entire frame rigid because I'd just taken a hit of ecstasy.

And it always felt this way...every single time.

She took a deep breath when she felt me stretch her, her fingers clawing down my back as she moaned into my mouth. She widened her legs farther and moaned as she started to grind with me, taking my cock with her usual enthusiasm. Her lips trembled against mine, shaking as she breathed.

My hips worked to thrust deep and hard, to pound that pussy and make it mine. This was the one thing always on my mind, all day, every day. When I walked in the door, I didn't want to make small talk with her mom or tell Helena what I wanted for dinner. I wanted to head upstairs and screw Sofia until she came around my dick.

It felt so good that it didn't seem real.

Fuck, how could pussy be this good?

Her hand moved to my ass, and she dragged me deep into her. "Hades..." Like we were back in time, two lovers that couldn't keep their hands off each other, we ground and moaned together, unable to get enough. She wanted me more than any other man, let me come inside her because I was the only one worthy of having the honor.

I pressed my forehead to hers and kept fucking. "Wife."

SOFIA

HADES WASN'T KIDDING ABOUT HIS DEMANDS.

When he walked in the door after work, he expected sex. If I wasn't naked on the bed or dressed in lingerie, there were always consequences. There was no deviation in his routine, never a day when he just wasn't in the mood.

He always wanted it.

He preferred to take me on the edge of the bed, my face down and my ass in the air. It was usually a quick fuck. He took out all his stress and frustration from the day on me, fucking me until I screamed.

Today I was on my back with my ass hanging over the edge, and he pumped into me deep and hard until his seed was resting between my legs. There was a distinct feeling of superiority about him, that he viewed this as an arrangement more than a marriage. He had never been this bossy with me years ago, but that was probably because he didn't see this as a relationship.

That ship had sailed.

When he was finished, he walked to his closet and pulled out a navy suit.

I lay there and relaxed, the endorphins swirling in my bloodstream from that climax. The sex was good, so maybe I should stop fighting him. Maybe I should be grateful I had a powerful businessman as a husband who knew how to fuck a woman. We would never love each other, but we could definitely respect each other. "You just got home. You're leaving again?" I sat up and pressed my knees together, feeling his heaviness inside of me.

He picked out a tie and tossed it on the table. "We're leaving."

"We?" I asked. "And where are we going?"

"Having dinner with a big client."

"That sounds like work...and I have nothing to do with your business."

"You're my wife. You need to make appearances." He opened my closet and picked out a black dress. "Wear this."

"I can pick out my own clothes, thank you."

He gave me a cold stare before he turned away. "Then get dressed."

"Now?"

"Yes. Now." He started to get dressed, not even washing off his dick before he pulled on a fresh pair of boxers. He put on each article of clothing then secured the tie around his neck. "Hurry and pick something."

I glanced at the closet then looked at the black dress. That seemed like the best option, especially since I was short on time.

Hades glared at me like he was trying to prove a point about what had just happened. He knotted his tie and then pulled on his jacket.

I refused to admit he was right, so I looked away.

"If you stopped being sensitive about everything, this would be much easier."

"Sensitive? I just don't like being told what to do."

"Then you need to start. You married a powerful man who gets shit done. If I tell you to do something, I'm right about whatever it is. Stop fighting it and see it as an asset. You don't need to think. Just listen."

I cocked an eyebrow. "Unlike your other girls, I actually like to think."

"Think on your own time." He grabbed a new watch from his drawer and clasped it around his wrist.

"How many watches do you have?"

"Too many." He sat in the chair and put his shoes on.

"Why do you collect them?"

"Most of them are gifts. Some are collectibles. It's something I've been doing since I can remember." He tied his laces then stood up, looking like he hadn't gotten hot and sweaty just minutes ago.

I pulled on my black dress and zipped up the back. The shoes that killed my feet came on next.

His hands rested in his pockets as he watched me. "You can wear flats."

"No. Doesn't look right."

"You'll still look beautiful in an ugly pair of shoes."

Sometimes I liked this man. Sometimes he drove me crazy. And sometimes that happened at the same time. "Who's the client?"

"He owns a shipping company. Has a high revenue and needs to launder millions."

"Someone else can't do that?"

"Not as well as I can."

I straightened in my heels then grabbed my clutch off the dresser. "So, it's just the three of us?"

"Five."

"Who are the other two?"

"His wife and Damien."

I'd never really talked to Damien before. There'd never been the opportunity to exchange more than a few words. But he was close to Hades, so he should be close to me too. We couldn't be strangers forever. "And what is my purpose in all of this?"

"To be beautiful."

I stared at him, unsure what that meant.

He explained further. "I want to show you off."

"Like a trophy?" My mother had explained this before, that a powerful man wanted the most beautiful wife he could possibly attain.

"Exactly. Except I don't want other men to want you." He moved until our faces were close together, our lips nearly touching. He loomed over me like a king stood over his subject. "I just want them to know that I have you."

<hr />

I SAT WEDGED between Damien and Hades in the back seat of the car.

"Why do I have to come to this?" Damien asked, looking out the window in annoyance. "Aren't you enough? I could be at the whorehouse right now or—"

"Damien." Hades quickly silenced him.

Damien glanced at me before he looked out the window again. "Sorry."

"You don't need to censor your conversation because of me." I didn't want to hear all the details of their criminal empire or their adventures in the brothel, but I wasn't offended by it either.

Damien turned back to me. "I like you."

I smiled then looked straight ahead.

Hades moved his hand to my thigh, his large fingers resting there possessively. His gaze remained directed out the window.

"You got any hot girlfriends to set me up with?" Damien asked. "I'm rich, fit, and I know a couple of jokes."

"You don't seem very funny to me." Damien was one of Hades's associates that didn't immediately make me uncomfortable. The other men who came into the hotel reeked of threat. Damien seemed harmless, but that was probably inaccurate.

"I can be when I'm trying to get laid. So...got a lady for me?"

I had the perfect lady in mind, but he'd ignored her at the wedding, so he wouldn't get his chance now. "No."

Hades smiled slightly, probably knowing I was lying about Esme.

"Come on," he said. "Maybe a woman from college that you experimented with?"

"I've only experimented with men," I said honestly.

Hades's fingers dug into my thigh a little harder.

"Damn," Damien said. "You're practically my sister-in-law. You're supposed to hook me up."

"You can't get your own dates?" I countered.

Hades smiled. "She's got you there, man."

"Obviously, I can," he said. "But I was hoping for a woman of your station."

"My station?" I asked.

He gestured with his hands, making an hourglass silhouette of a woman. "You know, with your level of beauty."

It was a compliment, but a stupid one. "It's not a club."

"Man...that'd be sexy if it were."

"Alright." Hades silenced him. "Stop harassing my wife."

"I'm not harassing her," Damien said. "I'm just getting to know her."

"Then ask me what my favorite color is," I said. "Or what my favorite drink is."

Damien rubbed his jawline as he considered my request. "Hades says you're usually drinking a vodka cranberry or wine...so I'm gonna go with the first one. As for your favorite color, I'll just have to guess. Red?"

I was surprised Hades had noticed so much about me. "You got both right."

"Of course I did. So now we need to move on to the more intimate stuff."

We arrived at the large estate just outside the city and stepped inside. Introductions were made, and the man Hades was hoping to acquire as a client was older, maybe in his fifties. His wife was half his age...no surprise there.

We gathered in the dining room and had dinner, where the men did most of the talking. Hades sat beside me, while Damien was on his other side. They talked about money, about ways Hades could handle the man's money so people couldn't find it. He didn't just launder money... he physically hid it so no one had any idea where it was. It was impossible to be robbed when you had nothing to be robbed of.

The wife was quiet, barely saying a few words to me. Whenever the conversation became boring, she wore the biggest frown... like the poor girl was miserable. She didn't like her husband whatsoever.

At least I respected mine...and he was good to me.

It was the second time I'd seen Hades in his element, and he was vastly different from how he was when it was just the two of us. Now he was cold, calculating, and he commanded the room while saying as few words as possible. If he was trying to secure this man's business as an addition to his company, it didn't seem like it.

It seemed like the opposite.

When it came down to business, Damien was serious too. All that bullshit in the car was long gone. He wore an expression as determined as Hades did. The two of them were loyal team-mates, communicating without even speaking to each other. They didn't even need to make eye contact. They just felt each other's energy.

It was a boring evening, but it was interesting to see this other side of Hades.

The monster.

The men excused themselves to talk in the other room so they could light their cigars and drink gin and scotch. The wife offered me dessert, but I turned her down. We were left to make small talk at the dining table.

"Your husband is young," she noted. "Whenever my husband's associates come over, they're usually around his age."

"Yeah...he's in his early thirties." He felt ancient to me since we were seven years apart, but I was certain all the other men my mother had in mind were decades older. Maddox was the exception to that. The thought of him made me realize I'd never asked my mother about the interaction, if he really had been a candidate.

She sipped her wine then propped her chin on her palm. "He seems to care about you."

"Why do you say that? He hasn't said much to me."

"I can tell by the way he looks at you." She drank from her glass again. "My husband only looks at me when he wants something. The rest of the time...he just ignores me."

Hades never ignored me. In fact, he paid too much attention to me. "I'm sorry."

She shrugged. "At least I'm rich, right?"

―――――

WHEN IT WAS GETTING LATE, I approached the drawing room. If I asked Hades to take me home, he would. The night had been stale from when I walked in the door, but now it was worse. I had work in the morning, and it was almost eleven.

There was a crack in the door, and I could see the three of them gathered in armchairs. Smoke from their cigars lingered at the ceiling, and their glasses of scotch had been depleted. I was just about to push the doors open when the potential client spoke.

"Hades, how's married life?" He shook his glass of scotch, letting the ice cubes roll around loudly. He didn't even take a drink, so his behavior was simply obnoxious.

Hades had his legs crossed, his elbow on the armrest and his fingers grazing the shadow of his jawline. His brown eyes matched the colors of the drawing room, the old wood, and the aged scotch on the table. "No complaints."

"I would assume so," he said with a laugh. "With a wife like that..."

"Yes, she's beautiful," Hades admitted. "She's also smart, compassionate, and strong. She runs the Tuscan Rose and does a great job of it. I'm very lucky to have her as a partner."

Whether he meant that or it was all bullshit, it touched me. He fought for me in his own way, showed the men in the room I wasn't just a trophy wife he fucked at night. I was also valuable to him with my participation in this marriage. If someone were to ask him about Damien, he would have given a similar answer because they were partners. And he talked about me like I was his partner too.

"But I doubt any of that is as important as her ability to fuck." The man laughed before he took a deep drink, as if he didn't believe Hades was being genuine at all.

Hades watched him for a long time, his eyes open and filled with a hint of hostility.

Damien glanced at him, like he knew Hades would explode if his buttons were pushed any harder.

The older gentleman refilled his glass once more. "My wife is good enough, but I can't say I'm not jealous. What's it like to fuck a woman like that? To own a woman like that—"

"Keep talking, and that's the last thing you'll ever do." Hades's words sliced through the air like a double-edged knife. His fingers slowly tightened into a fist, and his knuckles turned a slight shade of white. With unblinking eyes and a gaze full of ferocity, he stared down his own client like an enemy. "I came here to talk business, not discuss my private relationship with my wife. She isn't just the woman in my bed. She's my partner in life, equal owner of everything I do. Disrespect her, and you disrespect me. You don't own family—and she's family. So, unless the next thing out of your mouth is an apology, Damien and I will withdraw our offer and you can find a solution elsewhere."

The man stopped shaking his glass, stopped drinking his scotch.

He avoided eye contact with Hades for a long time before he finally mustered the courage. "I apologize..."

THIRTY MINUTES LATER, we finally left the house and walked to our car in the driveway.

I'd never interrupted their conversation and chose to pretend I had no idea what was said. I'd spent the next thirty minutes drinking wine at the table, suffering through the wife's mediocre conversation because I was in shock from what I'd just heard.

Hades stood up for me.

He was loyal to me—just as he promised.

I could have easily ended up like the poor woman in that house...treated with insignificance. But my husband respected me, defended my honor even when I was nowhere around. He was willing to walk away from a big deal if I didn't get the respect I deserved.

Now I was proud to be his wife.

Hades helped me inside the car first before he took the seat beside me. His hands stayed on his lap, and he looked out the window, clearly upset by the turn of events. He wasn't affectionate, and he didn't ask me how my night had been.

Damien seemed to be in the same foul mood.

Our driver took us back into Florence and headed to Damien's home. He also lived in the city, in a large building just like Hades.

My eyes kept glancing at Hades's hands in his lap, thinking of something I could do to show my gratitude. I could pretend not to know anything, and maybe that was smart, but I still wanted to show my appreciation for what he had done. We had a murky past filled with resentment on both sides, but we still had a future together.

My hand moved across his thigh until I interlocked our fingers.

He turned his head slightly my way, surprised by the unexpected affection. His fingers lightly squeezed mine in reciprocation, and his deep eyes looked into mine like he was trying to read my thoughts. Sometimes I forgot how handsome he was, how every woman in the world wished she could be me. But I had him all to myself...and I would have him for the rest of my life.

After a minute, he looked away again, our hands still joined together.

We pulled up to Damien's, and he got out of the car without saying goodbye.

We got back on the road and headed home.

It was dark in the back seat with the sun gone. It was just the two of us, his driver keeping his eyes on the road. My hand pulled away from his and rubbed up his chest, moving until my fingers could grasp his collared shirt and tie. I gave him a gentle tug, wanting him to turn toward me.

He turned his head my way, his eyes immediately focusing on my lips.

I tugged on him again and kissed him.

Our lips came together with the same explosive chemistry, with the same shocks that traveled down our spines. My fingertips went numb as I squeezed him harder. My mouth clung to his desperately, breathing oxygen into his lungs like he couldn't get it on his own. I moaned quietly as my mouth opened to take his, to take his tongue.

He pivoted his body and slid his hand up my dress, following the curve of my ass and fingering my thong underneath. His kisses turned more heated, became heavier. He unbuckled his safety belt so he could get closer to me, bring our writhing bodies together so we could feel each other as much as possible.

I didn't know why I wanted to kiss him so much... I just did. My heart softened for him, and my walls came down. He started to feel like a man I could really trust, someone who would have my back even when I wasn't in the room. That kind of loyalty was hard to find...even among family.

Since I'd never wanted to get married...maybe this was the best thing I could ever have. Maybe this was exactly what I wanted, a loyal man who would always take care of me, who would value me over money.

His hand slid into my hair, and he kissed my neck. "Baby..."

I rolled my head back and let him take all of me, let him conquer me. "Hades."

8

HADES

OUR NAKED BODIES FELL TO THE BED, AND I COULDN'T GET INSIDE her fast enough.

Her fingers dug into my hair as she kissed me, as she breathed hard into my mouth while she waited for me to slide deep inside her.

So fucking wet.

My cock throbbed inside her, surrounded by her slick warmth. My mouth paused against hers because my mind was overstimulated. Everything was good...everything. It felt the way it used to, unbridled passion.

She couldn't get enough of me.

I couldn't get enough of her.

I rocked into her and kissed her at the same time, my cock and my mouth deep in heaven. I could feel every inch of her, even feel her soul. The last few weeks had been strictly sex, getting off on each other's bodies. But now the old flame had been reignited, and we actually had emotion, actually had desire. Our hands shook as we gripped each other, and every kiss made our lips tremble with lust. It was exactly what I wanted...exactly what I'd longed for the last two years.

My woman was back.

I pushed her into the bed and fucked her fast, giving her as much of me as she wanted. The muscles in my ass ached because I was pushing my body to the limits, giving her the kind of good sex I never gave anyone else. With Sofia, I never met her halfway. I did all of the work, gave her a hundred percent.

And right now, she was giving me a hundred percent too.

"Hades..." She came right away, her pussy tightening around me like fingers into a fist. Her legs opened wider, and she rocked with my thrusts, her sexy lips parted as she moaned to the ceiling. "Yes...fuck yes."

I followed right behind her, caught off guard by the passion she showed me. My body was trained to last longer, to make a woman's toes curl before the grand finale. But I couldn't keep my body together, couldn't keep my urges under control. My cock exploded inside her, giving her a mound of come that would last until she showered the next morning. It would slowly drip down her thighs and splash to the stone tile below. It was impossible for her not to think about me, not when my essence was stuffed deep inside.

I rolled off her and let the sweat evaporate from my body. Our deep breaths slowly softened until they turned into gentle sighs. My hand rested on my chest, and I closed my eyes, so satisfied that my body immediately relaxed.

I had no idea what got into Sofia tonight. Our conversation at the table had been boring, and then she was stuck with a stranger for the rest of the evening. Seeing me do business might have been a turn-on. Or listening to his wife complain about how poorly she was treated might have made Sofia appreciate me. I saw how miserable that young woman was, and judging from the way her husband asked lustful questions about my wife, he wasn't a good man to be married to.

Maybe my wife finally realized how lucky she was.

She rolled over and turned her back to me as she prepared to go to sleep.

My hand stretched across the bed until my fingers rested against her back. I lightly grazed her skin, felt how soft she was. I started at the top of her spine and glided down to the top of her ass, right where her cheeks began. I could feel her back rise and fall with her deep breathing, feel her drift off to sleep and lose consciousness altogether.

I stared at her until my eyes couldn't stay open. Then I joined her.

I SAT in my office at the bank and took Damien's call. "I just got the money. They're putting it into storage now."

"We've got bigger problems, alright?"

I leaned back in my leather chair and looked out the window. "I'm listening."

"Maddox is in Florence. I've had a few guys tail him—"

"I told you to drop that shit, Damien. If you get on his radar, he might come after you."

"I'm sure he's wanted to come after me for years." His breath was shaky because it sounded like he was walking at a quick pace. "But that's not the point. I think he's staying in Tuscany and he's got business here—which is a problem for us."

"We've always known he's done business here. That's the whole reason we hate him."

"Well, we should take advantage of the situation and finish him off. Come on, this shit will finally be over."

"You know I want to kill him as much as you do, but we've got to be smart about this—"

"Being smart is taking advantage of opportunities."

"What if it's a trap?" I asked. "This guy is smart and empty. We killed his only brother, and he didn't care—at all. He's not like other men. So, stop putting yourself in danger. We'll take him out when it's the right time."

He was quiet.

"I need you, Damien. So drop this shit now."

I STEPPED INTO THE ROOM, while Sofia continued her meeting with the board. She stood at the front while her laptop projected her notes and reports, going over revenue reports as well as promotional ideas to increase occupancy of the hotel.

She stopped her presentation for an instant when she saw me, our eyes connecting before she continued what she was saying.

The rest of the men turned to me before giving Sofia their full attention once more.

I knew the men were behaving themselves, but I liked to drop by unannounced just to keep them on their toes. If they ever considered reverting to their previously disrespectful ways, they'd have to answer to me—and their own graves.

My eyes moved back to Sofia, who wore a black dress, pumps, and a navy blazer. She looked classy in the attire, but that jacket couldn't hide those sexy curves. Her ass begged to have my teeth sink into it. My tongue ached to taste her pussy. In all our time together, I'd never had the honor.

She was my wife; I should know exactly how she tasted.

I leaned against the back wall until her presentation was over. She took questions afterward, and it seemed like the meeting was a productive one. The guys weren't assholes anymore, and they actually listened to what she said. I influenced them to give her a chance, and maybe now they realized she really was a good leader.

The guys rose to their feet, shook my hand, and made small talk. When they filed out of the room, I walked up to my wife, seeing the way her eyes softened slightly as I drew near. She was definitely affected by my presence in a different way, like she was actually happy to see me.

"Your ass looks unbelievable in that dress." I leaned into her and gave her a soft kiss on the mouth.

"That's all you have to say about my presentation?" she asked, disappointed.

"You were awesome—like always. When someone is flawless, they don't get compliments or criticisms because it feels so natural. That's you."

Her eyes filled with warmth, as if that praise actually dug into her flesh.

"And you know me. I'm in love with your ass."

She smiled slightly before she rolled her eyes. But it was all playful. "Yeah...I've noticed."

"The guys haven't been giving you a hard time?"

"Not at all. Your presence seems to keep everyone on their best behavior..."

"Baby, did you just give me a compliment?" I hated her for what she did to me, but when our natural connection deepened, it made me forget how much she'd hurt me. It made me focus on what we had...since she could never hurt me again.

"Did you just call me baby?"

"Yeah. And I'm gonna keep calling you that." It was much more possessive than her first name, because anyone could call her Sofia. No one could call her baby...except me. "I think people are giving you a fair chance because of your new last name. They respect me—so they'll respect you. But the reason they listen to you is because of your skills. If you were wrong, they would come to me privately and say it. They don't."

Her eyes shifted down, breaking contact with me.

I liked this side of her, this insecure and vulnerable version. Her walls were usually so high that it was impossible to see. But she seemed to trust me enough to unveil her true qualities.

"Good to know..." She lifted her gaze again once the moment had passed.

"That's what you really want."

"Excuse me?"

"You don't want the hotel for the money. You want to be respected. You want to make this the greatest hotel it can possibly be...because that's what matters to you." It'd never been about financial security or power. Her ambitions had been much humbler than I'd ever realized.

She held my gaze, and after a long pause, she nodded. "When you walk into a room, it just goes quiet... I want that."

"That's because they're afraid I might kill them."

"No, it's more than that."

"I assure you, the room goes dead silent when you step into it too...because you're so damn beautiful." She was my wife, so I could speak my mind whenever I felt like it. I could tell her she was gorgeous every damn day. If she didn't like it, too bad.

"Well...I want to be more than just a beautiful face."

"You are."

She smiled slightly before she turned to gather her things.

I watched her lean forward over the table, her ass luscious in that tight dress. Her thick hair was pushed over one shoulder, and she collected her laptop as well as the extra notes she'd distributed to her colleagues.

I grabbed her by the arm and gently tugged her toward me.

Instead of twisting out of my grasp and giving me a burst of attitude, she let it be. She paused and waited for me to speak.

"I have to head back to the office." My hand slid to her elbow before wrapping around her waist. I positioned her close to me, making her forget about the supplies she needed to gather. My arm tightened on her lower back before it slid down to her ass and gave her a hard squeeze. "But when I get home, your ass will sit on my face. I'm gonna eat that pussy for dinner—and dessert."

She dropped her gaze, her cheeks filling with color as the image filled her mind.

My fingertips moved under her chin, forcing her to look at me. "Alright?"

She held my gaze, her face tinted in a mixture of arousal and embarrassment. "Alright."

9

SOFIA

I SAT WITH MY MOTHER ON HER PATIO, THE TWO OF US DRINKING decaf coffee after dinner. It was strange to live with her and my new husband because two different worlds had collided. When it was just her and I, it felt like old times. But when Hades walked into the room, I was reminded my reality was much different.

Hades stepped onto the balcony. "Something came up, and I have to run out. I'll be home later tonight." It was a nice courtesy that he came to tell me personally. He could have just left without telling me. Or he could have sent an impersonal text.

"Everything alright?" I got out of my chair and walked up to him.

"Yeah. Just bullshit." He was in a gray suit and tie, dressed to make a statement.

"Wake me up when you get home." I blurted out the request stupidly, not even thinking about what I said before it came out. It was desperate, clingy, and something lovers said to each other.

Hades took a moment to stare at me, like he was just as surprised by my request.

That night had changed my feelings to a strong degree. It made me appreciate him, made me want him to live a long and happy life. But I was also embarrassed by how transparent I was being, treating him like a wife would actually treat her husband. "Just be safe." I moved into his chest and kissed him goodbye.

Indifferent to my mother's presence, he slipped his hand into my hair and gave me a deep kiss. "I'm always safe." He rubbed his nose against mine before he turned and walked off.

I returned to my seat, prepared for whatever comments my mother was about to make.

"Now that is how you treat your husband." She added more sugar to her coffee and stirred it. "I'm glad you're warming up to him. He's a good man. I like him a lot."

"You hardly know him."

"He's gotten you to go soft—so he must be pretty damn remarkable."

I didn't want to roll my eyes at my mother, so I didn't.

"And he invited me to live with you. He's charming."

I kept my mouth shut about the truth. "He wanted to make me happy."

"Exactly. You have a good man. Appreciate it because not too many women can say the same thing."

I was beginning to realize that. Not only did he not hurt me, but he defended me. He gave me the independence I needed to be happy. He treated me as an equal...at least in a professional setting. And it was better that he wanted to have sex with me instead of every other woman in town. "Before Hades and I got married, a man came to my office because he was interested in marrying me."

"Another suitor?" she asked.

"Yeah. He said Gustavo had mentioned it to him before he passed away."

"Who is he?"

"His name was Maddox Stine. Never heard of him."

"Huh...I've never heard of him either."

"Really?" I took my coffee black, but I was a slower drinker so it was already lukewarm before it was halfway finished. "You didn't approach him before Hades?"

She shook her head. "Hades was the first and only man on my list."

"You think Gustavo would have gotten involved?" Gustavo wasn't my father, so I'd be surprised if he'd participated in planning my future marriage.

"He never mentioned it. The only thing I could think of is he was doing business with this man and mentioned you were single. Maybe this Maddox person decided to pursue it on his own. That must have been what happened because I can't see Gustavo shopping for a husband on your behalf."

"I can't either..."

"I'm guessing you didn't like him."

"He was young and fairly handsome...but he had a weird vibe to him. Kinda creepy. I told him I was marrying Hades, and he seemed pretty annoyed by the revelation. The whole encounter was strange."

"Does Hades know him?"

"I...I never mentioned it to him."

"Oh."

"I just didn't see the point. I picked him, so what does it matter if another man wanted to marry me?"

"Might make him jealous...and sometimes it's sexy when men get jealous."

"Mom." Now I did roll my eyes.

"Come on. You don't think it'd be hot to see Hades get jealous of another man?"

No. Because someone would probably die. "Hades isn't like that. I've never seen him jealous. He's too...confident to be jealous."

"Hmm...that's interesting."

"What?"

"Then why haven't you told him?"

IT WAS three in the morning when Hades came into the bedroom. His clothes fell on the floor, and his shoes were kicked off. The heavy sound of his metal watch echoed as he set it on the dresser.

I opened my eyes and stared into the darkness, seeing his muscular silhouette. He stripped down until he was naked then got into bed beside me. "You alright?" I mumbled, still half asleep.

He grabbed my arm and rolled me to my back so he could get on top of me. "I appreciate your concern, but you don't need to worry about me." He lifted up my pajama shirt and pulled my panties down my legs so he could get inside me. He separated my legs then pushed into my entrance, slowly sinking until he was completely sheathed. "You're always wet, aren't you?"

My hands dug into his hair as I pulled his face close to mine. "For you."

I STEPPED out of my office with a folder of papers that needed to be scanned and stored on our server. I'd made the mistake of wearing the shoes that killed my feet, and since the day wasn't even halfway over, it had been a really stupid idea to choose them.

I'd been staring at my feet, so I didn't notice the man I practically ran into. "Oh, sorry." I dropped the folder on the ground, the papers scattering everywhere. "I was looking at my stupid shoes and didn't notice." I bent down to gather everything.

The guy helped me. "Why are your shoes stupid?"

I recognized him right away—Maddox Stine. It was spooky because my mother and I had been discussing him just days ago. Now he was in front of my office again, even after our last tense conversation. "Because they're beautiful...but painful."

"That seems to be how everything is." He rose to his feet and handed me the papers he'd grabbed.

I returned them to my folder. "Nice to see you again, Maddox. Anything I can help you with?" Letting on about my discomfort was weak. If I wanted to be respected, I needed to seem fearless. If Hades was ever concerned about a situation, he hid it deep down inside, maintaining his rigid poker face. I did the same.

That was when Maddox gave me that eerie stare, that coldness that went all the way down to my bones. It was an unblinking stare, but it lacked hostility. He almost seemed mesmerized by my face, as if he were searching for my soul and all of my secrets.

I looked past his shoulder and saw Hades round the corner at the end of the hallway. He spoke to one of the girls in HR, but in seconds, he would realize I had been cornered by this creepy guy and handle it.

He would come to my rescue any minute...thankfully.

Maddox was unaffected by the lingering silence. He continued to stare at me, so confident in the situation that it made him seem more sinister by the second. "Two things." His deep voice was low, but the delicate volume didn't make him more welcoming. "I'd like to host an exclusive dinner at your hotel."

"Of course. I can arrange that." Maybe he wasn't that creepy at all. Maybe his external package didn't match the innocent person underneath. "How many guests?"

He ignored the question. "And secondly, what's a woman like you doing with a man like him?"

It wasn't a threat, but I certainly took it that way. All the air left my lungs, and my body tensed, like I had been cornered by

Lance once more, prepared to fight for my life. Maddox didn't say it in a flirtatious way, like a man trying to get me into bed even though I was a married woman. This seemed personal... even though he didn't know me.

My eyes glanced past his shoulder once more.

Hades finished his conversation and turned toward us. He was dressed in one of his luxurious suits, looking like a powerhouse who could kill any man with just a look. He oozed threat. I'd never been so relieved to see him, so relieved that this man was my husband.

His eyes met mine, immediately affectionate. Then he glanced at the man beside me, and that warm look instantly faded away, becoming an iceberg in the arctic. He even stopped in his tracks, staring at the man's backside like he knew exactly who it was. Less than two seconds passed before he moved forward again, this time ignoring me altogether because I wasn't important in the situation.

All he cared about was Maddox.

He moved toward us swiftly, and like a protective bear, he positioned himself in front of me, his large size obscuring me from view. He was the same height as Maddox, so the two men locked eyes, staring each other down with silent threat.

Once Hades was in front of me, I felt safe. I released the breath I'd been holding in my lungs as the relief washed over my body. Now that he was here, nothing would happen to me. Maddox would be disposed of, and he would be too terrified to ever return. I closed my eyes for a brief moment, clutching the folders to my chest.

The men continued to let the silence stretch, as if whoever spoke first lost all their power.

I stepped sideways slightly, so I could see the two men face off.

Hades finally spoke. "Leave."

Maddox's eyes shifted back and forth a little.

"I said, leave." Hades took a step forward, but Maddox didn't take a step back. "Don't come back."

Maddox showed a slight grin. "That's pretty hard to do...considering how beautiful your wife is."

Hades moved in closer. "You think I won't kill you right on the spot?" Hades discreetly pulled a blade from the inside of his jacket, pointing it right at Maddox's chest.

Maddox didn't glance at the weapon. "No."

Hades cocked his head slightly.

"Because if you do, you'll never see Damien again." A slow grin stretched across his lips, eventually taking up the entire bottom half of his face. Every tooth was on display, a grin so eerie he looked like a maniacal clown. His eyes widened to twice the size they'd been before.

Hades was silent, probably unable to process the terrible words he'd just heard.

Maddox gave me a final look and a subtle nod before he turned around and walked down the hallway. His hands slid into his pockets, and he walked with a powerful gait. Underneath those clothes was a fit man with endless tricks up his sleeve.

Hades didn't turn around until Maddox was gone from the hallway.

"Why aren't you going after him?" I blurted once we were alone. "He has Damien."

He slipped the blade back into his suit as he turned around to look at me. His face was pale, ghostly white like his strained knuckles. "Because I have to protect you first."

10

HADES

Damien was more than just a friend.

He was family.

He was everything.

So when I heard Maddox say those horrifying words, I was actually scared.

It was the first time in my life I'd been truly afraid.

So fucking afraid.

"Hades?" Sofia grabbed my biceps and gave me a gentle squeeze. Her fingers showed her concern, her eyes showed her devastation. She watched me fall apart, watched me panic. "Are you okay?"

My greatest enemy had my greatest friend. "No." I pushed down her hands. "I need to get you home."

She didn't try to touch me again.

What if I hadn't walked into the Tuscan Rose at that moment? I was supposed to have a meeting at the bank, but it had been canceled at the last minute. Maybe Maddox knew that, which was why he decided to make his move then. What if he'd gotten Sofia too?

What would I have done?

I grabbed her hand and pulled her with me to the outside of the hotel. I got her into my car and sped through the streets like a madman, trying to get her to the safest place she could be while I figured this out.

I should be hunting down Damien instead...but I had to keep her safe.

He would understand.

"What are you going to do?" she asked from her side of the car.

I ignored her.

"Hades?"

"Not now, Sofia." I'd warned Damien to back off, but he fucking did it anyway. Now he was hidden away somewhere, a prisoner about to be tortured until Maddox got what he wanted from me. I'd already killed his brother...would he do the same to me?

Sofia turned quiet, but she was still restless.

I got her to the house and made some calls. I moved more security detail to the property, making sure no one got in or out of the place. It was on lockdown. Snipers couldn't pierce the windows with their bullets because they were all bulletproof. Maddox would know I'd brought her here, but that didn't mean he could reach her.

When we were in our bedroom, I made sure the patio doors were shut before I made more calls.

Sofia sat in one of the armchairs, watching me pace the room as I interrogated my men to figure out the last place Damien had been seen. I gathered that he'd been in Florence, tailing Maddox, before he was dragged out of his car and taken away. No one had any idea where he went.

I hung up and slammed my closed fist into my chest. "Fuck."

Sofia's eyes moved back and forth as she watched me.

I didn't want to call Maddox because that was exactly what he was hoping for. He wanted to make a deal, making me trade Damien for whatever he wanted. But since I had no idea where Maddox took Damien, I couldn't save my best friend first. And if I waited too long, I knew Maddox would kill Damien.

What if he wanted Sofia?

What if that was the trade? What would I do? I couldn't live without him...but I couldn't live without her.

I finally looked at my wife, who was sitting in her dress, clearly afraid from everything that had just happened. She watched me with emotion in her eyes, like she was just as concerned about Damien's life as I was. "What did Maddox say to you?" I stood with my arms by my sides, wishing my phone would ring in my palm with news.

"I should have told you this before..." Her voice escaped as a whisper, broken with emotion.

I took a step toward her. "Told me what?"

She looked at the rug underneath her feet before she lifted her chin to meet my look. "A few months ago, he came to my office..."

Jesus.

"Gustavo had mentioned to him that I needed a husband, and he wanted to throw his hat in the ring. I told him I was already marrying you..."

I closed my eyes as the terror gripped me by the throat. My enemy had sights on my wife long before I even knew about it.

"He seemed angry, but I didn't realize he knew you. Then he left."

"Did you see him any other time?"

"No. Today was the first time. I'm sorry I didn't tell you before... I didn't think it was relevant."

I should keep my anger under control because it wasn't her fault, but I couldn't. "I'm your husband. You tell me everything, every minute detail that you think is insignificant. Maybe it's nothing to you, but it could be something to me. Don't you ever pull that shit again. You see anything even remotely suspicious, you tell me." I shoved my thumb into my chest. "You understand me?"

Her attitude didn't flare. "Yes."

I was so livid that nothing could keep me calm. Damien was probably going to die, and there was nothing I could do about it. "What did he say to you?"

"First, he said he was interested in hosting a dinner at the hotel...then he told me I shouldn't be married to you."

I wished I'd killed him a long time ago. None of this would be happening. Maddox was ready to wipe me out, probably waiting years to gather as much information about me as possible. "Anything else?"

"No...you walked over."

I started to pace the room again, my hand dragging down my face as I tried to figure out my next move. If I didn't know where Damien was, I had to play Maddox's game, regardless of what he was about to ask me.

I just hoped he didn't ask for the one thing I couldn't give.

Sofia rose to her feet. "What are you going to do?"

"I have no idea where Maddox is. My men don't have a location on Damien. That means I have to call him...which is exactly what he wants."

"He'll want something from you?" she whispered.

I walked to the window, my hands on my hips as I examined the city below. "Yes."

"What do you think that will be?"

I didn't want to tell her my theory...because it would only scare her. "Don't know. But I'm sure I won't like it." I typed in the number then pushed the phone to my ear, letting it ring as I waited for that creepy voice to erupt through the speaker.

"You've gotten your wife to a safe location, and you've had time to realize you have no idea where your dear friend is. You have no idea where I am. Now you're playing your one and only card...to listen to my demands."

My jaw clenched as the rage coursed through my veins. I felt like his little bitch, and that made my teeth grind together so hard that it hurt my roots. If this weren't about Damien, I would just hang up and leave him to his fate. But that was the difference between Maddox and me. To him, everything was disposable. To me, there were things I could never let go. That gave him the power...and that gave me nothing.

"Ready?" There was so much arrogance in his voice. He was already pissing on my grave even though he had yet to claim my life. I was in the palm of his hand, and he enjoyed squeezing the air out of my lungs.

I didn't want to answer, didn't want to play his sick and twisted game, but I couldn't abandon Damien. I couldn't let him be tortured until he begged for death. He would never let it happen to me. "Yes." I hated myself for caving, hated myself for submitting to this fucking tyrant.

"Good. Damien will appreciate it since he's a bit uncomfortable right now."

I closed my eyes, pain everywhere.

"Hear. Listen."

"No—"

"Agh!" Damien screamed when someone struck him.

My hand covered my face because it was torture, picturing him covered in blood and writhing in pain.

Maddox came back to the phone. "I've been torturing him all day. I knew it would take a while to crack him. Once he was ready to sing, I paid your wife a visit."

I'd been going about my day like everything was normal...oblivious to Damien's demise. "What do you want, Maddox?" I kept my voice steady, refusing to let the emotion in my chest escape into my throat.

"Can I give you some advice?" he asked, smug as ever.

I closed my eyes again.

"Just let me kill him. My demands aren't worth his life. In a twisted way, I actually respect you, Hades. You didn't want to kill my brother, but you did because you had to. You didn't cave... Admirable."

Disgusting. "You're an asshole." How could he say that about his own flesh and blood? His sister-in-law was a widow now, a single mother to two young children. She was abandoned...and all of that could have been avoided.

"Thank you," he said, a smile in his voice. "You should be an asshole as well. I know you've got a soft spot for this man, but he's not worth it. He shouldn't have been tailing me, especially when you told him not to. His ambitions are too big for his capabilities. Let him pay his punishment. He deserves it."

"Don't you want me to give you what you want?"

"Not necessarily. I'll get it no matter what, whether it's now or later."

I took a deep breath, making sure the air didn't hit the speaker on the phone.

Maddox sighed in disappointment. "Alright. I'll return Damien...if you retire."

It was far too much to ask, but I was actually relieved by the request. I feared he'd want something far more valuable...like my wife.

"I really hope you don't cave so easily," Maddox said. "I would much rather have a war than a simple conversation. Far too boring for men like us."

I'd have to give up my entire business, my billion-dollar empire, to save Damien's life. It was my life's work, something I was proud of. I'd built it from the ground up, made a respectable name for myself on the street. It had led to other opportunities. It made men afraid of me. It gave me everything I wanted... including Sofia.

"You're going to say yes, aren't you?" he asked. "You're really going to close up shop for one man." He sighed into the phone. "That's so disappointing, Hades. You're the only opponent who can challenge me, who actually gives me something to strive for. With you gone, I'll be bored. So, are you sure you want to do that? Come on. Friendship is just as stupid as love. Men like us need power, loyalty, and sex. That other shit is for pussies."

If it were anyone else, I would never cave. That made me realize how much of a liability Damien was, that I had someone I would do anything for. But it didn't change anything. My business wasn't worth his life. "I agree. Loyalty is everything...and I'm loyal to Damien. You should have been loyal to your own fucking brother."

The psychopath had the audacity to laugh. "He would have done the same to me."

"I doubt it." I remembered the relief on his face when I got Maddox on the phone. He thought he was free.

"Then I would have been disappointed in him."

This man really was the devil.

"That's your final decision?" he asked, talking like he didn't just shit all over his brother's memory.

I'd be lying if I said I wasn't upset I had to give everything up. Or that I wasn't annoyed with Damien for getting mixed up in this. Nothing about it was fair. But nonetheless, I knew my answer. "Yes."

———

TUSCANY WAS A LARGE PLACE. For hundreds of miles, there were small villages, wine estates, and countryside. It extended all the way to the west until you reached the sea. It was easy to hide in the beauty, to disappear off the face of the earth.

Maddox sent me the coordinates, and we drove our vehicles offroad until we were deep in the lush landscape, so far away from the nearest person that gunshots couldn't be heard by anyone within miles.

I sat in the back seat and saw Maddox leaning against the front of his truck, his arms crossed over his chest, his annoying grin on his face.

It was evening, pitch black with the exception of the headlights from the cars. The stars were bright overhead because the country was asleep, its lights dim. I sighed as I stared at him, wishing I could just blow him into a million pieces.

But that would be stupid.

I had to play his game.

I had to lose his game.

I stayed in the vehicle and examined the scene around me, watching my men hop out of their trucks with their rifles across their chests. Normally, Damien would be in the seat beside me, and we would be taking in everything as a team.

Now I was alone.

I knew he wouldn't reveal Damien until I showed my face, so I got out of the SUV and walked across the soft grass to the open space between us, no-man's-land. My suit had been replaced by a t-shirt, jeans, and a leather jacket. The watch Damien gave me for my birthday was on my wrist.

I stopped fifteen feet away from Maddox, my pistol snug in the back of my jeans. With my arms resting by my sides, I stared into the cold eyes that made me furious. Not only had he hurt my family, but he'd played me like a damn violin. He had me by the balls, and his squeeze only tightened with every passing second.

I hated that goddamn smile.

One day, I would kill him...just not today.

He pushed off the hood. "Drag him out."

Two men moved to a truck parked in the rear. They opened the bed and yanked Damien out by his feet. After he fell to the dirt with a quiet moan, he was pulled to a stand and then was marched toward us. With cuffed hands and a gag in his mouth, he was a bloody prisoner. His face was black and blue from the beatings that had happened throughout the day. One eye was swollen, and judging from the way he held his body, a couple of ribs were broken. When he was shoved to the line, his eyes moved to mine.

He wasn't scared. He was just sorry. This was all his fault—he knew it.

"You sure you want to do this?" Maddox asked. "Because this

asshole doesn't deserve a second chance. He's an egotistical idiot who thinks he's got it all figured out. That kind of arrogance will get you killed...and he would have been killed if he weren't valuable."

I couldn't hold Damien's gaze longer than a few seconds. It was too difficult to look at him that way, to see a strong man I admired reduced to blood and bruises. I'd murdered people in cold blood...but seeing the pain on his face made me sick. "We have a deal. Let him go."

Maddox moved to Damien's side, his eyebrows raised, a smile on his face. "You'll give up everything for this guy? Your entire drug business, everything you've worked for, just gone?"

Damien obviously had no idea what Maddox had asked for in return for his life, and his eyes widened in fury at what his stupidity had cost me.

Asshole.

"I already said yes, didn't I?" I wanted this deal to be over, to forget this god-awful night ever happened.

"Just want to make sure you'll keep your word," Maddox said. "Because if you don't...there will be consequences." He pulled a short blade from his pocket and sliced the zip ties that restrained Damien's wrists. Then he ripped off the duct tape plastered across his mouth.

Damien bolted for me, moving across the grass and returning to my side where he belonged. He struggled to move, his body beaten and bloody. Some of my men came to his aid, swung his arms over their shoulders so they could get him into the back seat.

I continued to stare at Maddox. "Sofia is my wife. Find someone else." I shouldn't bring her up, but I needed my adversary to stay away from the most important thing I possessed. "She's mine until I'm gone."

He cocked his head slightly. "When I was told she was available, she seemed unencumbered."

"I know Gustavo never told you that, so disregard your source. He's an idiot."

"It was Gustavo. You don't believe me?"

Would that man really betray me? Did he find Maddox a more powerful ally than me? Should I care about the opinion of a dead man?

"Now that you're finished, why would she stay? Her husband is now an ordinary banker, nothing special, easily forgotten. She's used to a powerful man, used to fine luxuries. One day, she'll get bored of you...and she'll look for someone better." He gave me a wink before he turned around and got into the car. His men followed suit, piling into their vehicles and driving away into the night.

I watched their taillights move all the way to the road miles away. The nighttime air was chilly across my neck, probably because my temperature ran at the heat of a furnace. My men piled into their cars, but I remained behind, unable to accept what had just happened.

It was over.

I SAT beside Damien in the back seat, but it didn't feel like old times.

I was so fucking pissed.

My eyes stayed out the window, my body pivoted away from him because I didn't want even his shape in my peripheral vision. I'd just thrown away everything for him, but I still wanted nothing to do with him.

Damien had always been a talker—but now he was dead silent.

Because he knew he fucked up.

We drove back to the city, made our way through the streets as we headed to his home.

My phone rang. I glanced at it with no intention of answering it. The last thing I wanted to do was talk, to say anything at all. My mouth would run, and I would make death threats to someone who didn't deserve it.

But it was Sofia.

Since my rage couldn't displace my concern, since it couldn't wash away my fear for the woman I loved, I took that call so damn fast. Damien had been taken from me, and I couldn't imagine how shitty I'd feel if she'd been taken too. "Baby, are you okay?" That was all I wanted to know, all I needed to know.

"I'm fine." Her quiet voice entered my ears, subdued like she was tired but too jolted to go to sleep. "You're the one I'm worried about."

"I'm fine. We'll talk when I get home."

"Is Damien okay—"

"I got him back. But we'll talk when I get home." I hung up.

Damien leaned his head against the window, breathing heavily because he was battling the pain all over his body. "Don't be a dick to her."

"Wow..." I kept my eyes out the window. "How about you try not being a dick to me?"

He sighed. "Just don't take it out on her. You've worked too hard to push her away—"

"Shut the fuck up." I turned my head and looked at him, my jaw so tight, I actually strained the cords in my neck. My eyes twitched from widening so far. Just looking at his goddamn face made the adrenaline pump through every inch of my body. "Don't tell me how to treat my wife. She can wait until I get home, wait until I'm calm enough to carry on a conversation. You're the one who needs to learn how to treat people, how to listen to what the fuck you're told."

He rested his forehead against the glass. "He almost killed me—"

"That's your fault. I told you to back off. Now look what happened. Everything we've built is gone." I snapped my fingers. "Like that."

He couldn't meet my gaze, the shame too much. "You didn't have to make the trade..."

I turned back to look out the window. "Now I wish I hadn't."

I ENTERED OUR BEDROOM, finding her sitting in the armchair by the window. She was in one of my t-shirts, her long legs crossed and one of her bare feet on the rug. Her dark hair was slightly messy like she'd been fingering it, pulling it over her shoulder because she needed to fidget. It was three in the morning, so the lights were off. She sat in the glow from the streetlight, the pale glow making her look like a black-and-white picture.

I stripped off my jacket and tossed it on the floor.

She rose to her feet. "Are you okay?"

"I'm fine." I kicked off my shoes then poured myself a drink, letting the booze soothe all the sore muscles in my core. It was always a kick on the way down, but a bigger kick once it was in my bloodstream.

She came up behind me, her hands touching my triceps, while she rested her forehead against my back. "You don't seem okay…"

I was still so angry at the turn of events, that my best friend ruined everything with his stupidity. But I remembered all that I would have sacrificed to garner this kind of attention from her, to see her vulnerable as she showed her concern. She held on to me like she didn't want to watch me slip away, like she wanted to be a crutch just as I'd been for her.

It somehow sheathed my anger… that simple gesture.

I abandoned my drink and turned around, letting my chin fall so I could look down at her. Her makeup was faded and smeared like she had been too anxious to notice her appearance in the mirror. But that kind of genuine devotion was so sexy…to know she'd been waiting all night for me to walk through that door… that she'd called to make sure I'd survived.

I'd wanted this for so long—and now I finally had it.

My hand moved to her neck then slowly migrated up to her hair. I brushed the strands away, showing the beautiful contours of her face. My eyes memorized the fullness of her lips, the sparkle of her eyes. Even on my darkest night, she could somehow make it day. "Damien is in bad shape, but he'll live."

"Good...I'm glad he's okay. Where is he?"

"Dropped him off at home."

"Who's going to take care of him?"

I shrugged. "Not my problem."

"You really think he should be alone right now? In that condition? He's probably traumatized. It's not like he has a woman to go home to."

True. There was nothing better than walking in the door to see this woman waiting for me. "What's he going to do here? I'm not helping him."

"I could help him." Her eyes shifted back and forth as she looked into mine. "That man is like your brother... Why does it seem like you hate him?"

"Because I do hate him." My hand slid out of her hair and back to her neck. "This is all his fault. If he'd just listened to me, none of this would have happened. That little asshole fucked up everything."

"I'm sure he didn't mean it."

"Doesn't matter. This is the real world. There are shitty consequences for shitty actions."

"It seems like he's the only one who was punished."

Not even close. "I had to make a trade to save his life."

"Oh..."

"I had to give up my company…and that's exactly what I did."

Her eyes softened as her hand slowly dragged down my chest.

"I built that organization all on my own. Now it's gone—because of him. I could have let him die instead. That's what most men would have done. But…" I shook my head. "I couldn't do it. I'm pissed at him. Want nothing to do with him. But I can't live without him, so I did what I had to do."

Her hands slowly moved back up my chest, her eyes still glued to mine. "You love him."

I refused to acknowledge it. That was pussy shit.

"That's sweet."

I dropped my gaze. Most people would find me weak, find me pathetic. But Sofia was different from all those people. She'd never been impressed by my power or my money. Only wanted it when she needed it. She valued the qualities underneath my suit—and that gave me hope for something more.

Her arms hooked around my neck, and she moved close to me, our faces almost touching. "I'm glad you're home…I was worried the entire time. I wanted to call so many times, but I knew I shouldn't. Then I got impatient."

I closed my eyes and felt my dick get hard. That was such a turn-on, to imagine her expecting me, checking the time as she anxiously waited for me to come home. She cared about me, needed me. "You can call me whenever you want. You're my wife —that's your right."

She rested her forehead against mine, her hands moving to my biceps. "So, it's over? Do we need to worry about that man again?"

He got what he wanted. He defeated me, humiliated me. Now that I was out of the way, nothing would stop him from taking everything he wanted. "No." My hand glided up her neck again, cupping her cheek because I wanted to feel those lips against mine. She sheathed my anger like it was a sword, drenched my rage with cool water.

She looked at me through her thick lashes, her lips parted in preparation for a kiss.

My hand slid into her hair, and my fingers dug deep as I cradled her head to mine, kissing her with a softness I didn't know I possessed. I breathed into her mouth, let the horrible evening wash away. It somehow seemed insignificant now that I was with her...like she was the only thing that really mattered.

Our relationship had changed so much in just a week. She had been indifferent to me, fiery and disobedient. She'd resisted my every request on principle, refusing to trust me. But then one night...all of that changed. Her walls finally came down, and instead of defying me, she wanted to please me.

She wanted to be my wife...finally.

It reminded me of the way we used to be, the untamable desire that consumed us both like a wildfire. We couldn't get enough of each other, couldn't satisfy our urges no matter how many nights we spent together.

Maybe one day we could be more. Maybe with enough trust, affection, and lust, she would see me as something more. Maybe she could allow herself to love a man for the first time.

And maybe we could break my curse.

I STRAIGHTENED my tie in the mirror before I turned to leave.

Sofia only had a towel wrapped around her waist because she'd just stepped out of the shower. Her wet hair settled across her shoulders, looking like a teenage fantasy. Her wedding ring was still on her finger because I asked her to wear it always, even if she was home alone. "Leaving?"

I clasped the watch around my wrist. "Yes."

"Where are you going?"

"Work." Where else was I going?

"I thought you didn't have a job anymore?" She walked up to me, her arms crossed over her chest.

"The bank still needs my attention." At least I had something else to fall back on. I had more money than I could ever spend in a lifetime, so financial gain wasn't my motivation to go to work every day. I did it because I enjoyed it. It gave me purpose; it gave me power. If I retired and lived a mundane existence, I'd shoot myself in the head.

"I see..." She lingered in front of me, something clearly on her mind.

"What is it?"

"I was thinking of stopping by Damien's place...to check on him."

"You don't need to do that."

"I know I don't. But if he's family to you, he's family to me, right?"

My mood soured. "Not anymore."

Her eyes softened. "I'm going to bring him over here. We have several guest bedrooms on this floor. He shouldn't be alone right now."

"You don't need to be his nurse."

"No. But I can be his friend."

I was a bit jealous that Damien was getting all of Sofia's attention. If I came home bruised and bloody, she would probably be attentive to me too. Maybe I should walk down a dark alleyway and pick a fight with somebody.

"Is that okay?"

"Does that mean you'll be staying home?"

"For a couple of days."

I preferred to have her here instead of at the hotel, so that worked out in my favor. "Alright." My arm hooked around her waist, and I pulled her in for a kiss. My fingers gripped the cotton towel, tempted to rip it off her and take that clean body on the bed. But I had shit to do, problems to fix. "I'll see you later."

Her hands cupped my face as she kissed me. "Be safe."

"Always." I left the bedroom and called Damien.

He answered after several rings had passed. "If you just want to yell at me, it can wait..." He took a deep breath between his words, like carrying on a conversation was too difficult. "Because I feel like—"

"Sofia wants you to stay with us until you're back on your feet."

"What?"

"Just get over here. Can you manage that?"

There was a long pause before his next words. "Yeah. I'm just surprised she wants me there."

"Says you shouldn't be alone right now. I couldn't give a damn, but she's the better one of the two of us."

"I don't know what to say…"

"Then get off the phone." I hung up.

11

SOFIA

Damien was in terrible shape.

When his men helped him into the house, I hardly recognized him. With swollen eyes and a face so discolored, he barely looked human, he had been beaten so badly that it was a shock he'd survived at all.

It left me speechless.

He was escorted to a spare bedroom on the top level, a few doors away from our bedroom. I had Helena prepare it, pulling back the sheets on the bed so he could slip inside easily. A vase of fresh flowers was on the nightstand, and the windows were open to reveal plenty of sunlight.

He lay back on the bed and sighed, fully dressed because he was too weak to get his clothes off. When his men tried to help him strip down, he kicked them away. "Are you kidding me? Get out."

The guys left.

I slowly approached the bed, looking at his remains as if I were at a wake. I stopped above him, staring down at a plum instead of a face. "You shouldn't have gone home alone in the first place."

With his eyes closed, he shrugged. "I just wanted to get home... get in bed." He took a deep breath, the exertion of conversation too difficult.

"You want me to take you to the hospital?"

"And give that asshole the satisfaction?" he asked bitterly. "I'd rather die."

"Well...they have something magical called morphine. That might defeat your pride."

He was quiet as if he was considering it. "No."

"How would he even know you're in the hospital?"

"Trust me, he'd know."

I dragged the armchair toward the bed and took a seat. "How about I help you get undressed? You seem uncomfortable."

"I'm not uncomfortable because of the clothes..."

"They aren't helping either." I got to my feet and pulled off his shoes and socks.

"That's the most you should do."

"Come on. Your clothes are dirty. You don't want that stuff in a fresh bed."

"Well, Hades will kill me if I let you see me naked. He's already pissed enough at me as it is." He opened his eyes and looked at the ceiling. Every time he blinked, the white color around his eyes was a stark contrast to his bruised eyelids. He wouldn't turn his neck to look at me. Any movement at all seemed too difficult.

"Relax. I'm not going to take off your boxers."

"Doesn't matter. He won't like it."

"If that's really the case, he needs to grow up. You do too." I undid his jeans then pulled them off his body, being as gentle as possible so I didn't strain something already injured.

He winced a couple of times as I got the denim over his ankles and away from his body. I folded them up and placed them on the dresser. "The shirt is gonna be a little harder." My eyes didn't linger on his physique, but his muscle definition was obvious. He had muscular legs and a tight stomach.

He closed his eyes as he prepared for the worst. "Just get it over with." He took a deep breath before he forced himself upright, cringing in pain as he lifted his arms over his head to get the clothing off.

I got it over his head as quickly as possible.

He fell back to the bed, breathing heavily in agony.

When I looked at his chest, I saw a chiseled body packed with strength and power, but I also saw endless bruises. His ribs had been wrapped with gauze to cover most of the damage, but the discoloration had spread everywhere. "How many ribs did you break?"

He held up three fingers.

"Did they give you any painkillers?"

He nodded to his jeans. "In my front pocket. But they aren't strong enough to mask the pain entirely."

"I'm sorry..." I grabbed the blankets and pulled them up over his body, tucking him in like a child going to bed. My fingers brushed through his hair to feel his temperature before I grabbed the remotes on the nightstand. "Want to watch TV?"

"No. I just want to lie here."

"Alright." I took a seat again. "Let me know if you're hungry or need anything."

"The last thing I want to do is eat..." He kept his eyes closed as he lay there, indisposed.

I watched him with sadness in my heart, but I also felt a twinge of guilt for my relief. Hades came home in one piece, not a single scratch. I was glad Damien was the one with broken bones instead of my husband. "It'll pass, Damien. Just stay calm. The calmer you are, the less intense the pain will feel."

"Yeah..." His hands rested on his stomach, and he was entirely still. "Is Hades home?"

"No. Went to the bank."

"How pissed is he?"

"Well...he's very upset. But he also allowed you to stay here, so he can't be that angry."

"Yeah. I guess that's true."

"And he wouldn't have made the trade in the first place if you weren't the most important thing to him."

His eyes opened, and he chuckled. "I'm not the most important thing to him. You are."

"Maybe it's both of us."

He stared at the ceiling. "I should have listened to Hades. I should have backed off when he told me to. Now we've lost our business...and I got my ass beat like a little bitch." He sighed loudly, wincing when he took a deep breath.

"We all make mistakes."

"But men like me don't make mistakes." He turned his head to the right; that way, I wouldn't be in his line of sight at all. "I hope he forgives me someday, but I wouldn't be surprised if he never did."

"He doesn't hold grudges."

"Yes, he does. His whole life is based on grudges."

"But not against someone he loves."

He rolled his eyes. "We're close, but we aren't pussies."

"I don't think loving someone makes you a pussy."

"Really?" He turned back to me. "Then why are you so scared to love him?"

The question put me on the spot, and it was so unexpected I didn't know what to say. I held his gaze as I tried to think. "I'm not scared to love anyone. It's a natural reaction that you can't control. That means you can't force it either. I just don't feel that way...and I doubt I ever will."

He held my gaze for a while before he looked at the ceiling again. "Why? You're going to spend the rest of your life with this man. That's a long time to be with someone without feeling anything."

"I never said I wouldn't feel anything. I feel a lot of things for him...like respect, trust, and affection. Those are more important to a relationship anyway. And I don't understand why you're concerned about it. This is a convenient relationship for both of us—nothing more."

Damien was quiet as he soaked in my words. Seconds turned to minutes, and he still didn't speak. The conversation seemed to be over.

Which was fine by me.

"Can I ask you something?"

I raised an eyebrow. "You can ask whatever you want. But I can't guarantee an answer."

"That's fair." He turned his head back to me. "Have you ever been in love?"

I had no idea how much Hades had told Damien about our previous relationship. Maybe he knew Hades had proposed; maybe he didn't. But that was a long time ago and had nothing to do with our current relationship. "That's a strange question for a non-pussy to ask."

"Just curious."

"Have you?" I tried to circumvent the question by forcing him to answer it himself.

"No." The answer left his lips like a bullet leaving a gun. "And you?"

I crossed my legs and got comfortable in the chair. "No."

"Never?" he asked incredulously.

I shook my head. "Keep in mind, I'm only twenty-four. That's pretty young to know what love is."

"Romeo and Juliet were still in their teens."

"And they were naïve children who only knew how to think emotionally rather than pragmatically."

His eyes narrowed. "You're cold as ice, aren't you?"

"You just said you've never been in love, but I don't judge you for it. Why are you judging me just because I'm a woman?"

"I've never been in love, but I don't mock anyone who has been."

"I wasn't mocking."

"It seems like you're repulsed by the idea. I'm just trying to figure out why."

I shrugged. "Maybe there is no reason why. I grew up watching my mother's loveless relationships, and that's all I've ever known. Friends who have fallen in love are always scarred by the relationship. Afterward, they're never the same. People confuse romantic love for lust. Two people aren't terrible for each other, but they have amazing sex. People can't distinguish the difference. Half of marriages end in divorce, and those that don't are still unhappy relationships. So, why would I be interested in that?"

Damien was quiet.

"I married Hades because I didn't have a choice. In order to get what I wanted, I had to make that sacrifice. But being with him has made me see all the perks of marriage, like having a strong partner who can help you reach your goals. Having someone to protect you. Starting a family. Being with someone with a foundation of loyalty. It's a great arrangement. Sometimes he pisses me off when he bosses me around, but I've learned to deal with it. And I'm getting good sex, so why would I complain? This is the best-case scenario."

He watched me for several seconds before he faced the ceiling. "I guess that makes sense."

"Do you ever think about getting married?"

"No. I'm not repulsed by the idea, but I can't picture myself meeting a woman I can't live without. I'm in my thirties, and I've never met a woman who can keep my attention for more than a day. If I met someone really special, that would be a miracle. And if that happened...then maybe I'd go for it. But it sounds like you aren't willing to keep an open mind about it at all."

I was tired of explaining myself. "It doesn't matter now anyway. I'm married, so it wouldn't make a difference if I met a guy who made me feel that way...because I'm loyal to my husband."

"How's your friend doing?" Mother asked me as she sat across from me at the dinner table. She was on her second glass of wine while we waited for Hades to come home and join us for dinner.

"Terrible."

"Maybe he would be more comfortable at the hospital."

"He probably would be, but he's too stubborn."

"Men..." She shook her head then drank from her glass. "Good thing Hades was there to save him."

Damien only needed to be saved because he was a drug dealer. If he did something legal, none of this would have happened. My mother was as enmeshed in the underworld as my husband, so I was just as immersed. I stopped fighting it.

Hades walked in the door a moment later, dressed in a deep blue three-piece suit. With his dark hair and shadow across his jawline, he was suave in appearance, both beautiful and deadly. "Good evening, Maria." He greeted her with a partial smile and a hand on her shoulder.

"Hello, Hades." Her face lit up at the sight of her son-in-law, visibly enamored of his presence. He was a man she loved having in the family, one she was proud to have under her roof. There was no one better to bring power to our family line. "Hope you had a good day at the office."

"No complaints." His eyes settled on my face, and he leaned down to kiss me on the mouth.

I kissed him back, feeling the warm affection in his touch. Our natural chemistry made us irresistible to each other. Our lust was combustive. Paired with our mutual trust and affection, it created a relationship that was addictive to both of us.

Once he pulled away, I felt cold, like summer had disappeared and the season jumped from fall to winter.

He sat beside me and poured himself a glass of wine. "How was your day?"

"Damien is in pretty bad shape," I answered. "I tried to get him to go to the hospital, but he wouldn't budge."

He drank his wine, indifferent to what I said.

"How was the office?" I asked when I realized he wouldn't talk about his friend.

"Just a bunch of bullshit and paperwork." He watched Helena place dinner on the table. "This looks amazing. Smells amazing too."

"Thank you, sir." Helena flashed him a smile, giving him all her attention and respect because he was the person she admired the most. He'd been her employer for years before my mother and I came along. While she was polite to us, she didn't bend over backward to assist us the way she did with him.

When she left, we settled into quiet conversation over wine and dinner. Hades was quiet, only answering direct questions that were placed to him. After a long day doing whatever he did at the bank, he was usually not in the mood for long-winded conversations, but he put up a front with my mother. The longer we lived together, the more I got to know him, and the more I understood his behavior.

When we finished dinner, we said good night then walked up the stairs to our bedroom.

Hades glanced at his watch to see the time as he walked down the hallway.

"You don't like my mother, do you?" My heels lightly tapped against the rug that led down the long hallway. Side by side, we approached our bedroom, his height towering over mine.

"I'm always polite to her. What more do you want from me?"

"I don't want anything. I'm just curious."

He stopped abruptly and faced me. "After all the shit I do all day, I don't want to come home to meaningless conversation with my mother-in-law. I don't want to listen to her talk about her day and pretend I give a damn. I'd rather come home to a quiet dinner with my wife then fuck her. That's it." He held my gaze for a few seconds, livid, and then started walking again.

It took me a second before I followed him. "We don't have to have dinner with her every night."

"It seems like it."

"We can cut it down to Tuesdays and Thursdays."

"Then make it happen." He passed Damien's door without glancing at it, then entered our bedroom. He kicked off his shoes and stripped off the pieces of his suit, letting the jacket slide off and then popping the buttons of his vest.

"For what it's worth, she thinks the world of you."

He loosened his tie then turned back to me. "I never said I disliked her. I just don't like the fact that she gets in the way of my time with you. I want to have dinner just the two of us so we can cut out the mediocre conversation and just be real." He unbuttoned his collared shirt and stripped it off until he stood in only his slacks. Unlike Damien, Hades had the most beautiful, unblemished skin. Tanned, with a strong tightness over his muscles, he had a physique that made any woman forget the last thing she said. "I want to walk in the door and fuck you without saying a word."

"You could have that every night if you came home on time."

He undid his slacks and let them fall open. "I come home whenever I come home. Period." Despite the aggressive tone of his voice, he pushed down his pants to reveal a definitive bulge in the front of his boxers. Those came down too and displayed a cock rock hard and ready to fuck.

"How can you be hard when you're in such a bad mood?"

He toed his socks off, then stared me down like I was his enemy rather than his lover. He took a few steps toward me, his chin tilting down to stare at me with hard possessiveness. "Look at you. That's why."

HE HAD one of my legs over his shoulder, while his hand kept my thigh pinned to the side. He moved inside me with forceful thrusts, slamming deep and hard with the occasional moan. His face hovered above mine, his jaw tight and his eyes filled with desire and satisfaction.

I'd already had my climaxes for the night. My body was spent and fulfilled, so now it was just about him. My pussy had no problem staying slick, not when he magically turned me on over and over again. My arms rested around his neck, and I held him close to me as he pounded into me, my pleasured sighs filling the room to the top of the high ceiling. "It's your turn." My fingers slid into the hair at the back of his neck, and I kissed him slowly, felt his deep breathing enter my mouth because he'd exerted himself enough. Coated in sweat, with fat muscles filled with blood, he looked like he'd been lifting heavy weights in the gym for the last hour.

He brought his body closer to mine and ground into me, getting his entire dick inside me as he made his final pumps. He rocked me into the bed with each motion until he reached his breaking point. He rested his face against mine and came with a loud moan, all the muscles in his body tightening as he let his seed explode inside me. "Fuck..." He ground against me as he finished, giving me his heaviness.

It was my favorite moment, feeling my husband come deep inside me. My fingers fisted his hair, and I moaned because it felt so good. It made me feel like a desirable woman, letting my husband claim me in such an intimate way. No other man had ever had the honor of filling me with as much come as he could fit.

After a few seconds of rest, he pulled his semi-hard dick out of me and rolled over. His heavy back hit the mattress, and his body relaxed as he closed his eyes. The sweat was shiny on his chest, reflecting the light from the lit candles. His breathing slowly wound down, gradually turning to a gentle rhythm.

I had been repulsed by the idea of this marriage, but I began to realize it was exactly what I wanted...even if I hadn't realized it at the time. The sex was good, better than I'd find anywhere else, so that alone was a good enough reason. But my husband was also an honest and loyal man. If he weren't, he would have left Damien to his fate.

After a few minutes, he opened his eyes once more. A foul presence followed him everywhere he went, a cloudy sky that was ready to storm at any moment. Ever since he'd brought Damien back, he'd been abrasive and cold. Now that bitterness had returned even though it had nothing to do with me. I could just feel it.

He got out of bed and pulled on a fresh pair of boxers before pouring himself a drink. It was late, and he should be getting to sleep. But instead, he grabbed his phone and his laptop and prepared to move to the patio through the double glass doors.

I propped myself up on my elbow. "What are you doing?"

His muscled frame slowly turned around to face me again, a bottle of scotch in his grasp. "I've got work to do."

"It's almost nine..."

"Doesn't matter. I've got shit to do." He turned around and kept walking.

"Hades." I pushed back the covers and sat upright.

He slowly turned back to me, not hiding his irritation.

"I've noticed you haven't visited Damien since he's been here."

All he did was stare.

"I know you're angry with him, but maybe you should—"

"Don't tell me what to do." His deep tone caused a terrifying vibration in the air. Instead of looking at me like I was his wife, he looked at me like I was someone who'd crossed him...like I was Damien. "If I want to talk to him, I will." Instead of turning away, he waited until he was certain I had nothing else to say.

"He's sorry. And he's been punished enough—"

"You have no idea what you're talking about," he said coldly. "He got his ass kicked because that's exactly what he deserved. That's not punishment. He hasn't been punished yet...but he will."

I was surprised Hades was this cold to his own friend. "Don't you think you're being a little harsh?"

His eyes narrowed, like I'd just crossed a line. The cord in his neck became visible because his body stiffened so tightly. The red tint to his face indicated that I had gone too far and should have kept my mouth shut. "I lost my business because of his stupidity, Sofia. I told him to back off, and he didn't listen to me. This is all his fault—because he always thinks he knows better. You're exactly the same way—and you don't know a goddamn thing."

12

HADES

I GOT READY FOR WORK WITHOUT ACKNOWLEDGING MY WIFE.

In mutual silence, we both got dressed and pretended the other didn't exist. I slipped my watch onto my wrist while rage made my blood boil. She didn't need to concern herself with my affairs, let alone give her opinion about it. She didn't know a goddamn thing and needed to mind her own business.

Instead of being apologetic, she was just as angry with me.

That was the downfall of having a sassy wife. She stood by her decisions and refused to apologize for her point of view. She was stubborn and argumentative. And she didn't scare easily. They were all traits I hated about her...but also loved.

It was a double-edged sword.

I put on my jacket and finally faced her.

She gave me a pissed look then ignored me again.

I had a bit of an ego so I didn't appreciate the way she treated me, but I also respected her for not putting up with my shit. "I'll be home late tonight."

"Or maybe just don't come home at all." She didn't look at me as she slipped on her heels.

My fingers ached to grab her by the back of the neck and bend her over the bed. My palm would smack that ass until it was swollen and red. Old-fashioned punishment should get her to change her tune. But that tactic wouldn't work on her. "Be careful what you wish for."

"WHERE'S DAMIEN?" The suits stared at me, ready to do business.

"Unavailable." I kept the truth as quiet as possible because it made us look like pussies. I still hadn't figured out what I was going to do about the deal we'd made. I had to honor it, but I was also tempted to give Damien back and cancel the agreement.

The meeting resumed, and we talked numbers. The men were brothers from the south of France, laundering their money through my channels every few months. Now we were in one of their estates in the countryside, beautiful women and whores all over the house.

Once the deal was made, we shook hands.

"As a thank you," one of the men said, "we brought your favorite girl." He snapped his fingers.

His men opened the door and chauffeured the woman inside.

She was in a black trench coat, but I knew there was nothing but lingerie underneath. Her dark hair was in soft curls, and makeup was painted on her beautiful face. She gave me a flirtatious look, batting her eyelashes as she gave me an air kiss.

The men left the room to give us privacy.

Vivian was one of my favorite whores, a woman I'd spent a lot of time with throughout the years. I paid a lot of money for her, but when the men wanted something from me, they loaned me to her for days at a time. She unbuttoned her coat and let the jacket fall from her body, revealing a black bodysuit that didn't cover her perky tits.

I was pissed at my wife at the moment, and she would have no idea if I fucked this woman or not. It would be easy for me to lead a double life, to make Sofia regret treating me that way.

Vivian came close to me, getting on her knees so she could suck my dick.

When I got a good look at her, I realized how similar she looked to Sofia. She had dark hair, full lips, and eyes so much like my wife's, it was eerie. I'd been with this woman many times, had great sex I'd paid thousands of euros for, but not once did I ever feel anything.

Why did I feel so much for Sofia?

Why did I love her so much?

When Vivian reached for my pants, I pushed her hands away. "I'm married."

She raised an eyebrow. "What does that mean?"

"That I can't do this." I got to my feet without any regret. Even when I was ticked at my wife, it didn't change how I felt. Even when I was in a dark room with a beautiful woman, I wasn't tempted to betray her. My dick wasn't even hard.

Why did my wife have so much power over me?

Why was she the only woman I wanted to be with?

Why did I feel like shit just for looking at someone else?

***

I CAME HOME LATER like I said I would. Sofia was having dinner with her mother in the dining room, but I wasn't in the mood for bullshit conversation. I wasn't even that hungry, so nothing sounded appetizing anyway.

I made it to the third floor, my mood sour from the events of my night. There was a part of me that wished I could betray Sofia, that I could be the cold monster I used to be. If she wasn't good to me, I would just find someone else. It would hurt her, but make her take me seriously.

But I couldn't do it.

I wished I were immune to her charms, immune to her potent beauty. I wished this curse had never been placed on my shoulders. My life would be much less complicated.

I passed Damien's bedroom, the door wide open. He was sitting up in bed with a dinner tray on his lap. His face still looked like shit, but some of his mobility had returned. He held his fork and took a bite of his dinner, moving slowly like every extension of his limbs was difficult.

Without looking up from his food, he addressed me. "How long are you going to pretend I don't exist?"

I stepped into the doorway, my hands resting in my pockets. I leaned against the frame and stared at my oldest friend. The anger was still potent in my body, but there was also a hint of sympathy. My wife had been taking care of him for days, and he had already improved dramatically. Parts of his skin were actually turning white again.

When I didn't answer, he took another bite. "I guess that answers my question..." He turned back to his food and waited for me to walk away.

I moved into his bedroom and shut the door behind me before I took a seat in the armchair by his bedside. I loosened my tie and popped the top button of my shirt before I relaxed into the cushioned chair. One ankle rested on the opposite knee, and my hands came together in my lap.

He set his fork down and abandoned his dinner.

"You can keep eating."

"Nah. I don't have an appetite when you look at me like that." He winced as he grabbed the tray and moved it to the side.

I should have helped him, but I was too stubborn. He deserved every single ache and pain as punishment for his stupidity. All of this could have been easily avoided, and his bruises didn't compare to the pain I felt at losing my life's work.

He breathed heavily for a bit before he recovered from the movement. "Go ahead. Yell at me."

I stared.

"You've been keeping it bottled inside for days. You're like a can of soda that's been shaken vigorously. The second that top pops off...pandemonium."

My eyes didn't blink as I examined his gaze. My anger didn't decrease, but it was hard not to feel comfortable at his side. Our friendship had survived so many battles, and we never held grudges against each other. It was hard to hold one now. "I'm not going to yell at you. You know exactly how I feel. No need to say anything."

His eyes softened. "I think I'd prefer it if you yelled at me…"

"You aren't worth my time."

"Ouch." He shook his head slightly. "Why don't you just give me back to Maddox and call the whole thing off?"

"If I were going to do that, I wouldn't have made the trade in the first place. Even when you betray me, you're still more important than everything we've built. Take it as a compliment."

"I can't…not when I feel like shit."

"Well, I hope you feel like shit for a long time."

"I will…even once these bruises heal."

I turned my gaze away because I couldn't hold my anger. Damien was pompous with an enormous ego. The rare times he showed humility reminded me why we'd been friends for so long. He was a good guy…just a little stupid sometimes.

"What are we going to do?"

"The only thing we can do—pull out."

He lowered his voice. "You can't be serious."

"I made a deal—your life for the business."

"But that doesn't mean we can't hunt him down and kill him. Problem solved."

Maddox was an unpredictable foe. He'd been in our midst for years but never actually moved against us. He enjoyed the competition, enjoyed having an equal enemy. That made him psychotic, difficult to understand. "That could backfire. He's impossible to track. He's made sure of that."

Damien was quiet as he considered an alternative. "We could get him to come to us..."

"How?"

"We could continue the business like nothing's changed."

I cocked an eyebrow. "And go back on my word?"

"What's the worst that could happen? He comes after us?" Damien asked. "It'll give us a chance to kill him."

"He'll have the element of surprise, so he'll have the upper hand."

"Then we'll always be prepared."

I shook my head. "That wasn't what we agreed to, Damien."

"Well, we're in the drug game. This isn't the same as operating a bank on good faith, on strong handshakes. This is about survival. When people find out you rolled over for Maddox, they won't take us seriously. We need to be the monsters men want in their corners. Just giving up isn't the solution. And frankly, I don't think Maddox wants that anyway. He wants us to take it a step further, to make the fire an inferno. He wants blood, guts, and war."

I couldn't refute that last part. "Seems shady."

"We are shady, Hades."

I stared at the painting on the wall, a piece of artwork a designer picked out for me a long time ago. I had no participation in the decoration of this house. Everything was foreign to me...but it still felt like home. "I'll think about it."

"Think about it all you want, but it doesn't change anything. Our entire network relies on our organization. All our allies, all our business relationships, everything. Men on our payroll will have to be let go, and firing someone is the best way to make an enemy."

Damien was talking sense, but I still didn't want to be dishonest. People trusted me because I always spoke the truth. The second I stopped, no one would be able to believe a word I said. But in this situation, I may not have another choice. "I said I'll think about it."

Damien faced forward again, turning quiet as he dropped the conversation.

"You've improved."

"Thanks to your wife," he whispered.

"I thought Helena was taking care of you."

"Yeah, but Sofia keeps me company during the day. We play games, have lunch, stuff like that...gets my mind off it. And she's nicer to me than Helena is."

"Because Helena knows you're a piece of shit."

"Well, Sofia knows that too, and she's still nice to me." He turned back to me.

I knew exactly why Sofia was that way. "She has a big heart."

"I don't know about that, but she is kind."

"What's that supposed to mean?"

He avoided my gaze for a long time. "Nothing."

"Doesn't seem like nothing."

He still wouldn't look at me.

"Damien."

"Just drop it, Hades."

"Then why did you make that backhanded compliment in the first place?"

He shrugged. "I guess I'm just angry about the whole thing."

They'd been spending a lot of time together, so they probably had a lot of heart-to-heart conversations while I was out of the house. "Tell me."

"You don't want to know. Leave it alone."

The more he tried to hide it from me, the more it bothered me. "Damien, I'm not gonna stop thinking about it until you tell me. So you may as well just man up."

He turned back to me, sympathy in his gaze. "You said things had been different recently."

Until I pissed her off. "Yeah."

"So I asked her a couple of questions...she answered."

"What kinds of questions?"

He shrugged. "Doesn't matter. But basically...she said she'd never love you." He turned his gaze away like he couldn't stand the sight of my pain. His words were fists that blacked out both of my eyes.

I absorbed his words with my usual calm exterior. My poker face was the best in the game, my thoughts impossible to read. The only person who could gauge my feelings was my wife...because I allowed her to really see me. My insides turned to lava and burned my guts, making my intestines black. The heat wasn't a byproduct of rage. It was just an intense wave of disappointment; of a truth I already knew but refused to believe. Our relationship had deepened and everything seemed perfect...but that opinion was one-sided. No matter what I did, she would never feel differently toward me. That was the devastating truth.

"Told you you didn't want to know..." He had the respect not to look at me, to give me some privacy while I digested the painful words. "Sofia is beautiful, smart, and kind. She balances out your asshole-ness. But you deserve better. Are you sure this is a good idea?"

"What do you expect me to do?"

"Divorce her."

So someone else could have her? Never. "I knew what I was getting into when I married her. I'm committed."

He turned back to me. "You're just going to get hurt."

"It'll hurt more to live without her."

"Geez...that's intense. Fuck, I hope I never love a woman. Not worth it."

It was the most pain I'd ever endured, but it was also the most passion I'd ever experienced. I'd never been so alive. "I saw Vivian tonight. The guys loaned her out to me as a thank you."

Damien's eyes widened. "Did you...?"

"No."

"That's restraint."

"No, it wasn't. I could have gotten away with it, and Sofia would never know. But I wasn't tempted at all...because there's only one woman I want to be with. Even if she doesn't love me, even if she's pissed at me, I'm a slave to her. It's depressing but also exhilarating at the same time. Sofia is the best vintage bottle of wine, and everything else is horse piss. Once you've had the best, you can never go back."

"Sounds intense."

"What else did she say?"

He shrugged. "She said she's never been in love before. Your relationship is perfect as it is because you're a good husband who's honest and powerful...and you're good in bed. And if she ever does fall in love with someone someday, she still wouldn't betray you."

That stung the most.

Fuck, that hurt.

It was the first time I couldn't control my reaction. I released a deep hiss from between my teeth, feeling the searing heat cook my insides once more. The idea of loving me was so ridiculous to her that it was more likely she would fall in love with someone other than me. My eyes dropped to the floor.

"I'm sorry," he whispered. "But if it makes you feel any better, it has nothing to do with you. We never should have walked into that purple tent in Marrakech. Maybe things would have been different...or maybe they would have been the same anyway."

I'd wondered the same thing. Did that fortune come true because she read it to me? Or would this have happened whether we visited Morocco or not? I slouched in the chair and felt the strength leave my limbs. The devastation was still potent in my blood, like I'd lost her for the second time.

"That's why I wonder if it would be better for you to just forget about her..."

"I can't forget about her." During the two years we were apart, I still thought about her on a daily basis. I wondered where she slept at night. Anytime I was with a brunette, I pretended she was Sofia to give me a better climax. Leaving her would only revert me back to that endless loneliness.

He shook his head slightly. "How could a woman be so cold? Is she cold because of this curse? If you weren't being punished for what you've done, would she be a different woman? Is she damned because of this too?"

"No idea."

He turned quiet as he considered all the possibilities.

The fortune reader told me this was punishment for the crimes I'd committed. I'd done a lot of terrible things, but I wondered if killing my father was the specific action that triggered all of this. I wished I could take it all back, to have a clean slate with Sofia, sweep her off her feet and make her fall for me.

Or would I never have loved her in the first place?

An idea came into my head. "You think she's still there?"

"Who?" he asked. "Sofia?"

"No. That woman in the purple tent in the bazaar."

He cocked an eyebrow. "No idea. We were there ten years ago, and she was kinda old. Why?"

"What if I went back and spoke to her?"

"What would that accomplish?"

"Maybe I could do something to fix it."

"Like pay her off?" he asked. "I don't think it works like that."

"But maybe there's something I could... Is there a ritual or something? A blessing. I don't know. Maybe she read my future as it would unfold at that point. But what if I could do something to change the rest of the story?"

He shrugged. "No idea."

"That's why I'm going to ask her."

"So you're going back to Marrakech?"

"Yeah. I'll leave in the morning."

"I'm coming with you."

I eyed all the bruises on his face. "You're in no condition, Damien."

"Yeah, but you can't do this alone."

"I can do anything alone."

"But we were together the first time we went. Maybe we need to be together the second time."

"You're just going to slow me down."

He stopped arguing, his eyes defeated.

"Why do you want to go so bad?"

He wouldn't make eye contact. "I guess I want to ask her about my fortune...if it's really going to happen."

I SAT on the patio in my sweatpants and finished work before bed. The doors were open, so I heard Sofia walk inside after she finished dinner with her mother. There was no way to miss me when she walked inside, so she chose to ignore me.

She was lucky she didn't have to witness my dark side.

I closed my tablet and brought it inside along with my glass of scotch.

She was already dressed for bed, wearing one of my t-shirts with her panties underneath. She pulled her hair over one shoulder, naturally sexy without even trying.

I was angry with her for being angry with me, but that didn't stop me from getting hard. Just hours ago, my favorite courtesan was on her knees and ready to suck my dick, but there was no blood between my legs. The sight of my wife in my t-shirt giving me the cold shoulder made me so hard it actually hurt.

Man, I had it bad.

She closed the drawer and turned toward the bed, choosing to pretend I wasn't standing there.

My patience evaporated, and I grabbed her by the arm.

She twisted out of it so fast, like she'd been expecting it.

But she was no match for me. I pinned both of her arms behind her back then forced her to bend over at the edge of the bed. My hand gripped the back of her neck and held her in place, the shirt riding up her stomach and revealing her perky ass in her panties.

She tried to fight me. "Asshole, let me—"

"Knock this shit off. Now." I kept her in place with no exertion because she was weak in comparison to my strength. "Treat me that way, and I'll treat you this way. Be pissed at me all you want, but don't fucking ignore me. You will show me respect every goddamn day. Understand?"

She tried to buck me off. "Fuck you."

I kept her down. "I had a meeting tonight, and my associates bought me my favorite whore."

She stopped trying to evade my hold.

"I used to pay a lot of money for her, fuck her in this very bedroom for an entire weekend. She would have done anything I asked, and you would have had no idea where my dick had been all night. But I turned down the offer and came home to you. I'm committed to this for better or worse. You need to start behaving the same way." I let her go and turned away, my cock still pressing against my shorts because I got off on restraining her. I was tempted to fuck her like that, keeping her under my clutches as she fought my hold.

I grabbed the bottle of scotch and poured another glass. My back was to her as I let the liquid slide down my throat and straight into my gut. It was potent because I had an empty stomach. I was tempted to leave the house again and head to a bar. Or better yet, I should get on a plane and fly to Morocco now.

I felt her palms flatten against my back, her touch slight and gentle.

I was about to take another drink, but I put the glass down instead.

Her hands glided up my back to my shoulders, massaging me lightly, touching me with remorse.

I closed my eyes and enjoyed her touch, slipping under her spell for the millionth time.

She grabbed my bicep and forced me to turn around.

I moved with the pull, wanting to forget about this fight and get naked as quickly as possible. Her immature behavior would have made me indifferent to her if she were someone else. I wouldn't put up with this shit. I still shouldn't put up with this shit. But there I was...fucking weak.

She looked up at me, her green eyes glazed and her lips slightly parted. Her palms started at my stomach and slowly slid toward my chest as she stepped in a little closer. Her face moved to my chest as if she was going to rest her forehead there, but instead, she kissed the skin over my heart.

I fought to keep my arms by my sides, refusing to allow myself to forgive her so quickly.

She lifted her gaze to meet mine again. "I'm sorry..."

My cock twitched in my boxers, wanting to slide between her lips as she whispered those words. I wanted to lie flat on her tongue and feel it move as she apologized again...and again.

"I just thought you were being harsh to your best friend."

"My issues with Damien are none of your business. Stay out of it."

"I'm your wife...your issues are my business."

I always got off on the way she said her title, the way she called herself my wife. "But you don't have the right to tell me how to feel about it. I spoke to Damien when I was ready. It had to be on my terms."

Her fingers continued to caress my chest. "Is that true? What you said…?"

"Would I lie to you?" My fingers ached to slide into her hair and brush it from her face, to pull her in for a deep kiss. But I had to keep my arms by my sides, keep up this pissed façade so she would remain apologetic. I never knew remorse could be so sexy. I pushed the front of my pants down so my cock could emerge, hard as steel. "Would I be this hard if I'd already fucked someone else all night?"

"I don't know. You fuck me all night and never have a problem."

"That's because I love…" I shut my mouth and stopped myself from making a dire mistake. "Because I love fucking you more than anyone else." I pushed my pants and boxers farther until they slid to my ankles.

She kept her gaze on me and didn't glance at my dick. She also didn't seem to anticipate what I was really going to say before I saved myself. Her arms circled my neck, and she rose on her tiptoes so she could kiss me.

My arms couldn't stay back for another moment, so I wrapped them around her waist and pulled her close, my lips burning at her touch. My hands slid under her shirt, and I pushed her thong over her ass, my cock thinking about that slick pussy.

I pulled the shirt over her head and revealed her round tits and flat stomach before I backed her toward the bed, stepping out of my bottoms in the process. Her panties got left behind too.

When the backs of her knees hit the bed, she prepared to lie down so I could get on top of her.

I had other plans.

I spun her around and forced her into the position she'd been in before, her face against the sheets and her ass in the air. Her pussy was visible to me, along with that little asshole I had yet to fuck. My hand gripped the back of her neck and applied pressure while my other hand pinned her wrists together at the small of her back. "You're going to show me how sorry you are."

I HAD to head to the airport, but Sofia was smothered into my side, her arm draped across my waist while her lips rested against my chest. Her hair stretched over my arm, the scent of her shampoo ingrained in my skin.

I wanted to stay there and watch her wake up.

But I had shit to take care of.

As gently as I could, I pulled my body from underneath hers and placed her on the pillow. I slipped from under the sheets and made it to the edge of the bed. My phone lit up with another message. I'd been getting them all morning.

When I got to my feet, she stirred. "What time is it?" She pulled the sheets farther over her shoulder and closed her eyes.

"Early."

"Then why are you getting out of bed?"

"I've got to catch my flight." I pulled on clean underwear and grabbed a t-shirt from the closet.

"Flight?" She sat up in bed and let the sheets fall. "Where are you going? When were you going to tell me?"

"Last night, but I never got around to it." I pulled on my jeans then grabbed my leather jacket.

She got out of bed, wide awake now that she knew I was leaving. "Where are you going?"

"Marrakech."

"And what's there?"

I kept my answer vague. "Business. I'll be back tomorrow." I pulled on my shoes then slipped my watch onto my wrist.

Standing there naked, she looked devastated by the news. "So, I'll be alone tonight?"

"My men will keep you safe."

"That's not what I'm worried about. It's just... I've never slept here alone." She grabbed the shirt she'd been wearing the night before from the floor and pulled it on.

"You can handle it." I grabbed my bag next.

She walked up to me. "Are you doing anything dangerous?"

"No. I'll be home tomorrow—I promise."

Her eyes scanned back and forth as she studied my gaze. "I'm sorry I said I didn't want you to come home... I didn't mean that."

"I know." How could she fuck me like a maniac but not love me? How could she be so upset about my departure but feel nothing? "Just don't say shit like that again. Because you never know if it'll be the last thing you say to me."

Her eyes softened further, like my words were bullets to her heart. "I don't want you to go."

I'd just gotten dressed, but now I wanted to strip everything off and climb back into bed with her. I wanted to get hot and sweaty with my wife and forget about the rest of the world. Listening to her beg me was such a turn-on. Watching her turn vulnerable for me, become clingy, was the sexiest thing in the world. "I have to."

"Alright. Could you call me before you go to bed?"

She was making it harder and harder for me to leave. "Yes."

She moved into me and slid her hands up my chest, the longing obvious in the emotion in her eyes. She'd been pissed at me yesterday, but now she didn't want to let me go. She rested her forehead against my chest and stood there, her hands resting at my stomach.

My hand slid into her hair, and I pulled her close to me, my chin resting on her forehead. I held her against me for a few minutes, ignoring my looming tardiness. It was my own plane so I could get there whenever I wanted, but I wanted to be in Marrakech before nightfall. Though nothing could pull me from here, not when I had her so close to me.

She didn't want to let me go...and neither did I.

I pressed a kiss to her forehead. "I have to go."

She slowly pulled her hands off me. "Alright...be safe."

"Always." My hand cupped her cheek, and I looked into her beautiful face, missing her before I was even gone. My thumb swiped across her bottom lip, and I inhaled a deep breath as I treasured this moment, felt grateful she was mine and not someone else's. "I'll miss you." It was a pathetic thing to say, pussy shit for someone like me. But I said it anyway...and I meant it.

Her eyes lit up, and a smile spread across her lips. "I'll miss you too."

IT'D BEEN ten years since I'd visited the bazaar. It was a massive place, and Damien and I had been wandering the alleyways and admiring the handmade pots and rugs as we killed time that night before the brothel opened at dusk. I didn't have a clear idea where that purple tent was located, so I kept walking in the hope I would stumble across it.

I bumped into various characters, gypsies who tried to pick my pockets and prostitutes who wanted a paycheck for the night. There were defanged cobras and magicians swallowing lit swords along the way.

Everyone knew I was lost.

I kept looking, knowing I would find it eventually if it was still here.

I turned to the right and headed down a new alleyway lined with gold pots. That was when I spotted it, a purple tent tucked nearly out of sight. It was a suspicious position for a business because it wasn't clearly visible. It seemed like it only wanted to be visited by people who already knew it was there.

I opened the flap and stepped inside.

It was exactly as I remembered it. Gold pots were on the ground with turquoise jewels, it smelled like scented oils, and there was a round table with a single chair. A purple tablecloth was over the surface, along with the cards the gypsy had read a decade ago.

This was the place.

But where was the woman?

I took a seat in the chair and waited. I was prepared to sit there all night if I had to. This was a stupid idea with close to nothing odds, but I had to try. Otherwise, I'd lose my mind.

Half an hour later, the flap opened and a woman stepped inside. Adorned with various jewels around her neck and a shawl around her head, she looked like the woman I'd visited ten years ago, but I couldn't actually remember what she looked like. This might be her...or just someone dressed in the same way.

She halted as she stared at me, her eyes taking their time roaming over every feature of my face. They drifted down and looked over my appearance, from my leather jacket to my black shoes. When her examination was done, she glided to the chair across from me and took a seat. "Only one fortune per person. That's the rule."

My eyebrows rose in surprise. "You remember me."

"I remember your presence. Very tainted...very disturbed." She grabbed the cards on the table and shuffled them until they were placed to the side. A low burning candle was in the center, the wax starting to drip onto the tablecloth. The musky air smelled like paprika and candles. "But I can only read your future once. Unless I can provide you direction, I'm useless to you." Her hands came together on the table with resignation.

"I'm not here for a fortune reading. The first one was bad enough."

Her eyes slowly filled with sympathy, as if she knew exactly what I'd been through. "Knowing the future is both a blessing and a curse. You accept terrible things easier when you know they are coming...but they are also all you ever think about until they happen."

Definitely. "I need to know if it can be reversed."

One eyebrow cocked to the ceiling of the tent. "The future has already happened. Now it's the past. I hope you aren't dumb enough to think the past can be changed."

"That's not what I meant."

"Then be clear, Hades."

Goose bumps sprinkled up my arms, and the air suddenly felt thicker than it had a moment ago. There was an energy I couldn't identify. This woman seemed like more than just a card-reader. She's like a full-on sorceress. "How do you know my name?"

"I can read you."

Even if Damien had said my name ten years ago and she caught it, there was no way she could still remember it. That meant she had to be telling the truth. "I'm married to the woman I love, and just as you said, she won't love me back. It's not prejudice or betrayal that causes her indifference. She just...doesn't."

She nodded slightly.

"You said I was being punished for the things I've done—"

"And the things you would do."

"Yes. I thought your reading was bullshit at the time, but now that everything you predicted has come to pass...I know it's real."

She nodded again.

"Help me change it."

"Hades, I already said the past can't be changed."

"But you said I was being punished for the crimes I've committed. If I were to be forgiven for those crimes, would that break this curse?"

Her eyes narrowed as she stared at me.

"I love my wife more than anything in this world...and it kills me that she feels nothing for me. It's the kind of torture I wouldn't give my greatest enemy. I can't live like this forever. There has to be something I can do." I bared my soul to this complete stranger, desperate to get what I wanted. Normally, I would just throw cash at my problems and make them go away...but not this.

"Well...there are two options. But neither one is good."

"Alright..."

"The first one is unpredictable. We could try it and hope for the best, but I can't promise you it'll work."

"Let's just try."

"Hold on. You don't even know what you're agreeing to."

"Then tell me." I was impatient, wanting this eternal night to end for good.

"There are two ways to approach your problem. The first one is, we could make you stop loving her. Make you forget about her. With your newfound freedom, you could divorce her and get back to the life you had before."

I didn't anticipate that being a solution.

"I can't promise it'll work, but it does have a chance. This is the easier option for you. The second one is...near to impossible to achieve. I suggest we do the first one and not even bother with the second."

I didn't come in here with the intention of forgetting Sofia. If I could stop these feelings, it would solve all of my problems. My heart would cease to ache for her, and all the torture would be over. She could leave, and I wouldn't give a damn about her anymore. It was exactly what I wanted...right? "Will the other option achieve the same thing?"

"The opposite. You could break the curse, and there's a chance she'll love you on her own. But like I said, it is much more complicated and I don't recommend it. We could do the first one right now and you could be on your way."

Now I was at a crossroads, and I had to decide what I wanted. To go back to my blissful life of whores, money, and drugs without a care in the world...or I could have the most intense relationship of my life with a woman who felt the same way. Loving her was a pain in the ass, but living a life without that seemed... bleak. Sofia brought so much happiness into my life. I didn't want to lose that; I just didn't want to be tortured anymore. "The second one."

She gave me a disappointed look. "You want to continue this torture?"

I nodded. "I don't want to stop loving her. That's never been the problem." That was the dumber choice. I knew it was an error in judgment, a decision made with my heart and not my brain.

She grabbed her cards and started to lay them out again. "That leaves option two..." She spread them out, lit a different essence, and then stared at the surface of the table.

"Which is?"

"We need to identify your gravest crime...and you have to make it right." She flipped a few cards over and moved them around, as if she were trying to solve a puzzle.

"I can save you some time."

She lifted her gaze.

"I killed my father."

She didn't blink, like she already knew what I'd done.

"There's no way to rectify something like that." I shot him in the head and watched the light leave his eyes before he fell to the ground. My actions were heroic to some, but they were sickening to me. My brother gave me a look I'd never forget, and I knew he would kill me if we ever crossed paths again. I destroyed our family...and even I couldn't forgive myself.

"That's why option number one is better."

"No. That'll never be an option."

"So you'd rather love her when she'll never love you?" she asked.

I nodded. "So we'd better make option two work."

She sighed before she looked at the cards again. "You have one sibling, right?"

"Yes." I didn't bother asking how she knew that.

"He was close with your father."

Right again. "Correct."

She moved some more cards around. "Earning forgiveness from your late father won't be the problem. He deserved his punishment, and I'm certain he knows that. Your brother, on the other hand, is a different story. He carries the grief, carries the resentment to this day." She lifted her chin and looked me in the eye. "Your best bet is to earn his forgiveness."

She was right—option two was pointless.

"A father wants his sons to be close. If he sees you and your brother together again, he'll absolve you of your crime."

"He'll never forgive me..." My brother was my father's ally. He took over the business once my father was dead in the ground. We'd always be enemies, always hate each other for our crimes. I had a better chance of getting Sofia to love me by myself.

"Option one is always on the table if you change your mind."

That wasn't even a last resort. I'd rather love Sofia until my dying day than live an empty existence without her. Our passion gave me incredible nights. My devotion made me care about her, made me appreciate something besides money. Our friendship made me feel less alone. She gave me everything I'd been missing. "I need to know something."

"I'm listening."

"Would she have loved me if this curse had never happened?" It seemed like she was incapable of love, so maybe her indifference had nothing to do with me. Maybe she was just empty like a jar.

She moved her cards around again, gathering her readings. "Absolutely."

"How do you know that?"

"Because she's your soul mate."

13

SOFIA

Damien lay in bed while I sat in the armchair at his bedside. A movie was on, so we watched it together, sharing a bowl of popcorn.

I kept glancing at my phone, wondering when Hades would call.

If he said he would call, he would.

Unless something happened to him…

Damien must have noticed I'd checked my phone for the twentieth time because he said, "Don't worry about him. He's fine."

"It's getting late."

"Late to you isn't late to him."

"After what happened to you, how could you not be worried about him?"

He grabbed a handful of popcorn and stuffed it into his mouth. "Because he's not there to do anything dangerous. Just a quick meeting. You're stressing over nothing."

"My husband is alone in a different country. Of course I'm stressed."

"Well, don't forget who your husband is." He kept watching the TV. "He's a powerful guy who can handle himself."

"So are you," I pointed out. "Now you're stuck in bed."

"That's the difference between Hades and me. I'm stupid—he's not."

"Come on. That's not true."

"If I were smart, none of this would have happened. So, no, it is true." He grabbed more popcorn.

I watched the movie and still felt anxious about Hades's absence. He said if I ever called, he would answer. I was tempted to do that now, but I didn't want to bother him. So I continued to withstand the torture and dread sleeping alone in that big bed tonight. "It's gonna be weird sleeping alone tonight."

"You slept alone before."

"But not in his bed...and now I'm married. I've been sleeping with him for months, and I've gotten used to it."

"I'd offer to let you sleep in here, but he'd murder me."

I chuckled. "No offense, but you aren't my husband. It wouldn't work."

"The guy is like my brother, so we're pretty similar. And I'm obviously more handsome."

I thought Damien was a good-looking man, but Hades was on a whole other level. I still remembered the first time I saw him... fucking gorgeous. I was just a teenager battling hormones, and he was the subject of most of my diary entries. "That means you know his real name."

He shrugged.

"What is it?"

"Like I'm telling you that."

"Come on, I've been taking care of you for a week."

"So you only did it because you had an agenda?" he asked coldly.

"No...but a favor would be nice."

"You know I can't do that. That's personal shit. When he wants you to know, he'll tell you."

"I don't see why it needs to be a secret in the first place."

"Because that's not who he is anymore." He handed me the bowl when he realized he was hogging it.

I pushed it away because I'd had enough. "What was he like when he was younger?"

"How much younger?"

"I don't know...he said you went to university together."

"He was what you'd expect him to be, an egotistical jackass that was addicted to pussy. He wanted to drop out first, said we were too smart to waste our time with textbooks. When he jumped ship, so did I. Not once have we looked back. He's a brilliant guy who knows how to get shit done. Those qualities have only intensified over the years."

And now that ambitious man was my husband. "Has he ever—"

My phone started to ring, and his name appeared on the screen. "Hold on." I took the call and walked out of the room. "Hey... Is everything okay?"

He was quiet over the line, like my question needed careful consideration. "Baby, I'm fine." Those three words were so simple, but he said them with such emotion, like he'd run two marathons in a row. "You have nothing to worry about."

"The later it got, the more stressed I became. I thought about calling you, but I didn't want to bother you."

"Baby." His commanding voice echoed over the line. "You can call me whenever you want. No one in the world has that luxury but you. Use it."

I sat at the edge of the bed, comforted by the sound of his deep voice. "How was your day?"

He sighed. "Bullshit."

"Why was it bullshit?"

"It just was," he said vaguely. "What are you doing?"

"Damien and I were eating popcorn and watching a movie."

"The two of you are getting close, huh?"

"He's pretty much my brother-in-law. I should probably get to know him, right?"

"Yeah, but you don't need to torture yourself," he teased.

"No, we're fine. He tells me things about you..."

"Must be a mixture of bad and good."

"Only good, actually. Other than the fact that you were an

egotistical jackass that was addicted to pussy in your early twenties…"

There was a long pause before his playfulness returned. "I'm still addicted to pussy—yours."

That shouldn't sound romantic to me, but it did. "I can't wait for you to be home. I don't like it when you aren't here."

"Nothing could ever happen to you."

"That's not the only reason I want you home…" I just missed him, even when we were angry with each other. It was comfortable…it was safe.

"Baby, I'll be there in the morning." Now, he called me baby all the time, and it just fit, like a new pair of shoes that were already broken in. He only seemed to call me by my first name when he was angry with me.

"Alright…then I'll let you go."

"Send me some pictures." He abruptly changed the subject, his voice deeper and full of command.

"What kinds of pictures?"

"Baby, you know."

"Right now?" I asked incredulously.

"What else am I going to jerk off to?"

"Didn't you bring your tablet?"

"I don't want to look at that. I want to look at you. The sound of your voice…that's all it takes."

"I've never done that before…"

"Well, learn. Because I want a million pictures of you."

IT WAS late afternoon when his car pulled onto the property.

"I think he's home." I went into Damien's room. "The gate just opened."

He stepped out of the bathroom, just a towel wrapped around his waist. "I'll see him in a little bit. I'm sure he wants to see you first."

I headed downstairs to the main entryway, and by the time I got there, Hades was already speaking to Helena with his bag on the floor beside him. One of the servants took it away, probably to wash his dirty clothes and return the possessions he brought with him.

I was grateful to see him in one piece, without a scratch or a single bruise. I walked up to him and waited for him to finish giving his orders to Helena.

He finally turned and looked at me, and for whatever reason, he took nearly thirty seconds to really examine me. It was like he'd never seen me before, never took the time to study all the features of my face. His black wedding ring was on his left hand, and he walked toward me slowly with his gaze glued to mine.

Sometimes I hated this man, but most of the time, I didn't know what to do without him. He'd become the most important person in my life, my closest friend. He was the man I confided in, the man who protected me, the man who always knew all the answers. The only family I had left was my mother, but now he was family too. "I'm glad you're home." I released the breath I'd been holding, feeling my entire body relax now that I knew he was home safe. After what happened to Damien, I never assumed he was untouchable.

"I can tell." His hands gripped my hips, and he pulled us close together, his forehead resting against mine as he enveloped me with warm affection. His arm wrapped around my waist, and he pulled me in for a hug, making me feel delicate in his strong embrace. His lips moved to my forehead, and he kissed me gently.

I closed my eyes because the touch felt sincere. "Are you staying home the rest of the day?"

"No. I have stuff to do. Just wanted to see you before I left again."

I couldn't hide my disappointment. My fingers slackened on his body. "Do you have time to come upstairs for a second?" I hadn't slept well with him gone. The bed felt like a hard ice cube, and I could never get comfortable. All the endorphins from sex lured me right to sleep, and without that usual hit, I couldn't drift off.

A slight smile moved onto his lips. "I always have time for that."

We passed Damien's room and went to our bedroom. The door shut and the clothes came off quickly, dropping onto the floor like raindrops on the windowsill. He scooped me into his arms then laid me on the bed, his body rolling with mine until we were tangled around each other, two bodies made to slide together.

His hand slid into my hair, and he looked me in the eye as he sank inside me, his hard cock stretching my channel as he went deeper and deeper.

When I felt him nice and deep, I dragged my nails down his back and moaned. "I really missed you..."

He propped himself on top of me and held my gaze for a long time. There was no movement from his hips, a steady rigidness he was keeping on purpose. He stared into my eyes for a long time, his thoughts on something besides sex. His fingers touched my hair lightly, and he sighed. "I missed you too."

"I SHOULD GET out of your hair. I've been here for over a week." Damien grabbed his bag off the floor and stood upright, but sometimes he cringed because his body was still sore. His ribs were still healing, so he couldn't do much on his right side.

"You know you can stay as long as you want."

"Yeah...but I can move again, so I'll manage. Besides, I need to get laid. I'm losing my mind."

"You're in no shape to have sex."

"Not if she's on top and doing all the work." He carried his bag as he walked down the hallway with me.

"And what stranger is going to be willing to do that?"

"Someone who gets paid a lot." He took the stairs slower than usual, holding the banister as a crutch to reach the bottom.

I rolled my eyes as I walked him to the front door. "You don't want to stay until Hades comes home?"

"No. He's seen enough of my ugly face."

"I thought you said you were handsome."

"I am—just not right now." He stopped at the front door to say goodbye. "Well, thanks for everything...and for encouraging Hades to forgive me."

"You know he would have done it anyway."

"But taken a much longer time." He wrapped one arm around my shoulders and gave me a gentle hug. "Let me know if you need anything. If you ever need a place to crash because he's driving you nuts, call me."

"I might take you up on that offer, so don't be surprised if I call."

He gave me a thumbs-up. "You know I'll always answer." He waved then walked out.

I watched him go, unsure what to do now until Hades came home.

14

HADES

"It's surprising she doesn't love you because she seems a bit obsessed." Damien relaxed in the chair, shirtless with the gauze wrapped around his midsection. He let me refill his glass of booze so he wouldn't have to exert himself by picking up the bottle.

"Yeah?"

"She couldn't wait for you to come home."

She had the foundation to feel something for me, but supernatural forces had placed a cap on her emotional endurance. That was the most she would ever feel for me, nothing more. My meeting with the gypsy made the situation easier to accept. "Good."

"So, what happened down there? I could talk about your wife all day, but if I say any more, I'll probably piss you off."

"Knowing you slept down the hall from her already pisses me off."

"Ooh...someone's jealous."

"No. Just territorial. You want to know what happened or not?"

He raised his glass.

"The gypsy said I had to earn my family's forgiveness if I want to break the curse. I need to atone for my greatest sin so the punishment will stop. Sofia won't be bound to her indifference, and then she'll have the ability to love me...if she wants to."

Damien shook his head slightly, like this was all a joke. "This whole thing sounds ludicrous."

"I know."

"I know it's true, but it's crazy. Who the hell would believe us?"

"No one."

He shook his head. "So why would your family need to forgive you? What did you do? I know you don't get along with your brother, but he's an asshole. I love money and breaking the law as much as anyone else, but he's crossing the line."

I'd never told Damien what I did. "The gypsy said I had two options. The first one was making me fall out of love with Sofia, but I said no."

"You could have made all this go away on the spot, and you said no?" he asked incredulously.

"Yeah." Now I stood by that decision more than ever.

"You want this torture to continue?"

"I want her to love me back...no matter what it takes."

"So getting your family's forgiveness is the second option?"

"Yeah. It's the only chance I've got to break this curse."

"But what exactly do you need forgiveness for?" he repeated. "I don't get it."

I couldn't keep this secret forever, not if I were going to accomplish anything. "About five years ago, my father was running the operation my brother now handles. We had words...tensions rose...one of his girls was a prostitute I knew...so I killed him." I couldn't look Damien in the eye as I said it, still full of shame for what I'd done. It didn't matter how much my father deserved it, it made me sick to my stomach. It didn't matter if he raped women and sold them...my actions destroyed my soul. I'd never been the same since.

In shock, all Damien could do was stare.

"My brother was close with my father, so naturally, we became enemies. We haven't spoken since the day...and it's been five years."

Damien's eyes were still wide. "Jesus...that's heavy."

"Now I need to make peace with my brother if I ever want to vindicate myself."

"What are the odds of that happening?"

"Pretty much none."

He drank his entire glass of scotch, as if he needed the booze in his blood to digest what I'd said. "Have you ever considered just telling Sofia about all of this? Maybe if she knew, it would be a much more convenient shortcut."

I gave him an incredulous look. "You literally just talked about how crazy we sound. What the hell is she going to think?"

He shrugged. "She trusts you."

"Even if she did believe me, what's that going to accomplish?"

"I don't know… Maybe she'd be more open-minded about giving you a chance."

"No. That's not how I want it to be. It'd be a much more romantic story if I won her over and then told her everything."

"Don't want to rain on your parade or anything, but you have no idea if that's going to happen. You just said you have to get your psychotic brother to forgive you for murdering your father…and that's not going to be easy."

"Telling her now won't help, so that's out."

Damien stopped arguing with me. "I'm surprised you aren't home with her now. She seemed anxious to see you."

If I had it my way, I would put my entire life on hold so I could stay in bed with her forever. "I've got shit to do. And I have to figure this out soon."

"We need to figure out what to do about Maddox too. Have you considered what I said?"

"Yeah…a bit."

"I think we should keep going. When he comes for us, we come for him harder."

I didn't like that idea, but I didn't know what else to do. Letting my company fall apart would affect every other part of my life. It would even affect my clients with the bank. If I looked like the pussy that got bested, I would never reclaim my reputation.

"Let's get all our resources together and prepare for war. We take him out once and for all."

"If it were that simple, we would have done it already…"

"But we've never really tried. We've been avoiding it for years because it's too challenging. But if we do put everything on the table, we could get everything we've ever wanted—"

"Or lose it all."

I was in the car on my way home when Sofia called.

I answered in the back seat, watching the ancient buildings pass as we drove down the narrow streets. "Hey, baby." I lifted my wrist to look at the time. It was almost nine, so I was much later than I usually was.

"I haven't heard from you all day...wanted to see if you were alright."

I liked it when she checked up on me. Made me feel like she loved me...even if she didn't. Now that I knew she was my soul mate, I was much more patient about the situation. Maybe she couldn't give me what I wanted right now, but she was the woman I was meant to be with, so I would bust my ass until I could free her mind from this mental cell. "I was at Damien's, talking about work."

"How's he doing?"

"Looks like shit. Nothing new."

"Will he be okay on his own?"

"He wants the privacy." Couldn't exactly bring hookers to my place, especially when my bedroom was so close.

"Yeah...he mentioned that."

"I'll be home in less than ten minutes."

"Alright. See you soon." Her dreamy voice disappeared, and the line went dead.

I kept the phone to my ear even though she was gone. I loved the sexy noises she made, the way she pronounced every word like she was making a speech. She was a woman of class, full of elegance that had been ingrained in her DNA. I finally dropped the phone from my ear, wishing I could tell her about everything...but I couldn't.

MY BACK WAS against the wooden headboard with my knees apart. My hands gripped the backs of her thighs, and I helped her rise up and down even though she seemed athletic enough to do it on her own. She rode me from the crown of my cock all the way to the base, pushing white cream around my balls before she rose again. With her shaking tits and bouncing hair, she was a fucking fantasy.

I kept coming...over and over.

Her tight body was covered in sweat because she was working hard to please me the way I pleased her. She never took a break or asked for a new position, as if she were trying to prove something to me.

Like she needed to prove anything.

The sweat coating her skin made it shine, made her tits glow. Her nipples would harden and soften over and over again as her desire reached critical heights then softened after a climax.

I never wanted this night to end because the sex was so damn good. We could go nonstop, so hot for each other that this flame could never burn out. We both ran on an infinite fuel tank, always ready to burn.

When I came inside her again, I couldn't go any longer. It was my third load, and no matter how sexy she was, I needed a break. My arms wrapped around her waist, and I pulled her closer to me, my face moving into her neck and the top of her tits. My cock softened, so the come dripped out of her entrance and smeared across the both of us.

After she caught her breath, she pulled away and looked at me. "I want to know something."

"Then ask." I couldn't get over how beautiful she was, how perfect she looked even after a hard workout. Her makeup was washed away and her hair was oily, but she still looked like the sexiest thing in the world. If I hadn't fought for her, she could have married someone else...my soul mate could have ended up with another man. The thought made me sick to my stomach, especially when I could see how perfect we were together. We were two pieces that fit together like we were made for each other. Ever since the first moment I saw her, I felt something. She felt something too. Now it all made sense. Other women never meant anything to me...but she meant the world.

Because she was my soul mate.

I would fight for this if it killed me.

Her hands slid down to my chest. "What's your real name?"

I didn't expect a question so personal. "Why do you want to know?"

"Because it's your name..."

"It's not anymore. That's my past. The only man you've ever known is Hades...so that's who I am."

Her hands continued to rub my chest. "Why are you so ashamed of it?"

"It's just not who I am anymore."

She pressed the argument with her intense eye contact.

"I don't want to be called by my birth name, so it doesn't matter. Let it go."

"Could you at least tell me why?"

I dropped my gaze. "If I answer you, will you let this go?"

"I'll let this go whether you tell me or not. I just wish you felt comfortable confiding in me."

"That's not the problem. You know I'm transparent."

"Then I don't understand..."

"Alright, I'll tell you. But I don't want you to ever call me by it."

"Okay, I promise."

"Andrew."

Her eyes softened. "Andrew...that's a good name. But you're right, Hades does suit you a lot more."

I would hope so. "Is the conversation over now?"

"Yes. I didn't mean to make you so uncomfortable." She moved her face to mine and kissed me, remorse in her lips.

I forgave her instantly. "Now I have a question. A very personal question."

"Uh oh. Maybe I should have kept my curiosity to myself."

"After we broke up, did you ever think about me when you were with someone else?" I missed her when we weren't together, and sometimes I pictured her face on a different body to get off.

"Wow. You weren't kidding about it being personal."

"No. Now answer me."

She ran her fingers through her hair as she stalled. She even dropped her gaze because the contact was too much.

"I'm not gonna let this go, baby."

After a deep sigh, she lifted her gaze. "Yes…"

"How often?"

"You're really going to grill me, huh?"

"How often?" I repeated.

She shrugged. "It was more common than uncommon…" She ran her fingers through her hair again. "Truth be told, you were the best sex I've ever had, so all my lovers were disappointments."

Then you should have married me.

"Not that I didn't enjoy them. They just weren't…the same."

An invisible crown was on my head, and I tried not to smile in victory. I didn't need to be jealous of the men who came after me because they never erased me. I'd always been there, always lived between her legs.

"What about you?"

"You already asked a personal question, and I answered."

"I can't ask another?"

"Then I get to ask another."

"Alright," she said. "Did you ever think about me?"

All the fucking time. "Yes. And not just when I was with other women..."

Her eyes narrowed in confusion, and then a red tint came over her face once she understood my meaning.

And I was fucking devastated when you left me. "Now I get another question."

"Alright..."

"Did you ever regret saying no?" Neither one of us had mentioned our previous relationship since we'd gotten married, but I broke our unspoken rule.

Her eyes immediately turned guarded once I mentioned the night everything turned to shit. I asked her to marry me, and she left me. "Sometimes. And now that I'm with you, I realize how lucky I am to be your wife. It's exactly what I needed...even though I was too stubborn to understand it at the time."

I'd asked her to marry me because I loved her—not for convenience. But I let it go. "I'm leaving tomorrow for a couple of days."

As if I'd slapped her across the face, she looked stunned by the announcement. "You just got home."

"Something came up."

"Where are you going?"

"Rome."

"Why?"

"I have to talk to my brother about a few things…I might be gone a couple of days or a week."

"Really?" she asked in disappointment. "That's a long time."

"I'd never leave you unless I knew you were safe. And you can call Damien for anything, and he'll be at your beck and call."

"That's not the problem, and you know it." Her attitude started to flare, the sassiness coming into her eyes.

"I'm sure you have stuff to do at the Tuscan Rose."

"But I don't want my husband to be gone for weeks at a time. I don't want that kind of marriage."

"What kind of marriage is that?"

"When the guy takes off and has mistresses and whatnot."

I cocked an eyebrow. "You think I'm leaving to have an affair?"

"No, but that's the kind of lifestyle you're talking about. You didn't even invite me to come with you."

"Because I know you have shit to do."

"The hotel survived before me, and it'll survive if I'm gone for a week."

"Two weeks," I corrected. "You missed this week too."

"I doubt the people running it would start slacking when they know Hades Lombardi could walk in at any moment."

I narrowed my eyes, feeling the rage start to ignite my temper. "Do you really think I'm looking for an excuse to sneak off and fuck around?" Her punitive mind had no idea how hard I was working just to keep her. It was fucking insulting.

"I didn't say that—"

"That's literally what you just said." I grabbed her hips and pulled her off me.

"Look, I was just upset about you leaving, and I blurted that out. I didn't mean it."

I pulled on my boxers, burned by the insinuation I would do anything like that. "If I wanted to fuck around, I would do it right under your nose. I wouldn't be a coward and run off to sneak around behind your back. I'd do it right to your damn face."

She leaned against the headboard, frustrated by the way this fight was unfolding. "I take it back, okay? I know you wouldn't do that."

"Doesn't seem like it." I moved to the patio doors and looked outside, repulsed by the image of her face.

"I just don't want you to leave, alright?" she whispered. "Or at least, let me come with you."

I didn't have a problem with her coming with me, but I didn't appreciate the way she went about it. With my arms crossed over my chest, I looked at the city with blind eyes, not taking in a single thing I was staring at.

When I ignored her, she got to her feet and came up behind me. Her fingertips stroked my back, feeling the muscles with her feather-like touch. "I'm sorry, okay? My mother told me my father had mistresses all his life and she never cared about it...

but I don't believe her. He would go on these bullshit business trips—"

"I'm not your father." I turned around and faced her, the anger tightening all the muscles in my face. I wished I could tell her how I really felt, that I loved her too much to even think about another woman. That all I wanted was for her to tell me she loved me and couldn't live without me. If only she knew the depth of my feelings, she would understand how ridiculous her insecurities were. "I would never do that. That's not the kind of man I am. End of story."

Remorse flooded her eyes. "I'd still like to come with you...if you'll have me."

I'd leave her at the hotel while I spoke to my brother. She'd be safe there, my men watching her. At night, I would have a place to unwind, to vent all my frustrations by fucking her senseless. "All you had to do was ask."

"How long will you be gone?" Damien asked in the entryway while my men packed the vehicle with our luggage.

"No idea. Depends on his reaction."

"So, you'll be there for a while."

Sofia walked behind me and gave one of the men her purse.

Damien glanced at her. "She's coming with you?"

"Yeah."

"Why?"

"She asked. I didn't see the harm."

When she was out of earshot, he spoke his mind. "You sure she doesn't love you?"

She just loved my dick. "It's fun to pretend sometimes."

He chuckled and clapped me on the shoulder. "I'll take care of everything here. Fix this shit with your brother. If you need help, let me know."

"Thanks." We said goodbye then headed to the car.

"You sure you want to spend all week with this guy?" Damien asked as he hugged Sofia on the sidewalk.

"He's my husband...so yes." She was in denim jeans and a white blouse, her hair pulled back in an elegant but sexy look.

He leaned toward her. "Between you and me, I don't know what you see in him. I'm much better looking." He waggled his eyebrows. "And I've got a bigger dick too."

"Then that must be uncomfortable," she countered. "Because if Hades were any bigger, he wouldn't fit." With her head held high, she got into the back seat of the SUV and shut the door behind her.

Damien's eyes were wide with shock, and he shifted his gaze to me, his mouth agape.

I winked before I opened the back door. "She's got a mouth on her, doesn't she?"

AFTER A SHORT FLIGHT, we landed in Rome then drove to our hotel.

A hotel I'd acquired through marriage.

Sofia examined every inch of the lobby, watching the employees behind the counter, checking the freshness of the flowers, and going over everything with a meticulous gaze.

After we checked in, we were given the biggest suite in the place, the presidential suite at the very top of the hotel. We didn't need five thousand square feet of space, especially when we would only use the room for sex.

We entered the room, and our luggage was placed in the walk-in closet. Then we were left alone, admiring the expansive view of the city from the top of the building. Sofia opened the back doors and stepped outside onto the enormous patio, walking by the private pool and hot tub to the iron railing. It was past noon in the city, so the sun was high in the sky and people flooded the sidewalks as they lived their lives. The Colosseum was visible in the distance.

I came up beside her. "Ever been to Rome?"

"A few times."

"Beautiful place."

"Yeah..." A slight breeze moved through her hair, pulling at the loose strands that didn't stay pinned back.

Rome was one of my territories for my operation. Or at least, it had been until I'd made that deal with Maddox. I'd been thinking about my dilemma every single day since I'd agreed to it, tempted to do exactly what Damien advised. But it was so dangerous...and could blow up in my face. I wanted to fight for what was mine, but I didn't want to lose everything either.

"What now?" she asked.

Nothing happened during the day, so I'd make my move this

evening. I didn't have a concrete plan for when I approached my brother. No matter what I did, he would be livid to see me, might even shoot me. But that was a risk I had to take. "We could go to lunch. Do some shopping."

She pivoted her body toward me, her head tilted to the side. "Hades Lombardi shopping? I can't picture that."

"I wouldn't be the one shopping. I would be the one taking you shopping. Buying you pretty things and holding your bags."

"I can buy my own things, and I can definitely hold my own bags."

"But why bother when your husband can do those things for you?" She turned me into a weak man, a guy who wanted to bend over backward to give her the world. I could pay someone to escort her around town, but I wanted to be the one to do it.

Her eyes narrowed slightly as she looked at me. "Because I want my husband for other things."

―――――――

WE HAD lunch at a small bistro then walked the streets to window-shop. It was the first time we'd spent the entire day together under the sun, doing something normal couples did on a daily basis. I watched her examine clothes and jewelry, rarely buying anything because she was selective in her purchases. Whatever she did buy, she held the bag and never asked for my help.

When we headed back to the hotel, I grabbed her hand and held it in mine.

Her fingers squeezed mine back.

A thrill went up my spine when I touched her, when I felt the pulse of her fingertips. Sometimes I forgot that this was real, that I really had the woman I'd wanted since the moment I saw her. Now that I knew she was destined to share half of my soul, I cherished her even more.

I'd been dreading this confrontation with my brother, but when I held her hand like this, I remembered what I was fighting for. "Still think I came here to have an affair?" I couldn't keep the smartass remark inside my mouth even though we were having a good moment.

She sighed beside me. "I told you I didn't mean that."

"I'm still going to make you regret saying that." We crossed the street and approached the entrance to the hotel.

"Well, I already do regret it." She tugged on my hand and made me stop in front of the large doors that led to the hotel. She looked up at me, her bag resting in the crook of her elbow. "I'm sorry, alright?" Sincerity shone in her eyes, and that apologetic look made her even more desirable.

My eyes shifted back and forth as I looked into hers, a suffocating feeling choking me. My heart had grown so much over the last few months. My hatred for her had been replaced by a love so deep that I would die for her without thinking twice about it. It was a secret that was getting more difficult to hide. I was tempted to tell her how I felt, even if she didn't feel the same way, just because I was her husband and had the right to say whatever the hell I wanted. "I know."

SHE LAY IN BED NAKED, her stomach against the mattress while her toes were pointed toward the ceiling. Her rounded ass curved down to the small of her back, luscious curves that were impossible to resist. Her hair was a waterfall of ink, and her makeup had been destroyed by all the sweat. "How long will you be gone?"

I pulled on my black t-shirt and grabbed my jeans. "Not sure."

"What exactly are you doing?"

"I just need to speak to my brother." I slipped on my watch then grabbed my leather jacket.

She got out of bed and walked toward me, her perfect tits practically hypnotizing. "What are you going to talk to him about?"

"Burying the hatchet."

She crossed her arms over her chest. "What brought this on?"

I couldn't tell her the truth. "We haven't spoken in five years, and he's all the family I have left...we need to move on."

"That's not true. I'm your family too."

My heart fluttered at the words, and for a moment, this relationship felt real. There was always this central divide between us, but when she talked like that, it was easy to forget it was there at all.

"Not to mention Damien."

"Yes...but he's my blood."

She took a deep breath, the worry spreading into her features. "Should I be worried?"

Anything could happen. I was catching him off guard, and that could piss him off. "If he wanted me dead, he would have hunted me down a long time ago."

"But you're walking into the lion's den now. That's different."

I knew he wouldn't be happy to see me...but how unhappy remained to be seen. "I've handled worse. I'll be fine."

"What if I came with you?" she whispered.

I stared at her blankly. "Is that a joke?"

"I'm his sister-in-law. Maybe he'd like to meet me."

Just to piss me off, he'd probably take her and sell her off to someone. "No."

"I won't discourage you from reconnecting with your family, but I'm not sure what you hope to achieve. A terrible tragedy is separating you both, and it's complicated because you're the reason that tragedy happened in the first place. The odds are slim...and I think your time would be better spent doing something else."

I couldn't agree more. Unless her heart was on the line, I wouldn't bother with this. But I had to earn his forgiveness so I would be vindicated, so this punishment would cease. Failure wasn't an option...even if success seemed impossible. "I have to do this..."

Her eyes dropped toward my chest, her disappointment written across her forehead as her eyebrows furrowed. "Please be careful."

"You know I always am."

She moved into me and cupped my face. With the softness of a cloud, she pressed her lips to mine, tasting like a springtime morning. She kissed me gently, embraced me like a woman cherishing the love of her life. It was easy to believe she loved me because she was such a good actress. "Come back to me." Her lips moved against mine as she whispered, her eyes lifting to meet mine.

My hand slid into her hair, and I breathed into her mouth. "I promise."

THE TRICK to success was hiding in plain sight.

My brother used this same principle. He owned a bar that was open to the general public. Tourists and naïve people visited it on a nightly basis, ordering rounds of booze and lining his pockets with cash. But the men with sinister motives discreetly headed to the back and entered the door next to the bathrooms.

I ordered a drink at the bar to seem inconspicuous then headed down the narrow hallway and approached the door. This was the path to the underworld, a deep cave that crossed into the realm of evil. I broke the law and killed people for the riches. But never did I consider the abuse of humankind.

That was a different kind of evil.

I took the long hallway until I reached the stairs. Down I went, entering one of the biggest underground human trafficking sites. It looked just like a bar, men sitting at the tables drinking booze while the large fire burned in the hearth. It was quiet, no music playing like it was upstairs.

The occasional moan was audible.

I reached the bottom of the stairs and surveyed the faces around me, not recognizing anyone. I walked into that bar alone and unarmed. If I seemed remotely threatening, my brother would be too provoked to have a reasonable conversation.

I ordered a drink and sat alone.

The sound of a man grunting reached my ears, accompanied by the gentle cry of the woman he'd paid for. Some would call this a brothel, but that wouldn't be fitting. These weren't free women who chose to be prostitutes for a living. They were women who had been kidnapped and forced into sexual servitude. They would be used until they were damaged. Then they would be killed.

I was ashamed to call this man my brother.

Faced with the disturbing reality, I didn't feel guilty for murdering my own father. His crimes were far worse than mine.

I drank from the glass and waited for my brother to appear. He may not be there at all, and I'd have to return on a different night. Or maybe he was in one of those rooms... The thought was disgusting.

One of the men walked up to me, suspicious by my isolation. I hadn't offered to buy a woman, so I could just drink upstairs. It made me look like one of the police. If you didn't commit the crime like everyone else, you looked guilty of something else.

"I've got a couple of girls available. Want to take a look?"

My wedding ring was still on my hand, but that didn't mean anything. Married men visited this place all the time. "I'm here to see Ash."

His body tightened as he felt threatened. "What's your business with him?"

"I'm his brother—that's my business. Now, go get him."

The man obeyed and disappeared into the hallway.

Now that I'd witnessed all of these horrors with my own eyes, I didn't want my brother's forgiveness. I did the world a service, and if I wanted to make the world an even better place, I would kill him too. My stomach filled with acid, and my chest tightened in disgust. If Sofia weren't the most important thing to me, I wouldn't bother with this bullshit. I was about to make amends with the most despicable guy on the planet.

Ash emerged from the hallway. He stopped once he was in my line of sight, staring at me with eyes that resembled magnifying glasses. The longer he absorbed my appearance, the harder he breathed. His hands formed fists until his knuckles turned white, and all the hatred he felt five years ago visibly returned in full force.

Shit.

He walked over to me, his powerful arms hanging by his sides as his sculpted shoulders remained rigid. His lips were pressed together tightly, and his eyes were clouded with a shade of violence. He shared similar features that we'd inherited from our parents, dark brown hair, deep brown eyes, and a rugged jawline that belonged in film. We both possessed the kind of dick the ladies wanted.

He reached into the back of his jeans and pulled out his pistol. He cocked the gun and aimed it right at my forehead.

I didn't flinch. "A bit dramatic, don't you think?"

He kept the gun steady in my face. "If you didn't want a soap opera, you shouldn't have come here."

I raised my hands slightly in the air, showing him I didn't have a gun. "Alright...a little drama is entertaining. But let's cut to a commercial break and calm the fuck down." I lowered my hands again. "I'm alone and unarmed. Just want to talk."

He didn't lower his gun. "I guess we could talk about your funeral arrangements."

I drank from my glass until it was empty. "If you were going to kill me, you would have hunted me down a long time ago. Cut the shit and take a seat."

"You don't know me, asshole."

"I'm your brother—I don't have to know you." I kicked the chair across from me so it slid away from the table.

"That didn't stop you from killing our father." He shoved his gun back into his jeans and fell into the chair. He was a few years older than me, approaching his midthirties with spectacular physicality. He kept in shape, kept his body tight.

A smartass comment came to mind, but I kept it back. My objective was to receive forgiveness. If I spoke my mind, I would only infuriate him even more. "It's haunted me for a long time. My soul split in two that day... It's never been the same." It wasn't a false speech to gain his pity. It'd been a weight on my shoulders every single day. I struggled to combat the guilt and the relief of my actions.

Ash was still livid. "I remember when you shot him. I remember the look on your face. There was no guilt there, no goddamn hesitation."

"Then you must not have seen my face afterward."

He crossed his arms over his chest and slouched slightly in the chair. His men stared at our interaction from their place at the bar, ready to come to his side if he snapped his fingers. "What the fuck do you want, Hades?"

"We're brothers. Not strangers."

"Enemies aren't strangers." His eyes were frozen like two pieces of ice.

"You're no enemy of mine."

"Really? You've had a change of heart about my operation?"

I refused to lie to get what I wanted. "No. But I already live with Father's blood on my hands. I can't live with yours too. It doesn't fix the problem, only causes more problems."

"So you still think I'm a piece of shit."

"Yes."

He smiled, as if the insult were some kind of joke. "At least you're honest."

"Then you know I really do feel like shit for what I did."

"And that's supposed to make it better?" he asked incredulously. "You betrayed your family—"

"And you're betraying humankind. Those women are daughters, mothers, sisters, wives...what the fuck is wrong with you?"

"And selling crystal is better?" he snapped. "People get hooked on that shit and ruin their lives. Most of the women here got here in the first place because they're on drugs—probably your drugs."

"Not the same thing and you know it."

"I don't know about that..."

"You're kidnapping women and raping them. My customers have a choice. That's the biggest difference between the two of us."

"Whatever. You aren't a saint."

"Did I say that I was?"

He tapped his fingers against his arm, growing impatient. "What do you want?"

"I already told you."

"To fix this relationship? Well, that's not going to happen. I don't care how many times you apologize, I'll always fucking hate you. What kind of sick bastard kills his own goddamn father?"

"A man trying to do the right thing."

He shook his head. "The world doesn't run on right and wrong. You know it."

"But it doesn't have to run on the blood of innocents either."

He shook his head again. "You came all the way down here just to waste my time?"

"No."

"Well, it feels like you're wasting my time."

The odds seemed even more unlikely now. My brother's exterior had hardened over the years. There was no light to his darkness. He was a man stuck in his ways. "Ash...let's bury the hatchet."

"Why?"

"Because we're the only family we've got left."

He glanced at my left hand. "That can't be true. Who's the lucky lady?"

"Her name is Sofia."

"Can I see a picture?" He waggled his eyebrows.

I played by his rules the second I stepped into his domain, but once my wife was mentioned, that respect went out the window. "I don't need a gun to kill you, Ash." My threat was as sharp as a knife.

His mouth slowly melted into a smile. "You think I'm gonna bring her down here and—"

"Don't fucking say it." I'd rather die than even think about something like that happening to her.

His smile remained. "My brother is in love..."

"I married her, didn't I?"

"Most marriages are shams. But maybe this one is real."

"It is real." At least, it was to me.

His smile slowly disappeared. "Congratulations."

I didn't accept the sentiment because I knew he didn't mean it.

"Had a wedding?"

I nodded.

"And you didn't invite me?"

I didn't need him until now. "I'm here now."

He relaxed his arms and let them rest on the table. "It's been five years since the last time I saw you. And you know what? I haven't thought of you once until now." He rose out of his chair. "So how about we go back to that arrangement? Pretending the other doesn't exist."

"If you really hated me, you would have killed me by now."

"I don't hate you. I'm just indifferent to you."

I RETURNED to the hotel and stepped out of the elevator onto the top floor. The double doors to the presidential suite were in front of me, and I dragged my feet as I crossed the hallway and slipped my card into the device.

The door unlocked, and I stepped inside.

Sofia was on the couch wearing my t-shirt, eating popcorn right out of the bag. "Good, you're home." She set the food on the table and got to her feet, greeting me the way most wives greeted their husbands. "You weren't gone long."

"Because it wasn't a long conversation." I headed to the bar and made myself a drink.

"That doesn't sound good."

"It wasn't." I turned around and took a sip, the alcohol having no effect on my mood. I didn't expect much when I faced Ash, but even that fell below my expectations. "He wants nothing to do with me."

"Maybe you need to give him some space…"

I couldn't give him that much space. I needed to get this shit done. I couldn't tell him outright why I needed his forgiveness because he would hold it over my head to further my punishment. "I have to make this happen...somehow."

"Can I help?"

God, I didn't want her anywhere near there. "No."

She took the drink out of my hand then ran her palms up my arms, trying to comfort me with her seductive affection. "You did your best. Let it go."

"No." I could never let it go. "It's hard to look my brother in the eye and not hate him. I stood in the bar and listened to the women service the men down the hall...women forced against their will. It only reminded me why I killed my father in the first place. Now my brother is continuing his legacy. It's disgusting."

"Then why are you trying to make amends with him?"

"Because...we're family."

"Sometimes water is thicker than blood." She looked at me through her lush eyelashes, a priceless jewel that sparkled in the darkest of places. "Damien is your brother. You don't need this one."

I needed him more than anyone else in the world.

"Even if he was receptive and you started to get along, would you want to be close to someone like that? You killed your father for a reason. Now you're just turning the other cheek."

"If I offer him something better than what he has now, maybe he'll walk away."

"Like what?" she asked.

"A cut of my business."

She raised an eyebrow. "The business you gave up?"

I nodded.

"I don't see how that could work. You made a deal with Maddox..."

"I know. It's just an idea."

She dropped her hands. "If you make a deal, you should honor it."

"I know. But the real world doesn't operate on right and wrong. It operates on survival. The biggest monster prevails...that's how things really work. If I let Maddox push me out, it could affect every aspect of my life."

She watched me with trepidation. "He could have killed Damien, but he didn't..."

"I know."

"You should really think about this, Hades. Because there's no going back."

SOFIA WAS ASLEEP BESIDE ME, her glorious body naked under the sheets. I kissed the top of her shoulder before I slid out of bed and pulled my boxers to my waist. I crept into the other room, closing the door behind me so I could have privacy.

I made the call.

Damien answered right away. "You're alive. That conversation must have gone well."

"The opposite."

"At least he didn't kill you."

"I guess..."

"What happened, exactly?"

"He's not receptive. That's the short version."

"Sorry, man. I know how much you wanted this."

"I'm not gonna give up. I'll try again tomorrow."

There was a pause over the line. "Hades, if you keep pestering him, he might change his mind about killing you."

"I have to make this happen."

"But maybe it's not possible."

"Don't say that to me," I said coldly.

"And even if it is, it's going to take more than a few days. Rome wasn't built in a day."

I didn't want to wait longer than a few days.

"I'm not trying to kick you when you're down, alright? I've got to be the voice of reason for you. You'll always get honesty from me."

"I know."

"You can keep trying, but realistically, this is going to take a while. You killed your father...he's not gonna get over that overnight."

I knew he was right.

"What if you brought Sofia with you?"

There was no fucking way I was bringing my wife anywhere near that place. "Fuck no."

"I just mean, she's persuasive. She's got this way about her—"

"I know. I married her."

"Just an idea..."

"This guy traffics women, and you think I should bring my drop-dead gorgeous wife around?"

"He wouldn't touch Sofia. If he wanted to hurt you, he would have done it already. You're off-limits."

"I don't know about that."

"You're alive, aren't you?" he questioned.

I slumped into the chair and rested my neck on the back of the couch. "What's going on over there?"

"Holding down the fort. I cranked up production and am getting ready for a drop."

I sat up on the couch, pressing the phone closer to my ear. "You did what?"

"I've got the cooks working around the clock."

"Damien, what the hell are you thinking?"

"What?" he asked innocently.

"We made a deal with Maddox."

"And last time we spoke, we agreed not to lie down and take it."

"No," I hissed. "We discussed that possibility. We didn't agree on anything."

"Well...that's how I took it."

"Then stop everything."

"Hades, you know I can't do that—"

"If he finds out, we're fucking done."

"Not if we kill him first. That's what we should have done a long time ago. Cut the head off the fucking snake. Come on, you really picture yourself staying home all day, bored out of your goddamn mind? That's not you. That's not me. We're going to fight this piece of shit and take back what's ours. I'm sorry I rushed into it, but I thought we were in agreement about that. We aren't pussies. I'd rather die the victor than live as a coward."

I RETURNED to the bar two nights later.

I expected the same outcome, but I had to keep trying anyway.

This time, the guys behind the bar recognized me. They didn't serve me a drink and went to retrieve Ash right away.

My brother stepped out of the hallway and looked at me, just as pissed today as he was a few days ago. His nostrils flared before he approached my table, fists swinging by his sides. He stopped in front of me and leaned over the table. "You think I won't kill you?"

"I know you won't."

"I guess I'm better-looking *and* smarter." He dropped into the chair. "Your false sense of immunity is stupid."

"You won't shoot unless I shoot first. And as always, I'm

unarmed." I raised my hands in the air so he could search me if he wanted to.

His eyes narrowed. "I thought we'd finished this conversation."

I lowered my hands.

"I have nothing left to say to you."

"Well, I have more to say to you."

He slowly sank back in his chair. "You're such a bitch, you know that?"

I ignored the insult. "You won't kill me for the same reason I won't kill you—because we're brothers. I don't approve of this disgusting operation you have running here, but I won't oppose you. I have enough forces to tear this place down in an hour, but I won't touch you."

"Careful, little brother," he said as his eyes narrowed. "Sounds like you're making threats."

"Just reminding you where we stand."

He drummed his fingers on the table. "What's your point?"

"You aren't indifferent to me. If you were, you would kill me. I'm not indifferent to you. Otherwise, I wouldn't be here now. You wouldn't either. So there's some allegiance between us." I placed my closed fist over my chest. "Even if it's buried very deep."

His eyes steamed with hostility.

"I'm sorry for what I did to our family. I mean that."

He continued with the same blank stare.

"I'd take it back if I could."

"Even the god of the dead can't bring him to life, so you can't take it back."

"I'm being sincere."

"I'm sure you are. Doesn't mean I care."

"Father would want us to have a relationship, even after what I did."

"We'll never know what he wanted—because he's dead."

My brother reminded me of Damien. Impulsive and emotional. I ground my teeth because he was so frustrating.

He leaned forward. "What the fuck do you want from me? When did Hades Lombardi become the biggest pussy in the world? Coming here, expecting a heart-to-heart like a fucking woman? Fuck off."

"I want to make you an offer."

"An offer?" he asked.

"You know I'm the biggest drug lord in the south of Europe."

His eyebrows furrowed. "Don't expect me to be impressed."

"But you do know. And I'm looking for a partner."

He couldn't hide his surprise. He didn't see it coming. "What?"

"My empire generates billions every year. Yes, billions with a B. Join me and leave this behind."

"Why would you offer this to me?"

"Because you can make way more money working with me than you ever could selling pussy."

He crossed his arms over his chest.

"And we can fix this." I pointed between the two of us. "Brothers again."

"Back to the pussy shit…"

"Ash, I'm being serious."

He shook his head. "I'm missing something, and you aren't telling me what it is."

My brother may be irrational, but he was smart.

"What is it?" he pressed.

"You aren't missing anything, Ash. This is genuine."

He doubted me with his eyes.

"I'm a different man than I used to be. I'm married now, and that's changed my entire life."

"So, you are a pussy," he said with a chuckle.

"Loving a woman with everything I have is the most courageous thing I've ever done. I take care of her, I provide for her, I keep my dick in my pants even when the offers pour in. I put all of my hopes and dreams into one basket. Loving something means you have something to lose… It creates more risk. Trust me, it doesn't make me a pussy. Maybe someday, you'll see what I mean."

He didn't make any more jokes. "Unlikely."

"Stop raping women and actually put in some effort."

Anger emerged onto his features. "I don't mix business with pleasure."

"You're still an asshole."

"Maybe." He shook his head. "But I don't rape women. Let's just get that straight. Father did that shit. Not me."

Maybe there was a chance he could be redeemable after all. "Then stop this."

"No. It's just business. Plain and simple."

"Drugs is a business, plain and simple. Not people."

"We're of differing opinions."

"It's not an opinion, asshole. What you're doing is wrong. If something like that happened to Sofia, I would put a bullet in my brain just to make the pain stop."

His face remained stoic. "She must be one hell of a woman to make you settle down."

Not just one hell of a woman... my soul mate. "She is. We're going to start a family. All the more reason you and I should work this out. We've lost five years. Let's not lose any more."

"You don't even like me, Hades."

"Not true. I just think you're better than this. Father poisoned your mind. You never would have gotten mixed up in this if he hadn't."

He shrugged. "Maybe. Maybe not. We'll never know."

I wanted to throw in the towel, but every time Sofia popped into my mind, I kept trying. "Meet me halfway, man."

He swept his gaze around the room, watching his men while his thoughts remained buried behind his eyes.

"Leave the past in the past."

"I'm an easygoing guy, Hades. Life is too short to hold grudges. But what you did isn't a grudge...it's a betrayal."

I closed my eyes and sighed. "I warned him to stop at least five times."

"What if he told you to stop selling drugs?"

"If it were that important to him, I would have."

"Bullshit."

"It's not bullshit. And I had to save those women. One of them was my friend."

"A whore you used to fuck."

"Doesn't matter," I snapped. "She was a fucking human being."

"She's doing the same thing now she was doing before—"

"Don't tell me you really believe that. I know you aren't that heartless. I know you aren't that stupid."

He shut his mouth.

I'd hit rock bottom with my brother and didn't know how to fix it. The cards in my pile were gone, and there were no tricks up my sleeve. This wasn't a problem cash could fix. It wasn't a problem threats could fix. I was fucking desperate. "Have dinner with Sofia and me tomorrow night."

Ash craned his neck awkwardly, like he couldn't believe the words that flew out of my mouth. "I thought you didn't want Sofia anywhere near me."

"I don't want her anywhere near *here*."

"And why would I want to spend the evening with you?"

"She's your sister-in-law. You don't want to meet her?"

"Just because she has my last name doesn't mean she's family. You certainly aren't."

Now I regretted killing my father even more. If I hadn't, none of this would be happening. "I get that you're angry, but I don't think you're as heartless as you pretend to be. You've been sitting with me for thirty minutes now, when you have a million things to do. You give me your time when you claim I don't deserve it. You threaten to kill me when we both know you can't pull the trigger. You have the right to be mad at me, but at least try to be my brother. That's all I ask."

15

SOFIA

"You want me to have dinner with your brother?" When Hades came home, he was in worse shape than his last visit. Making amends with his brother was pressing stress all over his body, making him more exhausted than he'd ever been. I'd do anything to help him, but I was surprised he'd asked.

"Yes." He sat next to me on the couch, his arm behind my shoulders. His body was pivoted toward me, his hand resting on my thigh. His fingers lightly grazed my skin, gently touched me as he inched farther up on my shirt to my panties underneath.

"I thought you didn't want that."

"I'm desperate."

"I can see that."

"I'm not taking you to his place of business. I would never put you in harm's way." His shadowed jawline was sharp as a straight line. His lips were full and kissable. And his brown eyes were very persuasive.

"I know."

"And he would never try anything either."

"What makes you so sure?"

After a long pause, he answered. "I just know."

"You know I'll help you in any way I can. I just don't know what you want me to do."

"Just be you. Damien is emotionally stunted, and he's an idiot. But he opened up like an uncorked bottle of champagne."

"That's different."

"You have that effect on a lot of people—including me. Just be yourself...maybe you could soften him up."

"I'm not sure how to do that, but I'll try."

"Thank you." He leaned into me and kissed the corner of my mouth, his large hand cupping the back of my head to keep me in place. His fingers moved up my hip until he grabbed the lace of my thong and tugged it down. "Is there something I can do to show my appreciation?"

I remembered the night he'd ordered me to sit on his face. He ate my pussy in a way no other man ever had. There was so much heat in his aggressive kisses, so much stimulation from that strong tongue. Just the thought made my ears feel warm, made me shiver like his mouth was pressed against me at that moment.

He got my panties to my knees and let them slide down to my ankles. "I know that look." He grabbed my hips and tugged me down, my head moving to the corner of the armrest. He pushed my thighs open, one knee pressed against the back of the couch, while the other hung over the edge. He slid to his knees and pushed up my shirt with his hands. Then his face moved between my legs, and his lips made contact with the places that ached the most.

My back arched on its own, and I released a deep sigh. "God..."

WE SAT side by side at the table, a small vase of flowers in front of us along with a basket of bread. I was in a one-strap black dress, my hair in loose curls with a diamond necklace around my throat.

Hades looked sexy in a black collared shirt with one button popped open at the top. His dark jeans were snug on his tight ass and muscular thighs. Even though he must be anxious about our company, he seemed calm like always.

I caught women in the restaurant looking at him. Sometimes, it angered me because he was clearly married. Other times, I couldn't blame them for giving in to the temptation of his appearance. If I were one of those women, I'd probably be doing the exact same thing.

"Are you alright?" He asked the question without looking at me.

I was about to meet a man who forced women into slavery. I wasn't looking forward to the acquaintance. But since this was important to Hades and he intended to get his brother out of the business, I stopped thinking about it. "Yes."

"Because you seem uncomfortable. I would never let anything happen to you."

"It's not that..."

"Then what is it?"

"I'm just annoyed that every woman in here keeps staring at you."

He slowly turned his head to me, an intense look in his eyes. He watched me like I was the only woman in that room, like none of them mattered. An arrogant smile slowly erupted on his face. "I didn't even notice because I'm too busy staring at you." His hand slid to my thigh under the table, and he leaned in to kiss me. It wasn't just a simple peck on the lips. It was a deep kiss that should only happen behind closed doors, one that had a bit of tongue and lots of breath.

Instead of being jealous of them, they were jealous of me.

"Should I come back?"

I pulled away and looked at the man who sank into the chair across from me. With dark hair and deep brown eyes, he looked similar to Hades because they were clearly related. He was a bit taller, with a musculature that rivaled his brother's. He gave me a quick smile before he picked up the menu.

Hades kept his hand on my thigh but turned his attention to his brother.

Ash continued to stare at his menu. "Red goes with steak and white goes with pasta...but what goes with scotch?"

"Anything goes with scotch," Hades said.

Ash set down his menu. "You know what? Maybe we are related after all." His elbows rested on the table, and he stared at me, ignoring his brother and turning all of his focus onto my face.

It was a bit creepy, but I refused to flinch under his stare. My husband was right beside me, so there was nothing this stranger could do to me anyway. Nothing to be afraid of. But I did feel repulsion toward him...because of the terrible things he did to earn money. I never liked the fact that Hades was a drug dealer, but at least he didn't hurt innocent people.

The waitress came to the table and took our drink order, but not before giving Ash a bit of special attention. It was subtle, just a gentle bat of her eyes, but I noticed it. Ash was handsome like his brother, inheriting the same masculine good looks and potent testosterone. But he was nothing compared to my husband.

Ash continued his heavy stare, hardly blinking.

"You got a problem?" I blurted, finding his attention over the top. "If there's something wrong with your eyes, you should get that checked out."

Ash's lips softened into a slight smile, and he glanced at his brother. "I like her already."

"I'm not looking for your validation," I said coolly.

"Ooh." Now he grinned. "Beautiful and sassy... My brother has great taste." He turned to Hades. "See, she and I could get along just fine. You should drop your last name and let her keep it. Or better yet, make her a widow."

Hades was as calm as always. His breathing didn't change, and neither did his rigidness. "Whether I'm dead or not, she's out of your league."

He grinned. "Good one, Hades."

The waitress returned with the drinks, two glasses of scotch and one bottle of wine for me.

I wasn't sure why Hades had wanted to bring me. My big mouth couldn't stop insulting his brother. I was supposed to be charming and persuasive, not difficult. But...that just wasn't me.

Ash took a long drink then licked his lips. "Tell me about your-self, Sofia."

"That sounds like an interrogation." I sipped my wine.

"An interrogation is when someone asks specific questions looking for specific answers. You can tell me anything you want." He relaxed in his chair, displaying a lazy posture, unlike his brother. "Tell me about your sex life with Hades...but only if you want this to be a boring conversation."

He was bold. "He just gave me incredible head on the couch before we left...and that definitely wasn't boring."

Both of his eyebrows jumped up his face, and he slowly turned his look onto his brother. "Damn." He slowly returned his gaze to me. "Take off that ring and marry me instead."

"Oh, I never take off my ring."

Ash nodded slightly. "Beautiful, sassy, and loyal...you're the whole package."

"Your brother is the whole package too...if you just gave him a chance." I steered the conversation where it needed to go and hoped it would stick.

He looked into his glass as he swirled the contents. "So that's why you wanted us to get together, Hades. You think your lovely wife can do some damage control." He set down his glass. "I'll make a deal with you." He leaned forward and looked at his brother. "Let me borrow her for the night and—"

"If you like your two front teeth where they are, shut your mouth." Hades didn't raise his voice because we were in public, but his message echoed off the walls anyway. "You don't have to respect me. But respect my wife."

Ash actually backed off, wiping that smile from his lips. "That's fair." He turned back to me. "I apologize...Mrs. Lombardi."

I drank my wine.

We returned to painful silence, and Ash stared at me again.

This was a terrible match, and I was a horrible referee.

"Back to what you were saying." Ash pulled his glass toward him. "Tell me about yourself."

"I'm the manager of the Tuscan Rose in Florence. My father founded our line of hotels twenty years ago, and now they belong to me and Hades. It's my life's work, and I'm proud of everything we do."

"Ambitious," he said appreciatively. "That's sexy in a woman."

I ignored his comment. "Hades and I live with my mother at his estate in the city. We don't really have a lot of hobbies right now because we're still newlyweds, but I enjoy golfing... Maybe we'll start in a few years."

"You golf?" Ash asked, his eyebrow raised. He grabbed his scotch and took a drink, his eyes staying on me. His throat shifted as he swallowed. The glass hit the table again with a quiet thud once he was finished.

"Why is that so surprising?" I kept my fingers around the stem of my wineglass. Hades's fingers still rested on my thigh, slightly touching me, slightly possessive. Copping an attitude wouldn't fix the situation with Ash, but I couldn't control my innate response to his sexist assumptions.

The corner of his mouth rose into a smile, practically a sneer.

"I don't know too many women who golf, let alone pretty women. What's your best score?"

"Whatever it is, it's lower than yours."

I could see Hades's slight smile on his lips, amused by the defiance I showed his brother, the most formidable man in the room other than himself. My husband appreciated my fire, my sass. And that made me appreciate him as a man.

Ash was visibly amused by me, his smile still prevalent on his handsome face. He glanced around the restaurant as if there was someone else to see before turning back to me. A quiet chuckle came from his throat, a raspy sound that mirrored his brother's chuckle. They were so identical that if I couldn't see Ash's face, I would've assumed that laugh belonged to my own husband. "Wow, you've got a mouth on you, don't you?"

"Why do you think Hades married me?" I sipped my wine and stared at him over the rim of my glass.

Ash turned his gaze to his brother across the table, his fingers lazily touching the rim of his glass. For most of the night, he'd been focused on me, but now he directed his attention to Hades, the reason he was there in the first place. His eyes showed an intimacy that wasn't there before, but they also showed his obvious distaste for his brother. A moment passed, and there seemed to be a sense of camaraderie between them. Maybe I just imagined it, or maybe it happened so quickly I wasn't sure if it happened at all. "I'm not sure why he married you. I didn't know you existed until a few days ago."

Hades met Ash's look, his fingers digging a little deeper into my thigh. The brothers faced off in a silent battle.

Ash turned his attention back to me. "But based on your looks, I can figure it out."

The waitress returned to the table, carrying the entrees we'd ordered for the evening. After she set them down, her attention went back to Ash, probably because he was available, unlike Hades. "Looks like you need a refill."

Ash raised his glass. "You know how to take care of a man."

The waitress grabbed the glass, gave a slight smile, and walked away.

When Ash turned his attention back to us, the quiet discomfort returned.

Hades had brought me to this dinner for a reason, and it wasn't to get chummy with his older brother. It was to build a relationship, to repair the damage. Their father's death had caused an irreparable rift between the two, making the two brothers strangers.

How was I supposed to fix that?

Maybe I couldn't. But maybe I could bring them closer together. "Why don't you tell me about yourself? I don't know anything about you."

Ash rubbed the back of his head, his fingers gliding through his short hair. "Glad to know that my brother talks about me," he said sarcastically. "When did he tell you I existed in the first place?"

I could lie and say something to make Hades look better, but the last thing I wanted to do was make Hades look like a liar. "A few months ago."

"And when did he tell you that he shot our father?" The hostility picked up in the air around us. Ash's gaze was already cold, but now it was arctic. A maniacal sheen was in his eyes, hatred oozing out of his pores like sweat. His fingers didn't have a glass to grip, so they made a fist on the surface of the wood instead.

I wanted to cross my arms over my chest, but I refused to let him know he was getting under my skin. I refused to blink. The second I showed weakness, he would prey upon it, choke me with it. "The same evening."

"Was this before or after you married him?" When the waitress returned with his drink, he grabbed it without looking at her. Without thinking about what he was doing, he brought it to his lips and took a deep drink. It was another trait the two men shared. They could drink like a horse and still survive.

"Before."

Hades stayed quiet. He didn't talk much anyway, but he gave me the stage tonight.

Ash's eyes were locked on mine like two missiles. "And you married him anyway?"

Now was the tricky part. I had to think about my answer carefully before I uttered it. It was clearly a sore subject for Ash. To be indelicate could push him away. "Yes."

His eyes dilated noticeably.

I kept going. "He told me what your father did, told me about his cruelty. Don't act like he was innocent—he was far from it. I don't blame Hades for his actions because his heart was in the right place. But I also saw how he struggled to accept the consequences of that decision, how it blackened his soul. I could see it in his eyes. He tried to do the right thing, and it cost him everything."

Ash hadn't blinked once.

I had no idea what was going on behind those brown eyes. Did I just provoke him? Or did I subdue him? "All I know is that he's sorry. If he could take it back, he would. Of course, I married him, and I stand by that decision."

Ash's fingers squeezed his glass. "You married a murderer."

"Better than a trafficker."

He tilted his head slightly. "If you're so repulsed by my career choice, why are you sitting here? Why bother?"

My eyes shifted back and forth as I stared at him. It was a good question, and I'd better have a good answer. "Because marriage is about being there for the other person, even if you disagree with the situation. His relationship with you is important to him. Therefore, it's important to me. The two of you need to work this out. You're brothers. You're blood."

He shook his head slightly. "I don't need to do anything, sweetheart."

"You wouldn't be sitting here right now if you felt otherwise." I steeled my resolve as I held the connection between our eyes.

That charming smile was long gone. "I'm just here for the booze." He took a long drink and set his glass on the table. "Not the company." He was like his brother, growing moodier with every sip. "But I admit you're lovely...even if your reasoning is a little off."

It didn't seem like I'd be able to achieve anything tonight, but I didn't want to get up and walk away. My husband had already tried his best to make amends, but he failed. If I failed too, we'd be out of options. "Ash, I can read people pretty well. I can see that you're angry with your brother, that you can't forgive him for what he did. But I can also tell that you care about him. You wouldn't be drinking your scotch and hating his company if that weren't the case. We aren't asking you to forget the past. We aren't even asking for your forgiveness. Just a chance."

Ash looked away from both of us. The steak he ordered was sitting in front of him, abandoned. No one had touched their food because none of us had an appetite. His eyes wandered around, taking his time as he considered what to say. The air was pregnant with tension, packed so tightly my muscles ached. "My brother is no saint. Neither am I. That's one thing we actually have in common. But we haven't spoken in years, and I like it that way. I say we go back to that."

"I don't." The emotion escaped in my voice because I wanted this to work. If this was important to Hades, it was important to me.

"I watched my father die. I saw his brains splash across the ground. I didn't even get a chance to say goodbye." His gaze dropped for a moment, reliving that memory. "It was winter, snow had fallen in the city. When his tissues and blood seeped from his body onto the concrete, I could actually see the vapor rise with steam. That fucking image was burned in my brain forever. You expect me to just forget that? That man wasn't only my father. He was my friend."

"But he wasn't a good man," I whispered.

"And neither am I." He turned his gaze and faced me head on. "Hades and I are the same. And in my eyes, your husband is no better."

The urge to defend my husband sparked in my veins like a shock of electricity. It was a compulsion to fight for his goodness, for the man who deserved more respect. Maybe Hades shouldn't have done what he did, but he was nothing like Ash. He was nothing like his father either. "Yes, my husband is better. His crimes don't affect innocent people. Yours do. There's no way you can sit there and excuse your behavior. Your father was an asshole. So are you." I refused to kiss his ass to get what I wanted. He wouldn't respect me if I did. "There's no way you could possibly disagree. You can't look at those girls every day and defend what you're doing. Stop acting like Hades did something terrible. You are the terrible one."

Ash turned to his brother. "I don't think your wife likes me much…"

Hades shrugged. "She has high standards."

I stayed quiet because I'd said everything I needed to say. I didn't want to win his brother over with lies and deceit. I wanted to be honest. Because a relationship without honesty wasn't a relationship at all.

Ash leaned forward, his elbows resting on the table. He pushed his steak aside. "What do you expect me to do?" He looked his brother in the eye, his hostility slowly radiating outward. It was like a nuclear star pulsating with energy. "Just walk away from everything I've built? Forgive you like nothing happened? Be two pussies who golf all day? You really think that's gonna happen?" He leaned forward even more, lowering his voice. "This is what I don't understand. It's been five goddam years. No calls. No texts. No fucking birthday cards in the mail. And then all of a sudden, you come out of nowhere? That doesn't make any sense to me. Why now?"

Hades kept the same stiff posture, remaining calm and confident despite being involved in the most intense conversation I'd ever witnessed. "What does it matter, Ash? I'm here now. This is an opportunity for both of us. We can hold on to the past and be consumed by it, or we could just move on. Mom is still alive but can't remember either one of us. We are all the other has. Just let it go."

Ash actually rolled his eyes, which was somewhat comical considering how intense he was. "Being married has really turned you into a pussy, hasn't it?"

"No," Hades answered. "Loving a woman has made me into a man. And a man rights his wrongs, admits his mistakes, preserves his family. I'm not asking you to change your stance overnight. I'm just asking for the chance to make things right. We can go back to pretending that the other doesn't exist, but I'd rather not. I don't think you would either."

Ash stared at his brother a moment longer before he turned to me. Conversations continued at the tables around us, but it was deadly silent for us. We were in a strange vortex, an alternate reality where anything could happen.

Hades turned rigid as he waited for his brother to say something.

Under the table, I rested my hand on top of his, keeping him close as we waited for his brother's decision.

When Ash reached into his back pocket and grabbed his wallet, I knew this night had been in vain. He took out a wad of cash and threw it on the surface of the table. "I'd rather be strangers than brothers. I'd rather be enemies than friends."

THAT WAS A FUCKING WASTE OF TIME.

My wife was asleep in bed wearing my white t-shirt. I should be asleep too, but I preferred to sit on the couch, a glass of scotch to keep me company. The curtains were pulled back from the windows, and I had an uninterrupted view of the cityscape. The suite was so large, she couldn't hear me cope with my thoughts, didn't notice the sound of the glass tapping against the bottle, didn't detect the loud sighs of regret escaping my lips. I pulled out my phone and considered calling the only real family I had left.

But I didn't.

Like he could read my thoughts from over a hundred miles away, his name appeared on the screen.

Damien.

I took the call and put the phone to my ear. "It's three a.m. Why are you calling me?"

Damien struck back with his spiteful attitude. "It's three a.m. Why are you answering?"

I dragged my hand down my face, feeling the stress across my skin. "Because I can't sleep."

"You can never sleep."

Untrue. After I got married, everything was different. Sofia became my dream catcher. She took away the nightmares I battled every day. It was always the same nightmare every time, smoke rising from the barrel as my father lay dying. But somehow, she took that all away. "Why are you awake so late?"

"You know, booze and whores."

"On a Tuesday?"

"Uh…like every day."

I'd chuckle, but my mood wouldn't permit it.

When Damien realized I wasn't going to speak, he carried the conversation. "Sooo…how bad was it? Like, there was a shootout? Or you know, just some wrestling in the middle of the floor? Maybe a bitch-slap? Maybe two?"

"I wish."

"For the bitch slap? I can do that for you."

I sighed into the phone. "Shut up, Damien."

"If I did, this would be a really boring conversation. I'd just have to sit here and listen to you stewing all night long. No thanks. So tell me what happened."

"Not much to say. Ash wants nothing to do with me. That's the bottom line."

"And Sofia had no pull?"

"No. She cast her spell, but it didn't work."

"Hmm…maybe he's gay."

"No…just stubborn."

Damien was quiet for a while. "So, you think this is hopeless?"

"Yes." I took a drink before returning the glass to the table. "But I can't give up. If he never forgives me, then I can never break the curse. That's a life I refuse to accept."

"Well, if your brother is anything like you, he'll always be stubborn. Maybe it's time to take a break. Come home, wait a couple weeks, and then try again. If you come at him day after day, you're not gonna wear him down. You're just gonna piss him off. Well…there's another option… But you'll never go for it."

"I'm desperate. I'll go for anything."

He released a sarcastic laugh. "Not this, man."

"What is it? Damien, just spit it out."

Damien released a long sigh into the phone. "Well, he hates you, but he doesn't hate beautiful women. Sofia is beautiful, and damn, she's persuasive. I'm sure the conversation would be much different if it were just the two of them."

"Yeah…you're probably right." I stared at my glass on the table, repulsed by the idea of leaving my wife alone with a man like Ash. But I couldn't deny Damien's logic. At dinner, Ash was noticeably different speaking to my wife. Softer. Calmer. Kinder. But once his eyes were on me, it was full-blown hatred. Sofia balanced my coldness, offset my rough exterior. She was an asset that could help me immensely. I just wasn't sure if I wanted to use her.

"I think that's your best bet. I know you don't like that idea. Neither do I. But maybe give it a chance. And if that doesn't work...throw in the towel. If your brother was gonna do something, he would've done it by now."

"But if I send her in there, I'll be sick to my stomach."

"Then have him meet her somewhere else."

"I doubt he'll even take my call at this point." Our relationship seemed to be worse by the end of that dinner rather than better. Sofia did all she could, but her charms couldn't fix what I'd done. I would just give up and go home, but there was too much at stake.

"That's why you have her call, idiot."

In any other situation, I wouldn't even consider it, but this had to be done...no matter the cost. "I gotta go, Damien."

His grin was audible through the phone. "Get that shit done."

WHEN SOFIA STEPPED out of the bathroom, she was dressed in a dark blue sundress, a gold necklace around her neck. Her hair was in soft curls, and she looked ready for the runway, not an average day. She ran her fingers through her hair and shifted her gaze to look at me. "Morning."

I stood in my black sweatpants, a coffee mug in my grasp. I took a drink, and I looked at her, marveling at how pure her beauty was. It was simple, easy, but so profound. Makeup or no makeup, it didn't make a difference. She was the most stunning woman I'd ever seen. I was so absorbed in the moment, so consumed by my own thoughts, I'd already forgotten what she'd just said.

As if she knew exactly what had happened in my head, she gave a bright smile. Her palm pressed against my bare chest, and she leaned in and kissed me. "It's nice to see you drink coffee. Your breath always smells like scotch."

"Your breath always smells like my dick."

She rolled her eyes playfully then turned away and poured herself a mug of coffee.

I watched her movements, one hand resting in the pocket of my sweatpants.

She added a splash of cream before she turned back to me. "Didn't sleep well?"

"What makes you say that?"

"Because you weren't in bed half the night."

Maybe I wasn't as subtle as I thought. The longer we lived together, the more she understood me, the more she picked up on my habits, my moods. The more she understood when to comfort me and when to leave me alone. She'd made the right decision last night. Giving me space was exactly what I needed. I didn't bother explaining what happened because she already knew. "I need you to do me a favor."

"You just told me I have dick breath. Not a smart thing to say before you ask for a favor." She stirred her coffee and smiled slightly, being playful in the way I liked. Last night was a shit-show, but instead of making the situation worse, she tried to lighten it up.

"I meant it as a compliment."

"Oh, I'm sure you did." She took a seat on the couch, both of her hands cupping the large mug. "You know you don't need to ask me for a favor. I'm your wife. Ask me to do anything, and I will."

I moved to the couch beside her, slightly taken aback by the loyalty she'd just shown me. Her submission was beautiful; her obedience was a fantasy. Just months ago, I couldn't even get her to let me rub her feet, couldn't even get her to take my phone calls, but now she responded to me like we were friends, partners. "It's about Ash."

She inhaled a deep breath, the sound slightly audible in the silence. She couldn't keep up her visage of joy at all when he was mentioned. She ran her fingers through her hair once more, her gaze tilted to the floor. "I'm sorry it didn't work out last night. I never knew a man could be more stubborn than you, but he is your brother...so I guess it's no surprise." She brought her steaming cup of coffee to her lips, taking a long drink, licking her lips when she was finished. "You want me to talk to him alone, don't you?"

Sometimes I forgot how smart she was. "Only if you feel comfortable."

She continued to stare at her coffee. "Do you trust him?"

I set my coffee on the table and shook my head slightly. "I don't trust anyone."

"I hope that doesn't apply to me." She set down her mug.

I turned my gaze on her, touched by the genuine hurt in her eyes. "You are the one exception."

The corner of her mouth rose slightly. "I trust you too...more than I thought I could trust anyone. So, if you think it is safe for me to go, I will. You would never put me in harm's way."

"No. I don't think he'd hurt you or take you. If he did, he knows I know everything about his operation. I'd burn it to the ground with everyone inside. And even if that weren't the case, I don't see him doing that anyway." My brother wasn't a good guy, but sometimes, I guess he was just misunderstood. He got into this business because of my father. If that had never happened, I imagined he would've done something much better with his life. When we were growing up, he was always curious and adventurous. If he found a stray animal, he always took it to the shelter. The only reason there was darkness in his soul was because our father put it there. "You should be safe."

"Alright. What do you want me to do?"

I grabbed her phone and typed in the number on the keypad. "Call him."

"You want me to fix this over the phone?"

"No. Ask to have lunch with him. Or dinner. Whatever. I don't give a fuck."

"And what if he says no?"

I gave her a hard stare. "Don't let his answer be no."

She turned her gaze back to the phone, and after a moment of trepidation, she hit the send button. She put the phone to her ear and let it ring.

I was close to her side, so every single sound over the line was audible. My elbows rested on my knees, and my hands were joined together. The sunlight came through the open window. It was a beautiful day at the end of summer. As newlyweds, we should be doing fun things, not trying to fix the past.

Ash answered. "Yeah?"

Sofia kept her confidence in her voice, never wavering even though she only knew this man as a formidable foe. "It's Sofia."

A long pause ensued over the line. "I'm never gonna get rid of you, am I?"

"I'm a lovely person, so I don't see why you'd want to."

"True," he said with a slight chuckle. "But you aren't lovely enough in this case."

Sofia continued the conversation. "Are you free this evening?"

His joy was palpable. "Asking me out? I'd be happy to take you to bed." His smile was so loud over the phone that I could picture all of his white teeth. "My brother isn't enough for you... No surprise there. I've had a lot more practice."

"I assure you that's not the case. I'd just like to have dinner with my brother-in-law."

"For pussy talk?"

"I wouldn't call it that...but yes."

"And you think a bottle of wine and a tight skirt will change my mind?" he asked.

"No, but maybe a bottle of scotch will."

There was a pause, as if he were intrigued. "You gonna drink scotch with me, sweetheart?"

"Yes...if you'll have me."

He was quiet for a while, suspicion creeping in. "Just you? He put you up to this?"

"Yes. You and me." She turned her gaze back to me, reading my expression as she kept the conversation going. "And yes, he put me up to this, but that shouldn't matter."

"I never say no to a beautiful woman, especially if scotch is involved. Maybe I can talk you into leaving him for me. Wouldn't be my first time."

"Never gonna happen, but give it your best shot."

"A devoted woman...that's hot." It sounded like he was walking as he spoke, the wind raspy over the phone. "How about we meet at a bar tonight? Eight o'clock. And don't bring that bitch with you."

"Fine."

I reached out my hand to take the phone.

Sofia handed it over.

I put the phone to my ear and made my usual threats. "Try anything and I'll kill you, Ash."

He gave a slight chuckle. "Don't trust me? Ironic. You're the one who murders people. I'm the one who shouldn't trust you."

"I mean it, Ash. This is my wife we're talking about."

"I'll have a drink with her and walk her back to the hotel like a gentleman. Is that what you want to hear?"

"Yes. And you better mean that."

"I do. I actually respect her...unlike you."

17

SOFIA

HADES WALKED ME TO THE BAR, HIS ARM AROUND MY WAIST AS HE kept me close. He stopped in front of the entryway but didn't walk inside. His chin tilted down to look at me, his brown eyes shifting back and forth as he stared into mine. A soft shadow had emerged along his jawline, a byproduct of not shaving for days. That rugged look was sexy on him. Not all men could pull it off. It would often be a bunch of uneven patches, not manly whatsoever, just lazy. There was unease in his eyes, like he couldn't bear the thought of leaving me alone.

"I'll be fine."

He stared at me in silence.

"I don't know Ash as well as you, but I think he's harmless."

"I do too. That doesn't make this easier for me."

My hands reached to his face and cupped his cheeks. Our foreheads came together, and I held him that way outside the bar. People passed us on the sidewalk, oblivious to our intimate connection.

He pressed his lips to my forehead then pulled away. "I'll wait here until you're done."

"You don't need to do that."

"I prefer it." His arms tightened around my waist, and he pulled me close, pressing a delicate kiss to my lips. It was an innocent embrace, just a simple touch, but it conveyed more affection than I'd ever felt from anyone else. He forced himself to release me and stepped back to lean against the wall. His hands slid into his pockets, and he looked the other way so he didn't have to watch me walk inside.

I entered the bar and immediately noticed Ash sitting in a stool near the bartenders, wearing dark jeans and a black t-shirt. He was the youngest and most handsome guy in the place. The room was crowded, but the stools on either side of him were vacant. Somehow people understood that it was smart to stay away from him. There were already two glasses of scotch waiting, one for him and for me.

As I walked toward him, he lifted his chin to look at me, one hand resting on the top of his glass. He was rigid with a perfectly straight back. He regarded me with a confidence that rivaled his brother's. After he gave a slight smile, he patted the counter beside him, silently ordering me to take a seat. His gaze wasn't friendly, but it wasn't hostile either.

I rose on my tiptoes to take the seat next to him. As if I had something to prove, I grabbed the glass and took a drink. It was hot against my tongue and throat, and it burned all the way down. I definitely preferred wine to this gasoline, but I could drink like a man for the night.

He gave me a look of approval as he held his glass to his lips. "Sexy." Then he took another drink. "I'm surprised my brother actually let you come here. I guess he doesn't think I'm a monster after all."

"You should take that as a compliment. But you should also know he's standing outside." I felt safer knowing that Hades was just feet away, that he could get to me with just a moment's notice. I didn't think Ash would hurt me or capture me, but I'd be lying if I said I felt perfectly safe with him.

"Saw him. Saw that pussy forehead kiss too."

"You throw *pussy* around like it's a weak word, but I think it's the strongest word in our vocabulary."

"It's definitely the most beautiful."

"Pussies give birth to babies. The most you can do is piss."

A boyish grin stretched across his face, somewhat similar to his brother's. He took a sip, set it down, and then pivoted his chair so he could face me. "What are you gonna say to change my mind, sweetheart?"

"Nothing. You're too stubborn." I had to force myself to take another drink, and I hid my usual grimace as it burned my tongue.

"Then why are you here?" he asked. "Other than to flirt with me."

"I'd like to get to know you—not flirt with you."

"What's there to know? I'm an asshole. That's the gist."

Coming directly at Ash wouldn't get me anywhere. He seemed to have made up his mind and refused to change it. But maybe if I could make him think of simpler times, his heart would soften.

There was nothing I could say or do to change his mind that evening, but maybe I could plant a seed.

And maybe the seed would grow.

"What was Hades like when he was growing up?"

"Nothing special. He was Father's favorite until he dropped out of university."

"Your father doesn't seem like a man who would value education."

He shrugged. "Our mother cared. She was always the good one. We were all shitheads. My father asked Hades to be part of the family business, and when he said no, Father took it personally. They bumped heads from that moment on. That resentment only grew as time passed. It built up until it exploded... And then my father was dead." He turned his gaze back to his glass, looking at the amber liquid that sat still.

"Were the two of you close?"

"A bit. But we fought like all brothers do."

"Did the two of you still speak when your father and Hades were on bad terms?"

"Not really. But that wasn't because we had a problem with each other." Ash was similar to his brother in appearance, having the same obvious good looks, but Ash was thicker in the arms and the chest. He had beautiful, fair skin, not nearly as tanned as Hades, but that was probably because he was inside more often than my husband. Thick cords ran down all the way to his hands, powerful veins that webbed over his defined muscles. He was a big man...someone I wouldn't be stupid enough to provoke. "We just never saw each other. I was loyal to my father, and he was off doing his own thing."

When I'd first sat down inside that bar, all heads turned my way. Most men probably hoped I was single, because that's what people did in a bar, looked for someone to make a connection with. I was used to those stares, had received them my entire adult life. But I noticed they halted once they assumed Ash and I were together. Just like his brother, Ash could chase away any man in my vicinity. "So, you guys were never close?"

"Not really." His fingers gripped the top of his glass, and he gave his scotch a slight shake. "We were when we were boys. Not men." He stared down at his glass, made another shake, and then took a drink.

"Hades mentioned that your mother lost her memory."

"I wouldn't say lost it… She just got sick." His visage didn't really change, but it seemed like the statement was difficult for him to say. "She's been in the home for a couple years now. I don't remember the last time I saw her."

I wanted to suggest that both of them visit their mother, but I knew it wasn't my place to say anything like that. I had no idea what it was like to watch a parent slowly fade away, to watch a parent forget you. "I'm sorry."

"Yeah…our lives are a sad story. But whatever. You get over it." He stared straight ahead, looking at his reflection in the mirror behind the bar. "But it looks like my brother got a happy ending." He turned his gaze back to me, his brown eyes so similar to his brother's that it was like I was looking at Hades instead of him. He lifted his glass and tapped it against mine. "I'm surprised because it seemed like my brother would never commit to one woman."

"Well...that wasn't until he met me." I debated telling him the truth, that this marriage was just an arrangement, just a way for both of us to get what we wanted. Our relationship had deepened into a foundation of friendship and trust, but not love. Since Ash wasn't close to Hades, I decided to keep the truth private.

Ash smiled slightly. "You're cool. I like you."

"Good. Kinda like you too." Feeling affection for this man was natural, although I couldn't explain why. Maybe it was because he was similar to Hades, maybe because I projected my positive feeling for Hades onto him. Somehow it was easy for me to forget the terrible travesties he committed on a daily basis. "But I would like you a lot more if you stopped what you are doing."

He shrugged. "It's just business."

"Call it what you want. People are never business."

He shook his head slightly. "I guess we'll just have to agree to disagree." He pushed my glass a little closer to me. "You still haven't finished that."

"I still have to walk back to the hotel."

"I can always carry you."

"Ha," I said sarcastically. "My husband would love that..."

"So, what now?" he asked. "You return to Florence and be the wife of a drug lord? We move on and forget this ever happened?"

"No. We could never forget you. If you reject Hades forever, we'll still never forget you."

He took another drink from his glass, making it empty. He tapped it against the surface of the wood, getting the attention of the bartender, and silently asked for a refill. "I feel like I'm missing something here, a piece of the puzzle I can't find. Hades wants to reconnect with me, but I don't really know why. Has he told you the truth? Do you even know what that truth is?"

I held his gaze, noticing the new glass of scotch in my peripheral vision. When Hades told me to make amends with his brother, I didn't ask a lot of questions. That's what families did; they stayed in contact. A request wasn't that difficult to understand, but in truth, he hadn't ever really explained to me this compulsive need to make things right. Why would he want to patch things up with a man who committed the same crimes as his late father? Why was he taking time out of our lives to win over a man who didn't give a damn? I'd seen my husband in action, and he didn't give a shit about anybody.

As if Ash could read my thoughts, he said, "You should ask him."

Ash and I walked outside together, reaching the empty sidewalk. It was getting late, so there was nobody on the streets. His hands were in the pockets of his jeans, and he stood close to me, as if he were guarding me like a dog. There was a protective nature about him, even though he was probably the most dangerous man I'd ever met.

Hades emerged from the corner of the building, his eyes immediately rolling over my body, making sure I wasn't harmed and was in the exact same condition he had left me in. Tall with a strong stature, he walked up to us, his eyes on his brother. Once he reached us, his arm automatically wrapped around my waist. With a gentle tug, he pulled me closer. It seemed like two men were fighting over me, but there was never a contest in the first place.

Ash had a more relaxed posture, his weight shifted to one leg. He was definitely more laid-back compared to his brother, as if he didn't care what anyone thought of him. When he looked at Hades, there was a slight smile on his lips. "You aren't gonna let me walk her home?"

Hades didn't respond to the playfulness. "That's my job. Not yours."

Ash's gaze held on for a bit longer before he diverted his attention to me. "Thanks for drinking with me, sweetheart." He looked at his brother one last time, giving a silent goodbye, and then turned around and walked away.

Hades watched him go, his arm loosening around my waist the farther he went. "Did he bother you?"

"No. He's a nice guy...when he wants to be."

"Can I assume you made no progress?"

I shook my head. "I can tell he cares about you. I can tell he still loves you as a brother. But there's just something missing...like he's been hurt. Sometimes I wonder if he's not only upset that you killed your father, but also you pulled yourself away from him too. You forced him to hate you, so he lost you too."

Hades hadn't taken his eyes off his brother. Now he was a distant figure two blocks away.

I watched my husband cycle through many emotions—regret, loss, hurt. But in all the amount of time I'd known him, there never appeared to be anything missing. Now there seemed to be a huge hole in his heart, a void he couldn't fill. Was that void Ash? Or was it something else?

"Hades?"

His eyes dropped down to mine.

"Is there another reason why this is so important to you?"

The only answer I got was silence.

"Because you never mentioned Ash in all the years I've known you, and now you're bending backward to make things right. You've taken weeks off work, and you seem intent on not giving up. Why is this so important to you now? Is there another reason?"

He slowly dropped his arm from my waist. He pulled away his affection, as if he were battling his own demons. He never said much, but now it seemed like he wanted to say even less.

I waited, practically holding my breath. Somehow, I knew whatever he was going to say was important.

His chin tilted down slightly as he stared at the concrete beneath our feet. His hands slid into the front pockets of his jeans, and unlike his brother, he stood so rigid and proud, like he was a rock in the desert. "There is another reason...but I can't tell you what it is."

18

HADES

I KNEW MY WIFE RESPECTED ME WHEN SHE DIDN'T ASK ANY QUESTIONS.

We had returned to Florence, and I sat on the balcony, letting the darkness wrap around me like a warm blanket on a cold day. My elbow rested on the arm of the chair, my fingertips against my chin. Summer was officially over; fall was on the way.

Accepting the truth was like swallowing an enormous pill. It didn't matter how much water I drank, I couldn't get it down. I always got what I wanted, never stopped until I was a victor, but this time, I couldn't win. Getting someone to obey you through force, torture, and money was easy. But getting someone to forgive you... That couldn't be forced.

So, I failed.

Without my brother's forgiveness, my life would be exactly the same. I would love a woman who would never love me back. Every day, my heart would grow for her, but hers would never change.

Fucking depressing.

But I had to accept it.

Loving a woman who didn't love me back was better than not loving her at all.

I stared at the buildings across the street, trying to think of a way to get what I wanted, a way to convince my brother of my sincerity. But if Sofia couldn't wear him down, then I never could.

The patio doors opened, and Sofia's bare feet hit the Italian pavers. She was in a black nightdress, ready for bed, but she looked so sexy that it didn't seem like she was ready to sleep. We hadn't said much on the flight home, and ever since we'd been back, we continued to let the silence fester. She didn't bombard me with questions. And I hardly said any words.

She glided toward me, the cold air making her nipples tighten through the silk material of her gown. Her long hair stretched past her shoulders, the curls coming loose after the long day we'd had. When she got to my side, her hand moved to my shoulder. With a woman's touch, she gently rubbed my tight muscles and the warm skin at the back of my neck.

I didn't change my position, but my fingers slowly moved to her thigh. The backs of my knuckles lightly brushed against her soft skin. Those subtle touches couldn't convey all the emotions in my heart. I was just a man very much attracted to his wife. Little did she know I couldn't stop touching her because I was obsessively, devotedly infatuated with her. I didn't adore her just for her looks, didn't worship her for her good soul. It was much more than that.

But I could never tell her that.

My hand grabbed the material of her dress and gave a slight tug. She lowered into my lap, both of her legs stretching over my thighs. My arms flexed as I scooped her closer to me, our faces so close that my nose practically touched her cheek. I took a deep breath as I inhaled her perfume, summer roses and white lilies. My hand rested on both of her knees because my hands were so large compared to her petite frame.

My lips lightly pressed against her cheek, a kiss so soft I wondered if she felt it. My mouth slowly moved to the shell of her ear, the back of her neck, and then along her jawline. I loved to kiss her just to kiss her. Didn't have to go anywhere. Didn't have to lead to sex. All I wanted was to adore her—because that was my right.

I was her husband—I should adore her.

Her arms moved around my neck as she turned her gaze to mine. Her makeup was gone, so her beautiful skin looked natural, real. When she stared at me like that, sometimes it seemed like she adored me as much as I adored her, like she couldn't live without me the way I couldn't live without her.

I looked into her eyes and somehow knew a question would erupt from her lips.

"Why can't you tell me?" she whispered. She'd kept the question to herself for the last two days, but when the curiosity became too much, she cracked. Her left hand fell from my neck and drifted over my shoulder. Her palm flattened against my chest, as if she were trying to feel my heartbeat.

I dropped my gaze for just a moment, wishing I could tell her the truth, the whole truth. I wanted her to know everything, every feeling in my heart, every confession in my soul. I wanted her to know that we were meant to be together, that she was the only woman I wanted to be with—because she was the other half of my soul. "Because I can't."

"Why?"

"Baby, I just can't."

Her eyes filled with disappointment. "Will you ever?"

"Yes."

"I know whatever the reason is, it must be important. I've never seen you work so hard for something, especially something that seems hopeless. I know you don't agree with your brother's choice of livelihood. I know it kills you inside. But whatever you need from him must be bigger than that."

Yes—it was the biggest thing in my life.

"If you tell me...maybe I can help you."

"No one can help me."

"But—"

"Drop it." I hated to cut her off so coldly. She was only trying to help me, but talking about this only made me feel worse. I wasn't able to save us, and my secret hurt her too.

She wasn't affronted by my coldness. Instead, her eyes were filled with pity. Her hand moved across my chest, and her fingers dug into the back of my hair. She slowly leaned in and pressed her forehead to mine, bringing our hearts, bodies, and souls close to each other. "Are you going to give up?"

I closed my eyes and whispered into the darkness. "Never."

I rose to my feet and lifted her with me. She was a stack of pillows, a soft cloud because she was so small. Like a husband carrying his wife over the threshold of their home for the first time, I carried her inside and laid her on the bed.

When her head hit the pillow, her hair naturally spread across the sheets. Her hands moved to her hips, and she pushed her panties down her legs, getting ready for me even though I'd just rejected her. Like a real husband and wife, it didn't matter if we disagreed. At the end of the night, we still wanted each other.

Watching her want me was sexier than watching any other woman want me. I could pretend that she loved me, that her feelings mirrored my own. It was so easy to do.

When she looked at me like that.

I got my bottoms off without taking my eyes off hers. Her legs automatically opened for me, letting me slide to the place where I belonged. It was a parking spot reserved just for me, the piece of her I owned exclusively.

Our bodies combined together, our heated breaths echoing in the bedroom. My hands slid into the back of her hair, and my eyes focused on hers. She was the only thing in the world that really mattered to me. I used to think money and power triumphed over everything else, but now I realized I could give all that away and live in a tiny house with her and be just as happy. My old life was a distant memory. I couldn't even remember the women I had been with before her. She had the power to erase my past, to make me forget there was a time when she didn't exist.

Maybe she would never love me—but as long as I had this, I would be okay.

I WAS SITTING behind my desk at the bank when Damien walked in. Papers were scattered around my desk, and my laptop was disorganized with a bunch of random shit I could never stay on top of.

Damien wore a midnight black suit, and he unbuttoned the front of his jacket before he took a seat. "Sorry about your brother."

I leaned back in the chair and brought my hands together. "It is what it is."

"You aren't the kind of man to give up easily."

"Actually, I'm the kind of man that doesn't give up at all."

He relaxed in his chair, his knees falling wide apart. His fingers interlocked at the back of his neck, like he was vacationing at a resort, not sitting in my office. "Then why are you giving up now?"

"I haven't. Just taking a break."

"Yeah, that's probably a good idea. You might annoy him so much he ends up killing you. Then nobody wins."

I didn't want to talk about the issue with Sofia anymore. It was all I'd been thinking about lately, and I needed a break from the suffocation. "How's the Newton account? You didn't fuck it up while I was gone, right?"

"Newton account?" he asked. "No idea what you're talking about."

I raised an eyebrow. "I'm not in the mood, Damien."

He chuckled. "Geez, you need to lighten up. Of course I took care of the Newton account. I do a better job running this place than you do."

"Bullshit."

He shrugged. "I was the one taking care of it while you were gone in Rome..."

"I did what I had to do. You know that." After everything that happened with Ash, I realized I may never get what I wanted. That meant I had to be careful, look over my shoulder because I had so much to lose. If I was willing to live in a shack with Sofia, then there was no point in me fighting for the money and power I used to care so deeply about. "I want to talk to you about something."

"I feel like all we ever do is talk. Let's do something else like... like parachuting."

I ignored what he said. "I've decided to keep my word to Maddox. We aren't going to start this corporation again. He gave me an ultimatum, your life or the business. I made my decision, and I stick by it. It sucks. It sucks that it happened, it sucks that he humiliated us...but we lost. It's time to walk away."

Damien dropped his hands from the back of his neck, his face slowly slackening as the horrible news hit him in the chest. He began to lean forward, his entire body indicating his opposition to what I'd just said. "Fuck no. It's never time to walk away. I'm not lying down like some kind of pussy. We've been working on this for a decade. Maybe he won that battle, but we'll win the war."

"Damien. No."

"Just because *you* say no doesn't mean no. Half of that business is mine. You can drop out of the race, but that doesn't mean I have to." He rose to his feet and slowly approached my desk. His hands slid into his pockets, and he looked at me with sheer disappointment. "Where the hell is this coming from?"

"It's not coming from anywhere. It's the right thing to do."

"There's no such thing as the right thing. There're only winners and losers. And, asshole, I'm not going to be a loser." He rested his palm on my desk, his hand slowly balling into a fist.

"I have too much to lose, Damien." I rose to my feet to meet his gaze. We were both over six feet, both powerful and strong. If our fists flew at each other's faces, it would be an even match. "I don't want to lose this business any more than you, but I have a wife to think about. If Maddox comes after her, it'll kill me. And if he just wants me, she'll lose me. Either way, she loses everything. I'm sorry, Damien. But that decision is final."

He cocked his head to the side, his eyebrows furrowed like that decision was questionable. "And what about me?"

The anger rushed in my veins, the memory of that night when I'd told Damien to listen to me and he refused. "We're in this goddamn mess because of you. Let's not forget that. If you would have just listened to me, none of this would have happened. So no, asshole, you don't get a say in this."

His rage slowly faded away, guilt entering his gaze. He'd gone after Maddox when I told him not to, and I'd paid for his mistake with our business. He couldn't argue with that.

"Alright?"

After a deep breath, he spoke. "Fine." He returned his hand to his pocket and stepped away from my desk. He started to pace in my office, examining my bookshelves and the art on the walls. "Well, we've got a problem."

Fuck. What did he do?

"While you were gone, I continued production. There's a bit of crystal on the streets." He stopped pacing and faced me once more.

I could feel the heartbeat in my temples, like I was fighting the worst migraine of my life. My body immediately went into fight-or-flight mode, but all I wanted to do was fight. I'd turned my back for one second, and Damien fucked everything up. He'd always been the irrational one between the two of us, the impulsive one. I suspected that would ruin me eventually. "You did *what*?"

"Look, I had already started right after you left. That crystal is in the hands of our distributors now."

"But I told you to wait."

"And I did wait, but I can't stop the distributors from selling our product. I kept production going because I didn't see the harm in that. I mean, how is Maddox gonna know if we're producing anything?"

Both of my hands planted against the sides of my face, and my fingers dug into my skull. "Because he knows shit, asshole. If he figures this out, he's gonna come at us hard. We aren't the least bit prepared."

"Chill. He's not gonna find out. I'll make some calls and get our shit off the street."

"It might be too late."

"But it might not be." He returned to my desk. "Let's worry when there's actually something to worry about. There're only a few kilos on the street. I'm sure he'll assume it's some rogue dealers since we're out of the picture. I'll make sure production is halted, and this will all go away."

"It better go away, Damien. Because this is over...for good."

He looked at the ground. "I'm happy you found Sofia. I really am. But if she weren't around, you wouldn't be scared of anything. You would be the king of the underworld, the man who would do anything to stay on top. Now you've just given up."

"Because I'm married now, Damien. What kind of husband would I be if I didn't put my wife first?"

"You'd be just like every other husband in the world. That's not why you're doing this. You're doing this because you're in love with her... That's the big difference."

19

SOFIA

HADES HAD BEEN IN A BAD MOOD FOR THE PAST WEEK. HE WORKED long hours, he came home late, sometimes skipped dinner, and the only time we really had together was when we were fucking. Then he went to sleep and was gone early the next morning.

He probably had to catch up on all the work he'd missed, but he didn't give me a lot of details. I tried not to ask because it seemed to put him in a worse mood.

When he admitted he had another reason to reconcile with his brother, I couldn't figure out what that reason could possibly be. And I couldn't figure out why it had to be a secret either. But I had to remind myself that this was his personal business, his family, and if he wanted to talk about it, he would.

But if he had told me the truth...maybe I could've helped.

I was sitting on the couch in the bedroom with my laptop on my thighs, a glass of wine beside me, and I was drinking earlier than I usually did. Every time I grabbed the glass, my wedding ring tapped loudly against the surface. I brought it to my lips for a drink just when Hades walked through the door.

He stepped inside, stealthy in a black suit and a matching tie. The color matched his brooding nature, matched his scruff along his jaw. The first thing he did was walk to his dresser and open the top drawer. On the surface was an assortment of watches he'd collected over the years. He unclasped the one he wore and placed it inside.

"You look like a serious collector." I set my glass down and rose to my feet.

He shed his jacket from his broad shoulders and tossed it on the chair. Next, he grabbed the front of his tie and loosened it.

I walked to the drawer and looked down at the collection of watches. All different, all unique. Some were white gold, some were black, and some had leather straps. "Did you buy all of these?"

He unbuttoned his shirt, undoing each button until the shirt opened and revealed his perfect physicality. "No." He pulled his shirt off his arms and tossed it aside. Now he stood with perfect posture, tight arms, and a core so strong he was nothing but lines and muscle. "Most of them were gifts." He reached inside and grabbed a white-gold one. He turned it over and showed me the engraving underneath. "Damien gave me this for my birthday a few years ago."

I could see the small letters. It read, *Happy Birthday, Asshole.*

"That was sweet..." The corners of my lips tugged into a smile when I read the message his closest friend wrote.

He returned the watch back to the velvet lining.

"Can I look at them?"

He turned to me, giving me that intense stare that always made me melt. "You can do whatever you want, baby. Everything you see, it's yours." He wasn't trying to be romantic, but when he wrapped his arm around my waist and pulled me tight for a kiss, it was the most romantic thing in the world. He kissed me with aggressive lips, giving me tongue the second he had me. His hand reached down to my ass for a tight squeeze then a gentle spank. When he was done, he grabbed my glass of wine and took a drink.

I looked down at the watches, my lips burning after the scorching kiss he'd just given me. My fingertips absentmindedly touched my mouth, and I swore I could feel the heat of his kiss. After the moment passed, I studied the collection of watches. There must've been at least a dozen. I picked up a dark one, a watch with a black face. It was simple, sleek, smooth; it seemed to match his personality well. I glided my thumb over the glass, seeing the second hand tick by. When I turned it over, I spotted another engraving.

Andrew

From, Dad

I stared at it for a moment before I returned it to the case. When I glanced at Hades, he had downed the entire glass of wine. His belt was pulled out of the loops, and he set it on top of his dresser.

I considered confronting him about the watch, but I suspected it would only provoke bad memories. I walked toward him and pressed my palms against his bare chest. "Long day?"

"What makes you say that?"

"You've been in a bad mood all week."

His brown eyes stayed focused on mine, conveying his annoyance and frustration, not at me, but at the situation. He seemed to soften at my touch, to be invigorated at my affection, so he slid his hand up my neck and into my hair. He lightly tucked a strand behind my ear and held me the way a woman wanted to be held. "I have to tell you something."

"Something good, I hope."

He didn't give me the answer I wanted to hear. "I don't think you should return to the hotel for a couple of weeks."

"Weeks?" I asked incredulously. "I've already taken so much time off."

"I know. But it's not the best time."

"Why? You go to work every day."

"That's totally different. And even if it weren't, I wish I could stay home with you all day. It's just temporary. I have to make sure the dust has settled."

"What dust?" I didn't know what he was referring to. I didn't know what he was afraid of. There seemed to be a world weighing on his shoulders, a world I couldn't see. "What's going on?"

His hand slid from my neck, slipped from my hair until he secured it around my waist. He brought our faces close together, so close it seemed like he might kiss me again. "Damien's a dumb fuck. That's what's going on."

"You're going to have to be more specific."

He sighed before he gave me the full explanation. "Damien and I had a misunderstanding. He decided to continue the drug business in my absence. I believe that it's not a good idea, that we need to let it go. Unfortunately, he put more drugs on the street and resumed production. I've been doing damage control all week. It's been quiet out there, so I think everything will be fine. But you know me, I'm a cautious man. I think it's best that you stay home."

"If things have been quiet, then why can't I go back to work?"

"Too risky."

"Couldn't you just send some men with me?" I knew he was trying to protect me, but being cooped up in this house all day was not the way I wanted to spend my time.

"A couple men wouldn't be enough. The safest place for you is here."

"Hades, you know I'm not the type of woman to sit on my ass all day."

"But you are now. It's not forever."

"What about—"

"I said no." He dropped his embrace, turning cold. "I know you don't like being told what to do, but I'm supposed to take care of you. It's how it's supposed to be. Just do as I say."

My attitude wanted to rise in force and demolish the area around us. I prized my independence more than anything else, and because of him, I no longer had it. Like bile was in my mouth, my tongue was coated in distaste. I wanted to spit it out and scream. But I knew this relationship was about compromise. Fighting would only make things worse, not better. And it always ended the same way—with me on my back and him on top of me.

He studied my face as if he were waiting for the explosion to happen.

I pressed my lips tightly together, venting my frustration the only way I knew. I finally released everything as a painful sigh.

When he was satisfied with my reaction, he relaxed his shoulders. "Thank you."

I cocked an eyebrow at the statement.

"Thank you for listening to me."

"It's not easy…"

"I know." He stepped closer to me again, his hands cupping my cheeks and lifting my gaze to meet his. "And that's why it means so much."

THE WEEK PASSED with painful slowness.

I did as much work as I could at home, but it wasn't the same as being at the hotel. I couldn't hold meetings with the board. I couldn't check the routine of the hotel, and I couldn't pick up on the details only my eyes could observe. I had to hope that the managers of the hotel were doing their job.

And I had to hope that people didn't think I was lazy.

A text message came through on my phone. It was from Hades.

I'm picking you up for lunch. The car will be there in fifteen minutes.

I knew Hades was busy taking care of the bank and the hotel, so he was making time just to get me out of the house. He knew I was bored, cooped up and alone. Technically, my mother was there, but I'd rather be alone than hang out with her all the time. He did sweet things like that once in a while…when I least expected it.

I texted him back. *I'll meet you outside. See you then.*

I changed my outfit, put some earrings into my lobes, and then slipped on a pair of pumps. I made my way down three flights of stairs until I stepped out of the entryway. A black car sat there, all the windows tinted pitch black. When Hades had a driver, this was how he got around town, invisible with bulletproof windows.

I walked to the back door, opened it, and got inside. When I turned to look at my husband and embrace him with a kiss, I realized it wasn't my husband at all.

An audible lock erupted in the car, making all the doors impossible to open. The driver immediately started to drive away. A center divider was between us. That way, I couldn't grab him. I looked at the passenger beside me again, recognizing his face, his blue eyes, and the pure look of evil on his mouth.

It was Maddox.

It only took me seconds to figure out what had happened. He'd hacked into my phone and impersonated my husband to lure me down right into his car. If he tried to grab me at the hotel, it would've been far too complicated. Instead, he tricked me into leaving the fortress and stepping directly into his arms.

How could I be so stupid?

The car was speeding away, and there was no time to call Hades. If I tried, Maddox would just snatch my phone away. So I did something crazy.

I tried to kill him.

I launched myself across the car and banged both fists against his face. He was twice my size, twice my height, but I didn't care.

This was the fight of my life—and I wasn't going to lose. My hands smashed into his face, beat into his chest, exploded into his stomach with all the strength I could muster. I had no idea I could move so quickly, but when everything was on the line, I could do extraordinary things.

He grabbed my arm and pinned it at my side before he wrapped his other arm around my neck. Despite the beating he took, he was calm about the whole ordeal, didn't even seem mad about the bruises I'd just put on his face.

Made him terrifying.

He squeezed my neck just enough so I struggled to breathe. "Wasn't expecting that." His other hand moved to my scalp, and as if he were my lover, he ran his fingers through my hair, as if his touch would calm me rather than repulse me. "But don't make me hurt you, sweetheart. I would hate to bruise that pretty face."

He grabbed a syringe from his pocket, and with his teeth, popped off the cap.

"Please don't."

He pressed his thumb to the top, squirting just a little bit of liquid out.

"Don't do this to me. I've done nothing to you."

"The innocent pay for the crimes of the guilty. That's how it's always been..." He spoke in a dreamy voice, as if his mind were elsewhere. He even seemed a little bored, like capturing an innocent woman and sticking a syringe in her neck was just part of an average Tuesday afternoon. "I did tell you that you could do better than him. Don't say you weren't warned."

"Why are you doing this?"

He fisted my hair then pressed my face hard against his knee, exposing my neck to the needle. "Because your husband doesn't listen." He stuck the needle in my neck, pressed the top with his thumb, and then I was gone.

$a_3 = x^2$

HADES

AFTER A TWELVE-HOUR DAY, I HEADED HOME. IT SEEMED LIKE Damien and I had resolved the problem his stupidity had caused. All the drugs were off the streets, distributors were put on hold in the meantime, and production had halted in the facilities. Our business was officially shut down. If this had been a few years ago, I'd be livid.

But it didn't seem so bad.

I was ready to start a new life, to be a different man.

When I walked through the door, I ran into Maria. She was still youthful in her appearance, reminding me of Sofia in many ways. They had the same eyes, same full lips, and same dark hair. "I hope you started dinner without me."

Maria leaned in and kissed me on the cheek, treating me like the son she'd never had. "Oh, I already ate. I assume you and your wife had plans since Sofia hasn't returned my calls."

We had no plans to my knowledge, but I hated these family dinners, so I looked forward to one-on-one time with my wife.

Maria always hijacked the conversation and bored us out of our minds. And it wasn't like I could fuck her daughter right in front of her. "Maybe she's under the weather."

"Maybe. Helena said she didn't answer the door. Perhaps she's in the bathtub." Maria continued on her way toward the kitchen, probably to get another glass of wine.

I turned rigid on the spot, my gut clenching tightly with unease. There was probably a simple explanation for Sofia's behavior, but my instincts told me otherwise. I was a paranoid man...and now I was even more alarmed.

As I headed to the stairs, I pulled out my phone and called her.

No answer.

My heart exploded with dread. Then I started to sprint up the stairs. I didn't even breathe hard as I sped up three floors and darted down the hallway to our bedroom. I practically broke down the door when I got there. "Sofia?" I stood in the open doorway, scanning the room for signs of her presence.

There were none.

I moved into the room and headed to the bathroom. "Sofia?"

No answer.

I turned back around and looked through the room, even checking the patio. When I realized she wasn't there, a huge bomb of panic and anxiety exploded right in my chest. I tried to breathe, but I couldn't—tried to get ahold of my emotions, but they were too uncontrollable. I paced in the bedroom, dragging my hands down my face as my mind raced a million miles an hour.

My mind deduced what had happened. Sofia wasn't in the

house, and I knew she wouldn't disobey me and leave, wouldn't ignore my phone calls. Someone had taken her from my fortress, stolen her right out from under me.

There was only one person who could do that.

Maddox.

With flared nostrils and white knuckles, I broke down in the middle of my bedroom. My fingers fisted my hair, and my ribs vibrated with every beat of my heart. My wife had been taken from me, and I had no idea where to find her. It was the most excruciating feeling in the world, to lose the thing you loved most. I had been devastated when Damien was taken...but this was a whole new level of bleakness.

Fuck.

Sweat poured down my forehead and burned my eyes. I had to combat my panic because I needed to focus with everything I had. I had to get Sofia back, no matter the cost, no matter the amount of blood and tears.

My phone started to ring.

I looked at it, hoping to see Sofia's name.

No. It was Maddox.

The timing told me everything I needed to know. My worst nightmare had come to pass. I didn't fix Damien's mistake quickly enough, and now my wife was gone, subjected to unspeakable cruelty.

It was my job to protect her.

I failed.

I wanted to ignore the call, but that wasn't an option. My wife's life hung in the balance, and I couldn't afford to provoke him. He probably had spies watching the place, and he was notified the second I stepped inside my home. He wanted to see me suffer, wanted me to know he had me by the balls. This was punishment for my disobedience, which meant there might not be anything I could do to get Sofia back.

He might've already killed her.

I hissed between my teeth and almost collapsed to the floor.

If she died, I'd die too.

I took the call and put the phone to my ear.

He overtook the conversation, as always. "I warned you, Hades."

I kept the speaker away from my mouth so he couldn't hear the emotion in my breathing.

"You gave me your word—you broke it."

Sweat coated my neck and dripped down my temples. I wasn't warm when I came home, but I was so terrified now that my bodily functions had gone haywire.

"You never deserved her."

I wanted to be strong and incorruptible, but I didn't have room for pride. I would beg, plead, do anything to save her. "It was Damien, not me. I can't control what he does. Leave my wife out of this." I steadied my voice as much as possible, but I couldn't keep the pain muffled.

"That wasn't the deal, and you know it."

"What do you want, Maddox?" I hoped there was something he wanted. Even me, anything I could use to trade for her.

"Nothing."

My heart plummeted into my stomach.

"I got what I wanted."

I lost all control and screamed into the phone. "Let her go, asshole! She's innocent. Has nothing to do with this. I'm the one you want."

"I don't know... She is beautiful."

I was going to hurl right in the middle of my room. "Give her back to me, or I will come after you. I will cut you apart, piece by piece, and keep you alive long enough to watch the pile grow. I will come at you with everything I have, and I won't stop until everything you care about is gone."

His sinister smile was loud in his voice. "I hope so, Hades. You know me—I like action."

"Asshole..."

He hung up.

Motherfucker hung up.

Once the line went dead, that was when I noticed the tears falling down my cheeks. I thought they were beads of sweat. But, no—they were drops of heartache.

SOFIA AND HADES'S STORY CONTINUES IN
THE NEXT TWO BOOKS

The highly anticipated sequel to Penelope Sky's critically acclaimed series.

I lost the only thing that matters to me.

My wife.

And I'm the only one to blame.

I will sacrifice my life, my pride, and everything else for the woman I love.

Whether she loves me or not.

Order Now

The conclusion to the insanely popular Betrothed Series by critically acclaimed author Penelope Sky. Hades has done everything for the woman he loves. Now it's time for Sofia to do the same for him.

I never broke the curse...I just changed it.

Now I'm forced into a partnership with Maddox, and since I can't kill him, I have to tolerate him every day.

So Sofia leaves me.

I've sacrificed everything for her, but it's never enough. My love for her doesn't change despite the betrayal. The torture continues.

What am I gonna do?

I have one option. I said no the first time, but I'm not sure I can say no again...

<u>Order Now</u>

Damien is getting his very own story! There will even be guest appearances from Hades and Sofia AND a crossover story featuring Heath, the new Skull King. It's just as unpredictable and riveting!

When Heath, Balto's brother, demands payment from Damien's business, things get out of hand...and a war begins. It's the first time a character from another series has become a main player in one of my books. And it's going to be quite a tale.

Hades retired from the business.

Now it's just me.

Look at me now...bitter...angry...depressed. I resent my former friend so much, even hate the guy, but I've never been the same since he refused to forgive me.

I meet a woman. She's like all the others...beautiful, interesting, good at the fun stuff, but I don't feel anything.

One woman will love you for you, not your money or your power, but you'll lose her. And once she's gone...she's gone.

That gypsy wasn't right about me too, right?

I've got trouble on my doorstep when the new Skull King shows up. He wants a cut of my business.

Like he's getting anything. This is all I have left.

Once again I become swallowed by the underworld.

Will I survive it?

Order Now

She's gone.

But the fortune can't be true because she means nothing to me.

Nothing at all.

But the doubt starts to creep in. My thoughts only focus on one thing. The other women no longer satisfy me.

It starts to drive me crazy.

When I finally confront her, the horror shatters me.

She's marrying someone else.

Order Now

She's mine once again but she's practically a ghost.

She's just using me...not that I mind.

But her indifference is suffocating. I mean nothing to her...less than what she used to mean to me. Admissions of regret and apologies aren't enough to fix it.

I have to return to the gypsy...and hope for the best.

Order Now